Encomiums

D1155350

"Sade's neglected masterpiece... can be [...]sive turning point in the author's development, but also a significant milestone in the history of the philosophy of emotion."

— Marco Menin, University of Turin

"For those of us who have been waiting a lifetime for a translation, *Aline and Valcour* is the final piece of the puzzle that is Sade, and a key work in French literature."

— Steven Moore, author of *The Novel: An Alternative History*

"Sade may be diabolical, but he is also devilishly adroit."

— Beatrice C. Fink, University of Maryland

"*Aline and Valcour* shows an epistolary novel that is very much in and of the Revolutionary moment, which only enhances its appeal. That Sade produced a book this good is an occasion for surprise and pleasure. *Aline and Valcour* has the capacity to not only deepen the popular conception of Sade but the popular-academic conception of him as influenced by Barthes and Foucault. I also greatly admire the translation, which is kept in period but is not at all a pastiche. It is both formal & direct."

— Prof. Nicholas Birns, New York University

"Jocelyne Geneviève Barque and John Galbraith Simmons have triumphantly met the manifold challenges of this fascinating, often prolix novel, rendering Sade's words into a sparkling English that never lapses into faux-'modern' anachronism or pedantic literalism."

— Christopher Winks, Professor of Comparative Literature, Queens College

Aline and Valcour will force readers on this side of the Atlantic to re-think everything they've ever learned, heard, or read about the Marquis de Sade. The translation of this formidable novel... is accurate, clear, loses nothing of the Sadean voice, and makes for compelling reading.

— Alyson Waters, PhD, managing editor of *Yale French Studies*

"This remarkable translation of this extraordinary novel, done into English with such talent and devotion, will be a landmark contribution to French studies in the English-speaking world."

— Donald Nicholson-Smith, translator, Chevalier des Arts et Lettres

afin que... les traces de ma tombe disparai
comme je me flatte que ma mémoire s'ef

"so that … all traces of my grave may disappear from the surface of the earth, just as I like to think my memory will be effaced from the minds of men …"

nt de dessus de la surface de la terre,
...a de l'esprit des hommes... D.A.F. SADE

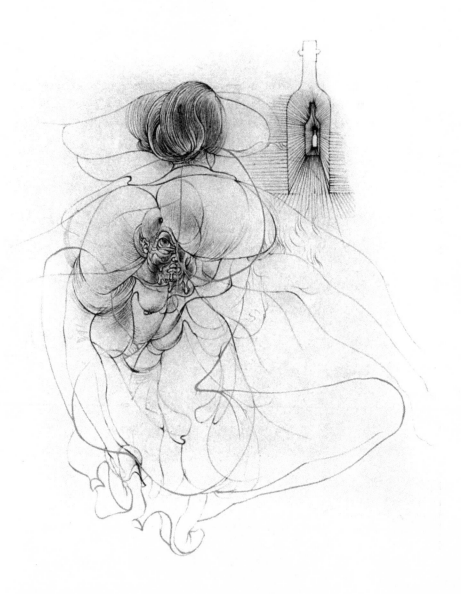

Hans Bellmer, *Aline et Valcour* (1968).

ALINE AND VALCOUR
or, the Philosophical Novel

by

Marquis de Sade

Vol. II

Translated by

Jocelyne Geneviève Barque

&

John Galbraith Simmons

Contra Mundum Press   New York · London · Melbourne

This translation is a recipient of a Grant from The National Endowment of the Arts.

NATIONAL ENDOWMENT for the ARTS
arts.gov

Letters I–V appeared in slightly different form in *The Brooklyn Rail* (February 2009) and *Fiction Anthology 2* (2013); "The Crime of Passion, or Love's Delirium" appeared in *The Brooklyn Rail* (September 2013).

First Contra Mundum Press Edition 2019.

Library of Congress Cataloguing-in-Publication Data

Sade, 1740–1814

Aline and Valcour, Vol. II / Sade; Introduction by John Galbraith Simmons

—1st Contra Mundum Press Edition
260 pp., 6×9 in.

ISBN 9781940625324

    I. Sade.
   II. Title.
  III. Simmons, John
       Galbraith; Barque,
       Jocelyne Geneviève.
  IV. Translation.
   V. Simmons, John
       Galbraith.
  VI. Introduction.

2019946562

Table of Contents

Introduction

Aline and Valcour

Endnotes

Illustrations

Translators' Note

In accordance with recent editions in French, our translation is based on the third state or printing of the novel in 1795. The text in English is complete and integral. Footnotes are Sade's own, added at the time of publication. At the end of each volume we provide contextual endnotes that gloss historic and unfamiliar events, names, and places.

ALINE AND VALCOUR
or, the Philosophical Novel

Written in the Bastille a year before the Revolution in France
by Citizen S***

Nam veluti pueri trepidant atque omnia cæcis
in tenebris metuunt, sic nos in luce timemus
interdum, nilo quæ sunt metuenda magis quam
quæ pueri in tenebris pavitant finguntque futura.
hunc igitur terrorem animi tenebrasque necessest
non radii solis neque lucida tela diei
discutiant sed naturæ species ratioque.

Just as children in the night tremble & fear everything,
so we in the light sometimes fear
what is no more to be feared than the things
children shudder at in the dark
and imagine will come true. This terror,
this darkness of the mind's eye must be scattered,
not by the rays of the sun & glistening shafts of daylight,
but by a dispassionate view of the inner laws of Nature.

— Lucretius, *De rerum natura*, Book III

Important Note to the Reader

The author must inform the reader that, having sold and submitted his manuscript at the time he left the Bastille, there was consequently no question of his being able to revise it. How then can this work, written seven years ago, remain fully current with the order of the day? He asks his readers to think back and recall the very extraordinary circumstances of that time; and he invites them to form a judgment only after reading from beginning to end. For a book of this sort, it is not the appearance of one or another character, or of some isolated system of thought, upon which an opinion may be based. One who is just and impartial will only ever pronounce upon the whole.

Principal Characters

Monsieur de Blamont	"The President," a magistrate judge and libertine
Monsieur Dolbourg	a banker, best friend & Blamont's companion in crime
Madame de Blamont	"The President," Blamont's wife
Aline	daughter of Monsieur & Madame de Blamont
Valcour	Aline's young suitor
Monsieur Déterville	friend to Aline, Madame de Blamont, & Valcour
Eugénie	fiancée then wife to Déterville
Madame de Senneval	mother-in-law to Déterville
Sophie	spurned mistress to Dolbourg
Sainville	young man & world voyager
Léonore	Sainville's wife & lover
Clémentine	Léonore's companion
Ben Mâacoro	King of Butua (a dystopia)
Zamé	Chief of Tamoé (a utopia)
Brigandos	Leader of Bohemian Gypsies

Letter XXXV
Déterville to Valcour

Vertfeuille, 16 November　　　　　　　　　　　　　　　　　　5

Part One — Sainville: His Story
Sainville began, telling the assembled:

By introducing the object that captivates him, a lover may　　10
hope to win indulgence for his faults. Cast a friendly gaze
upon Léonore and you'll see both the cause of my misdeeds
and reason to forgive them.

　　We were born in the same city, our families bound by
blood and affection; it was hard for me to see her without　　15
coming to love her. No sooner was she not a child than everyone talked of her charms. To my pride in being the first to
render homage was joined the delicious pleasure of realizing
that no one could infuse me with as much ardor.

　　Léonore, at the age of innocence and candor, listened　　20
as I confessed my love, indicated she was receptive; and the
moment her charming smile revealed she did not hate me, I
confess, was the sweetest of my life. We followed the customary path for delicate and sensitive hearts. We swore to love
one other, and to tell each other so, and to be soon united　　25
forever. But we were far from foreseeing what obstacles fate
was erecting to thwart our plans. Little did we imagine, as we
ventured upon these promises, that our cruel families were

---

* Any reader who would take what follows as a pointless episode, to be read or passed
　over at will, would be making a grievous error.

working to defeat them, like a storm brewing above our heads
— for Léonore's parents were arranging a union for her whilst
at the same time mine were about to impose a marriage of
convenience.

The first to learn of it was Léonore; she told me of our
misfortune and swore that if I was willing to stand firm, whatever difficulties to be encountered, we would stay together
forever. I need not tell you how pleased I was by this declara-
tion; my euphoria was complete.

Léonore, born to wealth, was introduced to Count de Fo-
lange, whose position and fortune would provide the happiest possible life in Paris; yet, despite the advantages of wealth
and, also, despite all the gifts with which Nature endowed the
Count, Léonore refused.

A convent was to be the price she would pay for her
rejection.

The same misfortune had befallen me with one of the
wealthiest heiresses of our province. She was on offer but I
refused with such harshness and determination that, when I
told my father I'd take Léonore as my wife or never marry, he
obtained for me an order to join and remain with my regiment
on duty without leave for two years.

"Before I obey, Monsieur," I said, casting myself at the feet
of my angry father, "allow me at least to ask the cruel reason
that compels you to disapprove of the only woman who can
make me happy."

"No reason whatever," replied my father, "for not approv-
ing of Léonore; but there exist several powerful reasons to
insist you marry another. For years I've done everything possible to prepare for your union with Mademoiselle de Vitri,
which would bring great wealth and put an end to a centuries-
old legal dispute that, were it lost, would completely ruin us.
Believe me, my son, such considerations are worth more than

all the sophisms of love. Life requires the means to live, while   o
we never love but for a moment."

"And Léonore's parents," said I, avoiding his last, "what
motives did they invoke for refusing consent?"

"The wish to make a much better match. Even if I weakened in my resolve, don't imagine for a moment they'll change   5
their minds. Else she must take the vows."

I stopped for now, only wanting to learn what obstacles
I faced in order to decide on a course to overcome them. I
begged my father grant me a week, promising that then I
would immediately leave for my place of exile. I obtained the   10
desired delay and, as you might imagine, took the opportunity to obliterate anything and everything that would prevent
Léonore and I from being united forever.

In the convent where Léonore had days before been
locked away, I had a religious aunt. This piece of luck allowed   15
me to formulate the boldest of plans: I recounted my misfortunes to this relation and was happy to find her compassion-
ate. But how could she help?

"Love can find a way," I said, "and I'll tell you how. I'll disguise myself. I'd fare not badly, as you can imagine, dressed as   20
a young woman. You'll introduce me as a visiting relative from
a distant province. Request authorization for me to stay a few
days in the convent. It shall be granted. I'll see Léonore and be
the happiest of men."

To my aunt, this daring plan seemed at first impossible;   25
she foresaw a hundred obstacles. But her head could not dic-
tate a single one my heart did not eliminate immediately, and
I managed to convince her.

Once we agreed upon the scheme and swore secrecy, I
announced to my father that I was exiling myself to the army,   30
as he demanded and, however difficult it was to obey his order,
I preferred it to marrying Mademoiselle de Vitri. I endured
further reprimands; every effort was made to persuade me,

but as my resolve was unshakeable, Father embraced me and we parted.

So I went away but no intention of obeying his wishes. Knowing that he had previously deposited in a Paris bank a considerable sum that he intended to settle upon me, I did not regard it as theft to obtain an advance upon such funds as would one day be mine. Furnished with a letter ostensibly from him, forged with my own reprehensible skill, from the bank I received the sum of one hundred thousand écus. Immediately thereafter, dressed like a young woman, I hired a clever soubrette and left for the city and convent where my dear aunt, inclined in favor of my love, awaited me.

The démarche that I'd just brought off was too serious to risk telling her about in any way. I indicated my sole desire was to see Léonore, with her present and, after a few days, to obey my father's orders. But because he believed me to be already in exile, I explained that we must be doubly careful. Learning he'd just gone to visit his estates, we felt more at ease and began our ruse straightaway.

My aunt received me first in the common room and astutely introduced me to some of her friends among the nuns. She made known her desire to have me stay at least a few days, and asked for and obtained permission. So I entered and found myself under the same roof as Léonore. One must be in love to understand the euphoria of it; my heart alone could feel what my head cannot describe.

The first day I did not see her; to rush things would have raised suspicion. We had to be cautious. But next morning, the charming young woman, invited by my aunt to come for hot chocolate, found herself sitting beside but not recognizing me; she breakfasted with other companions without suspecting, realizing her mistake only afterwards when my aunt kept her behind and, laughing, told her and introduced me.

"Here, my beautiful cousin, is a relative of mine I want you to meet. Please, look closely and tell me if it's true that, as she claims, you've seen her before."

As Léonore stared, she grew confused. Throwing myself at her feet, I asked forgiveness — and we gave ourselves over to the delightful prospect of spending at least a few days together.

My aunt believed she must be strict and refused to leave us alone. But I cajoled nicely, telling her a multitude of tender things that women, and nuns above all, so love to hear, and soon she allowed me to be alone with the object of my heart's desire.

"Léonore," I said to my beloved. "I come ready to urge you to fulfill the promises that we made to each other. I've enough money to last us both for the rest of our lives. Let's not waste an instant. Let us flee."

"Climb the walls!" said Léonore, frightened. "We'll never succeed."

"With love, nothing is impossible," I exclaimed, "Let it be your guide and tomorrow we'll be reunited."

The gentle young woman raised still more objections and made me aware of the difficulties, but I begged her to surrender, like me, to the feelings that inflamed us. She trembled — yet promised. We agreed to avoid each other's company and meet again only just before we started to execute our plan.

"Which deserves some thought," I said. "My aunt will pass you a note. You will follow its instructions to the letter. We'll see each other once more to arrange it, then we'll be gone."

I did not want to confide our plans to my aunt. Would she agree to help? Or betray us? Those considerations stopped me. But we had to act. Alone, disguised, knowing nothing of the place, neither its nooks and crannies nor its environs — all this made for great difficulty. But nothing stopped me — so let me tell you how I proceeded.

After spending 24 hours scrutinizing the situation, I came to understand that a sculptor came daily to a chapel inside the convent. There he worked to repair a large statue of Ultrogote, the patron saint of the place, whom the nuns, having witnessed her miracles and the way she granted their every wish, worshipped with profound veneration. A few simple paternosters devoutly recited at her altar and one could be sure of heavenly bliss.

Resolved to try everything, I approached the sculptor and, after preliminary genuflections, asked if he was as faithful and devoted, like the nuns, to the saint he was restoring.

"I'm a stranger here," I told him, "and would like to learn from you about some of the extraordinary deeds of this blessed lady."

"Well," the sculptor laughed, confident from my tone that he could speak more frankly, "Don't you see that these silly smitten sisters believe anything they're told? How can a simple piece of wood do such amazing things? The first of all miracles would be self-preservation and you can see it can't even do that because I've got to put her back together. Don't tell me you believe in all this nonsense, Mademoiselle!"

"Well, of course not," I replied; "but one must conform like the others."

Thinking that sufficed as an overture, I stopped there. But the next day, during our talk, once again in the same spirit, I went further, so playfully and solicitously that he became excited and I began to think that, if I kept it up, the very altar of the miraculous statue might become a throne of pleasure. When I saw he was in such a state, I seized his hand.

"Good man," I said, "look upon me not as a woman — but as an unfortunate man in love, to whom you can bring happiness."

"Heaven forbid! Monsieur! You'll get us both in trouble."

"No: listen to me. Do me this favor, help me, and you'll make a fortune." ○

In saying this, to lend my words force, I gave him a roll of some 25 louis, assuring him more if he agreed to help.

"Well, what do you want?"

"There's a young woman here I adore. She loves me, con- 5 sents to all. I want to take her away with me and marry her. But I need your help."

"What can I do?"

"Nothing could be simpler. We'll crack the arms of this statue. You then tell them that its terrible condition caused 10 it to break when you started repairs, that it would be impossible to fix here and absolutely must be taken to your studio. Being so attached to it, they'll do anything to save it, and so will consent. Tonight I'll come alone to finish the job, get rid of the pieces and envelop my love in the robes of the statue. 15 You'll drape her with a large cloth and, with the help of one of your apprentices, early in the morning you'll take her to your studio. There a woman will be waiting; you'll place under her care the object of my vows; when I arrive two hours later, you'll receive more proof of my gratitude. Later, you'll tell the 20 nuns that the statue crumbled to dust when you applied the chisel, and that you'll sculpt them a new one."

The fellow, not infatuated like me and infinitely more clear-headed, foresaw problems galore. I listened to none of them but sought only to convince him. Two more sheaves of 25 bills accomplished as much and we started work straightaway. Both arms of the statue were mercilessly shattered. Calling the nuns, they approved the plan to move the statue, which left only one thing to do — to act.

As agreed, I sent a note to Léonore advising her to meet 30 me that very evening at the entrance to the chapel, dressed most scantily because I had some saintly garments for her that could magically make her disappear from the convent. She understood none of it and immediately came to see me at my aunt's. As we had carefully limited our meetings, no one was surprised. The moment we were left alone, I explained the whole affair.

Laughter was Léonore's first reaction. Unsullied by narrow-minded dogmatism, she saw nothing but an amusing plan to change places with a miraculous statue. But reflection soon cooled delight. She must spend the night there — she might be heard. The nuns — at least those sleeping near the chapel — might take any noise as a manifestation of the damaged Saint's rage at the suite of events. All they need do would be to come, inquire, and discover — and we should be lost. How could she be sure to stay motionless while being moved? What if someone lifted the sheet under which she was hidden? What if? To her thousand objections, each one more reasonable than the last, I met them all by assuring Léonore that there exists a God for lovers and if we implored Him on our behalf, He would unfailingly accomplish our wishes — no matter the obstacle.

Léonore surrendered. Quite fortunately, no one shared her bedroom. I wrote the soubrette whom I'd engaged in Paris, sent her the sculptor's address, and requested she go to his studio early the next morning and bring decent clothes for a young lady who would be nearly naked; she was to take her immediately to the inn where we were to be lodged and call for a post-coach for nine o'clock sharp. I would be back without fail at that hour, and we'd depart just afterwards.

With all going so marvelously well on the outside, I was left only to deal with the interior plans — certainly the most difficult.

Feigning a headache, Léonore obtained permission to retire early, and as soon as everybody thought she was abed,

she came to the chapel, where I pretended to be engaged in   0
meditation. She joined me in ersatz contemplation. We waited for the nuns to retire to their holy couches, and once sure
they were held fast in sleep's embrace, we started to break
down and reduce the miraculous statue to dust — not difficult
considering its condition. I had at hand a large bag, in the   5
bottom of which were some heavy stones. We put the Saint's
rubble inside and I quickly dropped the whole thing down a
well. Léonore was barely clothed, dressed in the attire of Saint
Ultrogote, and I helped her assume the same position as the
sculptor had placed the statue in order to repair it. I bound   10
her arms to her sides while attaching the wooden ones we had
broken off the previous day, and after having kissed her — a
delicious kiss whose effect on me was more powerful than all
the miracles of all the saints in heaven — I left the temple of
my goddess and retired, overcome with adoration.   15

Early next morning, the sculptor arrived, followed by an
apprentice, carrying a sheet that they threw over Léonore with
such swiftness and dexterity that the nun providing the light
saw nothing. They all went away and Léonore was received by
the woman awaiting her at the inn as planned, with no further   20
obstacle to her escape.

To no one's surprise, I'd announced my own departure.
Amongst the nuns I pretended to be puzzled by Léonore's absence; I was told she was sick. Fully at ease by such indisposition, I showed hardly any interest. My aunt, quite convinced   25
we had exchanged our farewells in secrecy the day before, was
not surprised by my indifference, while my only thought was
to fly to the object of my every desire.

The dear young woman had passed a difficult night.
Amidst fear and hope, she was beset by extreme anxiety. Most   30
worrisome was the arrival of an old nun to bid the Saint *adieu*.
She had mumbled away for more than an hour, which all but

kept Léonore from breathing; and at the end of the paternoster, in tears, the old prude wanted to kiss the statue's face. But in the dim light, forgetting the statue's position was altered, her tender act of affection landed on the absolute opposite side of the one intended. Feeling that part covered and realizing her mistake, the old woman patted the place to better convince herself of her error while Léonore, extremely sensitive to be titillated on a part of her body that no hand had ever touched, could not avoid quivering — a movement the nun took for a miracle. She dropped to her knees, fervor redoubled; now better informed in her groping, she succeeded in planting a tender kiss on the forehead of the object of her idolatry, and at last retired.

After a hearty laugh around this adventure, we all of us left: Léonore, the woman I brought from Paris, a lackey, & myself.

But the first day nearly ended in calamity. Exhausted, after we'd gone no more than 10 leagues, Léonore asked that we stop in a small town. There at the inn, near dinnertime, a post-coach arrived. It was my father. From one of his chateaux, he was on his way back to the city, unaware of all that had happened. I still tremble when I think of it. He went upstairs and settled in a bedroom just next to ours. Convinced I could not avoid him, I made ready to throw myself at his feet to implore his forgiveness. But I didn't know him well enough to confidently foresee what he might decide; and such an approach might well mean giving up Léonore. I decided it was better to disguise myself and leave right away. I called for the innkeeper and told her that a man whom I owed 200 louis had by chance just arrived; and that, with neither the possibility nor the desire to repay him just now, I begged her to keep quiet and help me escape my creditor. The woman, with no interest in betraying me and generously compensated, enthusiastically took part in our scheme. Léonore and I exchanged

clothes and shamelessly walked past my father without his   o
recognizing us despite the attention he seemed to show. The
risk we had just run made Léonore decide we need not tarry
and, as our intention was to cross over into Italy, we drove to
Lyon without stopping.

                                                               5

As heaven is my witness, until then I had respected the virtue
of the woman whom I wanted for a wife; I considered that the
prize desired would be diminished if I permitted love to break
the hymen. But an incomprehensible difficulty destroyed our   10
mutual restraint, and grossly imbecilic behavior on the part of
those whom we importuned to help prevent the crime positively plunged us into it.* *O! Ministers of Heaven! Will you
ever realize that it's far better to accept a lesser evil than to
occasion a greater one, and that your worthless approbation,*   15
to which we would readily submit, has nevertheless far fewer
consequences than all those that result from your refusal?
The Vicar General of the Archbishop, from whom we
requested benediction, harshly dismissed us; and three other
priests in the city subjected us to the same unpleasantness.   20
Léonore and I, rightfully annoyed by obnoxious prudery, resolved to take God as our only witness, in the belief that by invoking His name before His altar we would be married just as
well as if the whole Roman priesthood had sanctified us with
all the formalities; it is the soul, the intention, that the Eter- 25
nal One desires. When devotion is sincere, a mediator serves
no purpose.

---

* It is appropriate to remark in passing that in no city in France is the clergy more
detestable than Lyon. If it be rightly said that the priesthood of Paris comprises the
most honest assembly of men in the capitol, one might say the exact opposite of Lyon,
whose members are characterized by guile, greed, ignorance, and debauchery.

⁰ Léonore and I betook ourselves to the Cathedral. There, during the Eucharist, I took the hand of my beloved and swore to belong forever only to her; she did the same. We both submitted to heaven's vengeance should we betray our oath. We declared our union confirmed and that same day the most charming of women made of me the happiest of husbands.

But the same God we had just so zealously invoked had no desire to prolong our happiness. You will soon see what awful disaster He decided upon to disrupt its course.

We reached Venice without further incident. I considered settling in that city, in the name of *Liberty* and as a *Republic* that always appeals to young people; but we quickly realized that if some cities in the world merit to be so qualified, Venice is not among them — unless one so credits a state characterized by the severest oppression of its people and the cruelest tyranny of the wealthy and powerful.

We took lodgings on the Grand Canal in the house of a man named Antonio, who ran a comfortable enough place, *Aux Armes de France*, near the Rialto Bridge. Thinking only of pleasure, we spent the first three months just visiting beautiful sites in the floating city! The pain to come was entirely unforeseen. Whilst we believed we were walking amidst flowers, wrath was preparing to break above our heads.

Venice is surrounded by many charming islands where the aquatic city-dweller, away from its stinking lagoons, betakes himself from time to time to breathe a few atoms of less insalubrious air. In imitation of this habit, with Malamocco village more pleasant and cooler than any other we visited, and more attractive, we dined there several times a week. We preferred the house of a widow who came highly recommended and who for a modest price offered an honest meal and the use all day of her charming gardens. A superb fig tree cast its shadow over a portion of the charming promenade.

Very fond of the fruit, Léonore took singular pleasure in an o
afternoon collation, right there beneath the tree, choosing
those that seemed ripest.

Then one day — fatal moment of my life! — as I watched
her so intently absorbed in that innocent springtide pursuit, I
asked her permission to leave for a brief while to visit, out of 5
curiosity, a renowned abbey nearabouts where famous works
of art by Titian and Paolo Veronese were carefully preserved.
Moved in a way she could not control, Léonore stared.

"Well!" she told me, "no sooner you are my *husband* than
you crave pleasures without your *wife*. Where are you going, 10
my friend, and what painting could be worth as much as the
original you already possess?"

"None, most assuredly" said I, "But I also know that it will
take me just an hour and such objects interest you but little.
These magnificent gifts of Nature," I added, pointing to the 15
figs, "are preferable to the subtleties of the art I wish to briefly
admire."

"Go then, my friend," said the charming lass. "I can stand
one hour alone without you. She added, looking to her tree,
"Go, hurry to your pleasures, I'll taste my own." 20

I kissed her, she wept. I decided to stay, she objected. It
was a brief moment of weakness, she said, that she could not
quell. She demanded I go where curiosity led; she accompanied me to the gondola, watched me climb in, stayed by
water's edge while I slipped away, weeping again as the oars 25
touched the water; then she disappeared from view in the garden. Who would have said that this was the instant that was
going to separate us! Or that our pleasures would be swallowed up in an ocean of misfortune!

"And so" — *here Madame de Blamont interrupted* — "you've just recently been reunited?"

"For three weeks, Madame," Sainville answered, "after having quit our native land three years ago."

"Go on, Monsieur; please continue. This catastrophe signals two stories that promise to be most interesting."

Sainville resumed: My trip was brief. Léonore's tears had so disturbed me that I could take no pleasure in my perusals. My heart's desire was my sole concern and I could only think of her. Returning, I dashed off the boat and flew to the garden. But instead of Léonore, the widow who owned the lodge threw herself at me, weeping, telling me how sorry she was, and that she deserved my anger. When I'd left, no more than a hundred yards from shore, a gondola had approached, filled with men she did not know. Six of them, their faces masked, came off. They took hold of Léonore, wrested her back to their gondola, and rowed fast away toward the open water.

My first thought, I admit, was to hurtle myself at the poor woman and knock her down with a single blow. I held back, she being of the weaker sex, and contented myself with grasping her by the neck and angrily screaming that she must bring back my wife or I'd strangle her straightaway.

"Execrable nation!" I cried. "So this is the way of justice in the famed Republic! Let heaven annihilate both me and Venice itself if the one so dear to me is not returned immediately."

Hardly were those words out of my mouth before I was surrounded by a squadron of constables; one of them stepped forward to ask if I did not know that a stranger in Venice must not criticize the government in any way.

"Scoundrel!" I replied, beside myself. "One can only say and think the worst when the right of refuge and rights of men have been cruelly violated."

"We know nothing about that," replied the constable. "But kindly oblige us by boarding your gondola, and returning immediately to your lodgings, where you will remain under house arrest until the Republic issues further orders."

Struggle was useless, anger impotent; my tears moved nobody and my screams melted into air. They dragged me off. Four loathsome rogues escorted me to my room at *Aux Armes* and left me in Antonio's custody; they then went off to report their perfidious intervention.

Words fail to adequately portray my predicament! How describe what I experienced and what became of me when I again laid eyes on the apartment that Léonore and I had quit a few hours earlier? Then a free man, now I returned as a prisoner, and without her. On the heels of rage came a sentiment that was terribly painful and dark. My gaze fell upon my lover's bed, her clothes, her dressing table; coming upon her things, my tears streamed down. Betimes I regarded them with dull stupidity only the next instant to throw myself upon them with wild delirium. *Here she comes,* I told myself: *here she is — resting — and she will dress — I hear her.* But cruel illusions only exacerbated my pain and I wallowed in the middle of the room, flooding the ground with my tears, my screams resounding beneath the vaulted ceiling. *"O Léonore! Léonore! Shall it be thus? Shall I never see you again?"*

Rushing out of the room as a man demented, I thrust myself upon Antonio, begging him to end my life. My pain moved him but my despair frightened him. With seeming sincerity, he entreated me to be calm. At first I rejected his comforting words; my state of mind could bear nothing. But at last I agreed to listen.

"As to yourself, be reassured," Antonio told me. "I would expect an order to expel you from the Republic will be issued within 24 hours. It shouldn't be more severe than that."

"I don't care about myself. Léonore — I want Léonore."

"Don't imagine she is still in Venice. The misfortune to which she has fallen victim has happened to many another foreigner, and even to some from the city itself. Turkish barques sneak into the canals, disguised so no one can recognize them. They prey on young women, abducting them for the seraglio; and no matter what precautions the government takes, such piracy can't be stopped. This must be what happened to Léonore. The widow in Malamocco village is guiltless, for we all know her to be an honest woman; she was sympathetic to your plight and without your outburst you might have learned more. These isles are always crowded not only with foreigners but also spies in hire of the Republic. Your words alone were the only reason for your arrest."

"Such detentions are wrong and your government knows what happened to the woman I love. O! my friend! Bring her back to me and I'll be heart and soul forever in your debt."

"Tell me frankly: Did you spirit the young woman out of France? If that's the case, what just happened could be the combined work of the courts in both countries, a circumstance that would completely change the situation." Seeing me stammering, Antonio continued: "Hide nothing. Tell all. I must hurry off to learn more. You can be sure that when I return, you'll know if your wife was abducted by government orders or owing to ill luck."

"Well!" I replied with that noble candor of youth which, though honorable, may nonetheless tumble us into the traps that crime likes to set, "She is my wife but, I confess, without her parents' consent."

"Good enough," Antonio told me. "In less than an hour you'll know everything. Don't leave the house, it would only make things worse, depriving you of the explanation you've every right to expect."

My man left and shortly returned.

"Nobody suspects your secret," he said. "The ambassador knows nothing and our Republic, with no grounds to inquire into your conduct, would have let you alone had you not blasphemed against the government. So, Léonore must have been abducted by Turkish freebooters who probably spied on her for a month. There were six small armed boats sighted in the canal as escorts, and by now they're 20 leagues distant. They were seen and our men gave chase but they were too far gone and escaped. Next for you will come orders from the government. Obey them; remain calm and believe me, I've done everything I possibly could."

Hardly had Antonio ended his cruel explanation than the arresting constable returned. He ordered me to leave the country next morning, adding that were it not for the legitimate character of my complaint, I would not have been treated with such leniency. However, he was willing to certify that the abduction was not committed by a Venetian criminal but by pirates of the Dardanelles, whose boats had stolen off into the Adriatic and whose activities could not be stopped despite every precaution.

These civilities complete, the fellow took his leave after asking for a few sequins in consideration of his kindness in having only confined me to my lodging instead of taking me off to prison.

Infinitely more tempted, I confess, to pummel the scoundrel rather than provide a gratuity, I was about to do so when Antonio, guessing my intention, entreated me to comply — and so I did.

After everybody left, I was again plunged into painful, soul-destroying despair. I could hardly think: not a single clear plan could fix my imagination; ideas came twenty at a time but each one, no sooner conceived than rejected; they quickly gave way to a thousand others, impossible to execute. One must endure such a situation to understand and wax more eloquent than I in describing it. At last I decided on a plan to pursue Léonore, reach Constantinople ahead of her if possible, use all my assets to pay off the barbarians who'd robbed me of her and, even if it cost my own blood, to rescue her from the awful fate that awaited. Asking Antonio to charter a felucca, I discharged the maidservant we'd brought with us and paid her in return for her solemn assurance that I never need fear her indiscretion.

The felucca was made ready by next morning and you can imagine with what joy I sailed away from those perfidious shores. Fifteen sailors were with me, the wind was up; and in the early morning two days later we caught sight of the famous citadel on Corfu Island, proud rival of Gibraltar, and perhaps as impregnable as that celebrated passage to Europe. The fifth day we rounded the Cape of Morée, entered the archipelago, and on the seventh evening we reached the shores of Pera.

No vessel, apart from a few dinghies belonging to Dalmatian fishermen, did we sight during our crossing; we vainly scrutinized the horizon in all directions but came upon nothing of interest. She must be too far ahead, I told myself, and long since landed. Great heavens! She must already be in the arms of some monster from whom, I feared, I would never succeed in rescuing her.

The Count de Fierval was then French ambassador to the Sublime Porte. I was in no wise acquainted with him — and would I have dared come forward if I were? Yet he was the only person to whom I could turn to in my misfortune and from whom I might learn something. I went to meet him; evincing despair, hiding nothing regarding my adventures, concealing only the true names of my wife and myself. I begged his compassion and requested his help, whether by action or advice.

The Count listened with all the openness and interest I might expect from a man of quality.

"Your situation is frightful," he said. "Were you receptive to wise counsel, I would tell you to return to France, make peace with your parents, and tell them about the dreadful tragedy befallen you."

"How could I, Monsieur? How could I live without Léonore? I must find her or die."

"Well, then," said the Count, "I will do everything in my power — perhaps more than my position permits. Do you have a portrait of Léonore?"

"Here is one rather good likeness, at least to the extent that art can aspire to what Nature made perfect."

"Let me keep it. By this time tomorrow I'll tell you if your wife is in the seraglio. The Sultan honors me with his generosity; I will depict for him the despair of my countryman; he'll tell me whether he possesses the woman. But consider carefully. You might be unhappier still if he has her, for I cannot promise he will give her back."

"For God's sake! She might be within those walls yet I will not able to free her? What are you saying? It might be better not to know."

"You must choose."

"Then take action, Monsieur. Since you take an interest in my suffering, take action; and if the Sultan possesses Léonore and refuses to give her back, I shall die of grief outside the walls of his serail. You'll tell him that the price of his conquest was an unhappy man's life."

The Count shook my hand, ready to share, respect, and attend to my pain. Far different was he from ordinary ministers, bursting with vainglory, who barely grant a man time to express his grievance before harshly dismissing him, counting as wasted the time that charity obliges them to lend an ear to the unfortunate.

Men of high position, see yourselves. You think you fool us in endlessly alleging a multitude of tasks, the better to prove the impossibility of our seeing or talking with you. Oft-used excuses and evasions only make you the more despised, speak ill of the nation and degrade its government. O France! One day, let us hope you shall be enlightened. The energy of your citizens will break the scepter of despotism and tyranny by crushing underfoot the scoundrels who serve either one. You will see that a people, free by Nature & by their own genius, can only govern themselves.

The same evening Count de Fierval sent for me and I hurried to meet him.

"You may be perfectly certain," he told me, "that Léonore is not in the seraglio, nor even in Constantinople. Shameful actions such as Venetians attributed to this Court no longer occur. In fact, there's been no privateering here for centuries. A little more reflection, had I not been preoccupied with the pleasure of being helpful, and I might have told you as much. If the Venetians did not lie to you, however, Léonore was indeed carried off in a vessel under false colors belonging to the Barbary States, which do engage in this kind of piracy. Only there might you learn more. Take back the portrait you lent me; I shan't keep you longer in the capital. If your parents inquired, if orders came down, I'd be forced to exchange my real satisfaction in serving you for the displeasure of arresting you. It would be wiser to go back to France and more advantageous to make peace with your parents instead of continuing to upset them with your prolonged absence. But should you decide to carry on with your search, leave here and pursue it along the coast of Africa."

When he finished, while sincerely thanking the Count, I felt it might be more prudent to conceal rather than expose my plans; and he might prefer it. After showering him with

gestures of gratitude and assuring him I would fully reflect on   0
his recommendations, I left.

I had neither paid for nor returned the felucca, so now
I asked of its owner if he would take me to Tunis.

"Most certainly," he replied, "to Algiers, Morocco, the
whole African coast. Your Excellency has only to ask."   5

Only too happy to find help amidst despair, I embraced
the boatman with all my heart.

"Good man!" I cried enthusiastically. "Either we perish
together or find Léonore."

It was impossible, however, to leave the next day or the   10
day after; season and sea were unpredictable, the weather terrible, and we had to wait. I thought it useless to pay another
visit to the French minister. What could I tell him? Not to see
him might stand as a favor. At last the sky brightened and we
put to sea; but the calm was deceptive. The ocean resembles   15
fortune itself: when it smiles upon us, we must always beware.

Hardly had we left the Archipelago before an impetuous
wind hampered the oars. We were obliged to unfurl the sails.
But the tempest quickly made the light vessel a toy upon the
waves, and we were only too happy to safely reach the coast   20
of Malta the next morning. We entered beneath Fort Saint
Elmo, in the harbor basin of Valletta, the city founded in 1566
by the great naval commander of the same name. Had I been
able to think of anything besides Léonore, I would certainly
have noticed the beauty of the fortifications by which art and   25
Nature made the place wholly impregnable. Instead, I immediately sought lodgings from which we could depart on short
notice but, finding nothing, resolved to spend the night where
we'd stopped, in a tavern.

Near nine o'clock in the evening, as I was trying to take   30
a short rest, there was noise from an adjacent bedroom. As
only a few loosely-joined planks separated the rooms, I could

see and hear everything. I listened — I observed. A singular spectacle took place before my eyes! Three men, who seemed to me Venetian, carried into the room a large wooden case covered with oilcloth. As soon as it was set down, the man who appeared to be in charge locked himself alone in the room, and he lifted the oilcloth — to reveal a coffin.

"O! It cannot be!" he exclaimed, "How awful — she's dead. She lies all still."

Was the fellow mad? How could he be surprised to find someone dead in a coffin? Why else a coffin if a body lay not dead within!

My thoughts gave way to the greatest surprise when I saw the man open the coffin and take up into his arms the body of a woman. The way she was clothed made me think that she must have simply lost consciousness and been placed inside the coffin while alive.

"Ah! I knew it," the man continued. "She could not survive the tempest. Why did I keep her confined once we were sure we weren't being followed? O! Great heavens!"

And so saying, he lay the woman down on the bed. He felt for her pulse and must have perceived a heartbeat. He jumped for joy.

"Happy day!" he exclaimed, "Just a swoon! Charming girl! You shan't deprive me of pleasure. I'll call upon you to keep your vows. You shall be my wife and my efforts shan't go for naught."

From a small chest the man took out flasks and lancets; he readied to bring every kind of help to the unfortunate woman, whose features I could not make out.

There I sat, most eager to follow what would transpire when the owner of the felucca suddenly rushed into my room.

"Your Excellency," he said, "don't go to bed. The moon is rising, the weather favorable. Tomorrow we shall dine in Tunis if Your Excellency agrees to hurry."

fig. 5

Too preoccupied by my love, overfilled by my desire
to find its object, I could not afford to waste time in some
strange affair at the expense of my search for Léonore. So I
quickly left her there — the beautiful woman in a swoon —
and made for the boat. The oars groaned, the weather grew
cooler, the moon shone bright and the sailors began to sing.
Soon we were far from Malta. How unlucky I was! Where will
our star of destiny lead that we will not follow? Like the unfortunate dog in Aesop's fable, I left my prey to chase its shadow.
I was about to encounter a thousand new dangers — all to
find the one whom chance had just placed within my grasp.

"Great God!" *cried Madame de Blamont.* "What are you saying,
Monsieur! The beautiful dead woman — was she Léonore?"

"Yes, Madame, and I shall leave it to her to later recount
for you what brought her there. Permit me meanwhile to continue. Once again you'll see how hostile fortune treated me
so capriciously and how, though still weak and in constant
and profound pain, I fled where hope glimmered to sail where,
in spite of all, harsh destiny awaited."

At sunrise we caught sight of land. Cap Bon peninsula had just
appeared when a furiously rising east wind nearly kept us from
passing along the coast but, rather, sped us with incomparable
impetuosity toward Gibraltar. Our light vessel made easy prey
for the storm and in a trice we found ourselves athwart the
straits. Our sailors, with little experience of swift speeds on
so frail a boat, feared we were lost; maneuvering in such waters was out of the question. We were only able to hastily furl
a torn and defective sail, abandoning ourselves to the will of
the heavens and a God who was, as ever, little embarrassed

by men's wishes and ready to sacrifice them, no matter their useless prayers, to anything inspiring one of His inexplicable whims. We passed like this through the straits, at risk of running aground any moment and, like so much flotsam, errants of chance and sorry toys upon the waves, striking one reef after another. Though we managed not to sink along the African coast, it left us only more fearful still of the Spanish shore.

The wind shifted as soon as we sailed out of the straits and battered us back against the east coast of Morocco. As that empire was one in which I'd planned to continue my search should the other Barbary states prove fruitless, I decided to land there. With my exhausted crew there was no choice; and the ship's owner informed me that once we reached harbor at Salé, unless I wished to return to Europe, he could no longer be of service to me. He maintained that his felucca, hardly equipped to leave Italian shores, was in no condition to go further, and that I'd have to either pay him or sail back with him.

"Go back!" I exclaimed, "Don't you realize that I'd prefer death than return to my country without my beloved?"

An argument crafted for a sensitive heart could little affect such a sailor's soul, and the dear mariner, unmoved, told me that, in that case, we must part company.

What was to become of me! How in the Barbary States could I seek legal redress against a Venetian sailor? Men like him were to be found from one end of Europe to the other. I had no choice but to submit, pay, and dismiss him.

Determined not to waste my time in the kingdom but to continue my search, I rented mules in Salé. Reaching the city of Meknes, where the royal court was located, I pleaded my case to the French Consul.

"I sympathize," he replied after hearing me out, "all the more if your wife has been put in the seraglio; to find her would be impossible, even for the King of France. However, such an unfortunate outcome is quite unlikely. Moroccan privateers seldom navigate the Adriatic; not for more than 30 years have they come ashore. The merchants who furnish the harems buy the women in Georgia or, if it's a question of abduction, steal from the Aegean Islands because the Emperor is fond of Greek women. He'll pay their weight in gold for girls under 12 years of age brought to him from those countries. But he is quite uninterested in women from elsewhere in Europe, and for that reason alone I can tell you, as surely as if I had visited the seraglio myself, that your goddess is not there. Whatever the case, get some rest. I promise to inquire; I shall write all ports of the empire, and perhaps we'll at least learn if she's been seen in these parts."

That seemed reasonable and so I took his advice and tried to rest — if possible amidst the tumult in my heart.

For a week I heard nothing. At last, the Consul came to see me.

"Your wife," he told me, "certainly did not enter the country; I have physical descriptions of all the women who landed since the date you mentioned; none resembles her. However, the day after your arrival, a small storm-battered English ship dropped anchor for 10 hours at Safi. Later, when it sailed off toward the Cap, there was a young French woman aboard, of the same age as you describe — with beautiful brown hair and superb black eyes. She seemed to be in a state of extreme distress; nobody could tell me who she was traveling with or why. Such meager substance is all I could obtain, and I've hurried to report it to you, with no doubt that this woman, so like the portrait you showed me, must be the one you're looking for."

"Ah! Monsieur," I exclaimed, "you grant me at once life — and death. I shan't breathe nor rest until I find that cursed vessel and learn the reason it carries aboard the woman I infinitely adore."

⁰ At the same time, I asked this upstanding gentleman to provide me with several letters of credit and recommendation for the Cap. He complied and before we went our separate ways he also explained how I might rent a light ship for a good price in the harbor of Salé.

⁵ Thus I returned to the celebrated harbor in the Moroccan empire, where I soon located a fifty-ton Dutch galley. To make myself out as a merchant doing business, I purchased a small consignment of oil, which I was told could be readily sold at the Cap. Twenty-five sailors, a good pilot, and my valet — such was my crew.

Our vessel not suited to the high seas, we sailed along the coastline, not further than 15 to 20 leagues out, and landed now and again to take on fresh water and food purchased from the Portuguese of Guinea. All went beautifully until, as we approached the Gulf, halfway on our journey, a sudden violent north wind propelled us in the direction of the island of Saint-Mathieu. I had never seen the sea in such wrath. The fog was so thick that from stem to stern it became impossible to see your hand in front of your face. Lifted skyward one moment by the fury of the waves, the next precipitated into the abyss by their impetuous fall and inundated by swells and tumult, there arose a frightening cacophony with the dreadful roar of the waves and creaking of the sculls. Exhausted by the violent roiling of the gusts and unspeakable agitation, we saw death on every side and expected it any minute.

Here a philosopher might profit from the study of man, observing with what rapidity a change in atmosphere drives him from one state to another. An hour ago our sailors were drunk and cursing. Now they raised their hands to implore Heaven's protection. Fear is truly the wellspring of religion and, as Lucretius said, the mother of all cults. Were man gifted with a better constitution and a nature less prone to disorder, we'd never hear talk of gods on earth.

So it went: danger pressed hard and our sailors feared   0
most the shallow reefs surrounding the island of Saint-Mathieu. We had absolutely no way of avoiding them. Still they
struggled arduously until a sharp gust of wind rendered their
efforts fruitless, striking the boat with such fury that it cracked,
crumpled in the torrent, and sank.   5

All through the dreadful uproar of the wreck and awful
tumult of foaming, roaring waves and gusting winds could be
heard the splintering of the doomed ship. Beneath the raised
scythe of the Grim Reaper, I seized a wooden plank — lucky
to have it for protection from dangers all around — and, hold-   10
ing it tight, gave myself up to the waves. None of my people
had the same good fortune and I saw them all die in front of
my eyes.

Alas! In my cruel situation, threatened by all the mis-
adventures that can assail a man, as heaven is my witness, I   15
asked not for mercy for myself. Was it courage or a failure
to believe? I don't know, but I cared only for the unfortunate
men who perished while serving me. I thought of them alone,
and of my dear Léonore, where she might be and in what state,
deprived of her husband and awaiting rescue.   20

Luckily I salvaged my entire fortune, protected by precautions I'd taken in exchanging a letter of credit for some
money at the Cap in Morocco. My bank notes were in a leath-
er wallet always carefully attached to my belt and so remained
with me; we could only perish together. But in my condition,   25
what consolation that!

Pitched along on my plank, alone and exposed to the
furor of the elements, I realized another awful impending di-
lemma, entirely unanticipated. My urge to survive had blinded me to the necessities of life; I was without supplies of any   30
kind. But there is a god for lovers — so I'd told Léonore, and I
was still convinced. Ancient Greeks were right to believe in it;

and even if, amidst such a dreadful situation, I never dreamt of invoking one deity or another, it remains that to that one I owe my survival. Or at least I assume as much because I've at last emerged from so much danger to be reunited with the woman I adore.

The weather gradually calmed. A cool breeze floated my plank on a tranquil sea with such plain sailing that, by evening, Africa was again in sight; but I was carried well down the coast while approaching land. Next day I was between Bengal and the land of the Jagas, along the coast of the latter kingdom and not far from Cape Negro. My plank, virtually thrown upon the shore, reached the land of those cruel and untamed peoples, of whose customs I knew nothing. Exhausted and famished, no sooner did I reach the beach than I sought to gather roots and wild fruits from which I made an excellent meal; then to my second need, a few hours of sleep.

After acceding to those demands of imperious Nature, I observed the course of the sun. It seemed to me that by walking inland, then turning southward, I would reach the Cape after passing through the region known as Cafrerie and the land of the Hottentots. I was not mistaken — but by such a route, what dangers awaited! Clearly, cannibals inhabited the country; the better I oriented myself, the less I could doubt it. Clearly, too, as I penetrated inland, would not the dangers multiply? I well knew that Portuguese and Dutch possessions lined the coast to the Cape; but, spiked with rocks, the coast offered no way forward. Instead, a vast and beautiful plain spread before me as if beckoning me to follow it. I thus held to the plan just described, determined, whatever the consequences, to walk west into the interior for two or three days, then shift straightaway south. Let me repeat: I calculated aright — but at what peril!

Armed with a thick length of wood that I carved into a o
bludgeon, I started out, my clothes slung over my shoulder
rather than on my back due to the extreme heat. The first day
went off without incident; I walked nearly ten leagues. Exhausted by the heat, feet scorched by the burning sand into
which I sank over my ankles, I watched the sun drop beneath 5
the horizon. After refreshing myself in the cold clean waters
of a stream, I decided to spend the night in a tree. Climbing
up into my fortress, I assumed a comfortable enough posture
along a branch to which I bound myself, and slept for several
hours. Blistering rays from the morning sun struck me despite 10
the foliage, warming me to the fact it was time to move on,
and I did so with the same plan in mind.

Hunger pressed once more but I found nothing to satisfy
it. Loaded with riches but unable to find life's basic necessities,
I said to myself: *Would not vegetables sown upon this plain* 15
be far preferable to filthy lucre of no real worth? It's the man
who goes off to extract gold from the earth, abandoning land
far more suitable that could feed him with so much less toil,
who is extravagant and deserves contempt. Ridiculous human
conventions: how many more errors do you admit not yet dare 20
beat back into the void whence they came?

I had walked hardly five leagues on the second day when
I came in sight of a group of men. With my extreme urge to
seek help, my first impulse was to approach them; the second,
when I recalled the terrifying idea of a country inhabited by 25
cannibals, impelled me to climb a tree and await what fate
had in store.

Great God! How can I describe for you what was hap-
pening! Never in my entire life, I can truly say, had I encountered a spectacle more frightening. 30

The Jagas, whom I'd just glimpsed, were triumphantly returning from a battle that with savages from the neighboring

Kingdom of Butua. The detachment halted beneath the very tree in which I'd just taken refuge; there were approximately 200, with about 20 prisoners chained together with bindings made from tree bark.

The Chief, surveying the poor captives, made six of them step forward. He brought them low with his bludgeon, taking pleasure in striking different parts of the body, showing off his dexterity while killing each with a single blow. Four of his followers chopped up the bodies and their bloody parts were handed out to the group. It is not even butchery when an animal is shared out with such rapidity, as were those sorry victims at the hands of their victorious rivals. They uprooted a nearby tree, stripped its branches, laid a fire, and over burning charcoals, lightly roasted the dismembered human flesh. No sooner were pieces passed over the flames than they were gulped down with a terrifying voracity. They accompanied their meal with droughts of some clearly inebriating drink — or so it seemed as I witnessed their postprandial frenzy and rage. The tree they'd chopped down they now planted upright in the sand; to it they tied the last of the prisoners, then began dancing around him while, armed with an iron blade, they skillfully cut strips of flesh from his body, killing the hapless fellow by slowly pulling him apart.* Pieces of flesh were swallowed raw no sooner were they sliced. But, before putting them in their mouths, they had to smear their faces with the dripping blood. This was proof of their victory. I must confess

---

* We recoil with dread from this story, awful to be sure. But if it is a crime to be vanquished among such barbarians, why should they not have the right to punish them by torture, just as we punish ours in essentially the same way? If two nations employ the same horrors, one of them has no right to inveigh against the other just because it operates with a little more ceremony. Only the philosopher, who accepts few crimes and himself kills no one, has the right to condemn both.

that fear and terror now so assailed me that my strength almost deserted me; but survival depended upon courage, and I held fast and forced myself to overcome that moment of weakness. The whole day, devoted to those awful rituals, was one the most dreadful I ever spent.

At sunset they decamped at last and a quarter hour later, with nobody in sight, I climbed down from my tree to search for food, so necessary given my state of exhaustion.

Assuredly, had my tastes been those of the cruel Jagas, I would've found an excellent meal right there on the ground; but such an idea, despite hunger and want, brought me such horror than I couldn't bear even to pluck roots from the soil surrounding the horrible place. So I went away from there and after a sorry and insubstantial meal, spent the second night the same way as the first.

I was starting to dearly regret my decision to walk inland, where it seemed I'd certainly be devoured, realizing it would have been much better to follow the coast, however impractical; but I was by now so far from it that retracing my steps would be as dangerous as continuing ahead; so I kept going. The next day I crossed the site of the previous day's battle and saw that a feast similar to the one I'd witnessed also seemed to have taken place there. The very idea made me tremble anew and I hastened forward.

Only — great heavens! — soon to be stopped.

I must have been about 25 leagues from the place where I'd first landed when, passing a thicket where they lay in wait, three savages suddenly fell upon me. They spoke a language of which I understood not a word, but their gestures and actions together indicated cruelty and there was no question of the dreadful fate they had in store for me.

Now a prisoner and knowing only too well how savagely they treated their captives, try to imagine my state of mind.

"O, my Léonore!" I cried out, "You'll never see your lover again! He is become prey to monsters, lost to you forever; never again shall we see and love one another." But those expressions of anguish were far from touching the souls of these barbarians who, of course, simply didn't understand. They bound me so tightly I could barely walk. For a moment I felt disgraced to be fettered; but reflection revived my courage: ignominy unde-served, I told myself, dishonors those who inflict it far more than those who receive it; the tyrant has the power to put one in chains, but the wise and sensitive man has the far more precious right to despise his captor and, offended though he might be by his chains, he smiles at the despot who crushes him — "his brow touches heaven's vault while the proud head of the oppressor falls mired in mud and muck." *

I marched with those barbarians for nearly six hours, fettered as I've described, before coming to a small village. It was regularly laid out; the main house seemed vast and rather beautiful, although constructed of branches and rushes tied to timber poles. This house belonged to the monarch; the village was his capital. In short, I'd entered the Kingdom of Butua, home to man-eaters whose habits and cruelties sur-pass, in their depravity, anything said or written about this most ferocious people. Until now no European has ever far reached these parts — not even the Portuguese, despite their desire to control and intent to establish a route to their own colonies in Benguela as well a way to reach Zimbawbe and nearby Zanzibar and Monomotapa. Just because, there exist no reports of any kind concerning these territories, I imagine

---

* Sublime reflections from the magnificent introduction to the immortal work by Abbé Raynal, which both covered in glory the writer who composed it and con-demned the nation that dared undermine it. O *Raynal, your century and your country did not deserve you!*

you'd be interested in learning a few details concerning the   o
way these people live. I shall understate some things when it
comes to introducing indecencies; but, to remain truthful I'll
sometimes be obliged to reveal horrors you'll find revolting.
How otherwise could I describe the cruelest and most dissolute people on earth?   5

At this juncture Aline made to retire, my dear Valcour; and I'm
pleased to remind you of her fine modesty; she blushes at the
least insult to decency. But Madame de Blamont, suspecting   10
she'd be disappointed by missing Sainville's intriguing story,
enjoined her to stay; she added that she relied on her young
visitor's honor and noble manners, confident he'd invest his
narration with requisite purity and gloss over anything that
was too strong.   15
    "As for purity of expression, the more the better," inter-
rupted the Count, "but to draw a curtain around details too
potent, Mesdames, I quite disagree. Concern over women's
sensibilities kept us in the dark while if sailors had spoken
more frankly in their recent reports, we'd all be familiar with 20
the customs of the South Seas islanders of whom today we
have only the sketchiest accounts. This is no obscene vignette:
Monsieur is not about to recount some fiction but to portray
a part of human history. If you wish to profit and learn something of the genesis of customs and mores, they must be pre-   25
cise in ways they cannot be etherealized. Only impure souls
are easily offended.
    "Monsieur," continued the Count, addressing Sainville,
"these ladies are too virtuous to let historical recitations stir
their imaginations. *The more the infamy of vice is revealed*   30
to the world (writes a famous man somewhere), *the greater*
the dread of it is summoned by a virtuous soul. Even where

o obscenities occur in what you are about to tell us, such things
may revolt, disgust, and instruct but never arouse." Fixing his
gaze upon Madame de Blamont, the honest old military man
added: "Remember, Madame, that Empress Livia, whom I always compare to you, liked to say that *for the chaste woman,*
5 *naked men are statues.* So talk to us, Monsieur, let your words
be decent; all is acceptable with proper terms; be honest and
truthful, and most of all hide nothing. What you've seen and
experienced seems to us so very interesting that we don't want
to miss a thing."
10

The palace of the King of Butua, *resumed Sainville,* was guarded by women — black, yellow, mulatto, and light-skinned Negroes;* except for the latter, who were small and stunted, the
15 rest, as far as I could see, appeared to be tall, strong, and 20 to
30 years old. They were completely naked, not even wearing
the loincloth that by decency partly covers the bodies of other
African peoples. All were armed with bows and arrows; as
soon as they saw us, they lined up on both sides to let us pass.
20 Although the palace was single-storied, it was vast. We passed
through several apartments furnished with straw mats before
reaching the king. Female troops guarded the rooms through

---

* Negro monarchs keep such women, however frightful they seem, in their palaces
as luxury possessions and they enjoy them as a form of elegant refinement. All men
are not excited to the act of pleasure by the same features; thus, what is singularly
beautiful, just as that which is excessively ugly, may equally excite, owing solely to the
different sex organs. There is no definite rule and beauty itself has no objective reality,
none that could not be contested. It may be viewed in one climate one way, but differently in another. As the earth's inhabitants do not unanimously agree, it is possible
that some people of the same nation find a frightful thing very beautiful while others
might find it ugly. All is a matter of taste and organization, and only fools, as to this
and everything so related, insist on pedantry of the *rule.*

which we passed. A further detail of six guards — taller and   0
infinitely more attractive — led us through a woven wicker
door that brought us to the monarch. He could be seen at
the head of the room, on an elevated platform, half-lying on
cushions made of leaves covering highly crafted mats; about
30 women surrounded him, much younger than those I'd seen   5
engaged in military duties. Some were still children, most
from 12 to 16 years of age. Facing the throne was an idol upon
an altar, 3 feet tall, a dreadful bloody figure, half-man and half-
snake, with female breasts and the horns of a goat. Such was
the God of the kingdom. On the altar steps before my eyes   10
was the most horrible scene. The King had just committed a
human sacrifice; this palace was also his temple. His just-
murdered victims were still palpitating at the feet of the idol.
Lacerations covered the wretched victims and blood flowed
everywhere, with heads separated from bodies — all of it   15
combined to chill my senses. I flinched from horror.

The King asked who I was, and when informed he pointed to a tall white man, wiry and sunburned, about 66 years
old. The fellow, whose approach he ordered straightaway, addressed me in a European tongue. After I replied in Italian   20
that I did not know his language, he immediately answered in
fluent Tuscan and we became acquainted. He was Portuguese;
his name was Sarmiento. Some 20 years ago he'd been captured like me. He had become attached to the Court and no
longer thought about Europe. With him as interpreter I told   25
my story to Ben Mâacoro — such was the name of the King,
who seemed eager to learn all the details; I omitted none.
When told that I put up with all these dangers for the sake of
a woman, he laughed uproariously.

"Two thousand within my palace walls," he said. "Yet not   30
one would make me budge. You Europeans are insane to worship the female sex. A woman is made for pleasure, not adora-

tion; it insults the Gods to confer upon simple creatures the status of cult. It is absurd to grant authority to women and dangerous to become subservient to them; it debases your sex and insults Nature; it is to become enslaved to human beings who are beneath us."

With no chance to refute, I asked the Portuguese fellow where the King had acquired such knowledge of our countries.

"He has formed his opinion on the basis of what I've told him," answered Sarmiento. "He's never met a European apart from you and me."

I solicited my freedom; the King bade me approach. I was naked: he examined my body. He touched it everywhere, much as a butcher examining a steer, and he told Sarmiento that I was too thin to be eaten and too old for *his pleasures.*

"For his *pleasures!*" I cried. "What! Aren't there enough women?"

"It's precisely because there are too many; he's had his fill," replied my interpreter. "O Frenchman! Don't you know the effects of satiety? It depraves; it corrupts tastes and proclivities, all the while seeming to elevate them. When seeds germinate in the soil, and fertilize and reproduce, isn't that a form of corruption? Isn't corruption the first law of generation? After you've spent time here discovering the customs of our country, perhaps you'll become more the philosopher."

"Friend," said I to the Portuguese, "nothing I see or have learnt from you instills in me any desire to remain here. I should prefer to return to Europe, where we don't eat men or sacrifice girls, where we do not *use* boys."

"I will ask on your behalf," he answered, "but I seriously doubt it will help."

Indeed, he talked to the King and the answer was negative. Although my chains were removed, the monarch told me that as his explainer was growing old, he was designating me

as his intended replacement. With his help I'd easily learn the   o
language of Butua. The Portuguese would show me my duties at court. My life would be spared only on condition that I
fulfill them. I bowed and we went out.

Sarmiento instructed me in the nature of his duties. But
he began by explaining what I needed to know about the coun-   5
try itself. The Kingdom of Butua was larger than it seemed,
he told me; it extended all the way south to the border with
the Hottentots, a neighboring territory that intrigued me and
might offer the hope, I thought, that by passing through it I
might reach the Dutch possessions, as I so ardently desired.   10

"To the north," Sarmiento continued, "the country stretch-
es to the Kingdom of Monoèmugi; it reaches the Mountains
of Lupata to the east and borders the land of the Jagas on the
west. It's the size of Portugal. Each month brings a tribute of
women to the monarch from all regions of the kingdom. You   15
will be inspector of this particular levy; but you'll only examine their bodies; they'll never be shown to you except veiled;
keep those with the best physique and reject the others. The
tribute usually comes to five thousand in number; you will
always retain a full complement of two thousand. That is your   20
duty. If you love women, you'll certainly suffer, unable to see
their faces and obliged to give them up without enjoying them.
But carefully consider and remember what the King told you:
Do or die. He might not be so generous with others."

"But why," I asked the Portuguese, "did he choose a Euro-   25
pean for these duties? A man from his own country, it seems
to me, would be more sensitive to the kind of beauty that
suits him."

"Not at all. According to him, we're better judges in these
matters than his subjects. A few thoughts that I communi-   30
cated to him when I arrived here convinced him my taste
was excellent and my ideas judicious. So he assigned me the

task and I acquitted myself nicely. Now I'm getting old and he wants to replace me when another European turns up with, as he supposes, the same aptitude. Nothing could be simpler."

I drew a clear conclusion: to succeed in my planned escape, I had first to acquire his trust. With the means to earn it on offer, how could I refuse? Also, I guessed that Léonore might be on the African seas; I was coming from Morocco. Could chance itself not bring her to this empire? Even if veiled, would I not recognize her? Could a lost love escape detection?

"But at least," I said to the Portuguese, "I hope such dainty snacks upon which the king seems to feast will not be submitted for my inspection. I shall quit if I have to deal with boys."

"Never fear," replied Sarmiento. "He has confidence in his own judgment concerning such prey. Few such tributes arrive at the palace and he alone chooses."

While we talked Sarmiento led me from room to room and I saw the entire palace save for the secret harems that included the most beautiful of both sexes, but in which no mortal might set foot.

"The 12,000 women belonging to the King," Sarmiento went on, "are divided into four classes. He himself decides their status when he receives them once they're chosen. The tallest, strongest, and best-built women he assigns to the detachment guarding the palace. Others, whom we call the *five hundred slaves,* represent a type of individual inferior to the first class; most are 20 to 30 years old and service the palace within, take care of the gardening, and perform general chores. A third category includes women from 16 to 20; these are used for the sacrifices; from among them are drawn victims to be immolated for the sake of his god. Finally, the fourth category includes the most delicate and beautiful, including children and young women up to 16 years old. These are the ones who serve his pleasures, white women among them, if there are any."

"Have there been some?" I eagerly interrupted.

"Not yet," replied the Portuguese, "but he ardently desires them and makes every effort to procure them."

Hearing those words sparked hope in my heart.

"Despite these categories," he resumed, "the women from every group must satisfy the tyrant's brutality. When he desires one, he sends an officer to give any woman he desires 100 lashes. Not unlike the Sultan's handkerchief in Byzantium, she thus learns of the honor accorded her and then is brought before the King. Because he often makes use of a large number in a single day, each morning a great number of women are forewarned as just described."

Here I trembled — *O Léonore!* I told myself, *should you fall into the hands of this monster and I could not save you, would it be possible that the charms I adore be so shamefully despoiled? Great God! Take my life rather than expose you to such a tragedy; let me be turned to dust a thousand times over than see the one I love so cruelly abused!*

"Friend," I said, overwhelmed by the awful thought that the Portuguese had just put in my head, "carrying out the refinement of horror you've just told me about — it won't concern me, I hope?"

"No, no," said Sarmiento, bursting into laughter. "The chief of the seraglio takes care of all that; your duties have nothing in common with his. You choose. Of the 5,000 women who arrive each year, 2,000 will come under his authority. Once you choose, nothing further is required of you."

"Good," I answered. "Because if I were obliged to cause those poor young women to weep and moan — I warn you — I'd immediately desert. I shall fulfill my duties while thinking only of the woman whom I adore. These creatures will receive from me neither punishment nor favor; the privations jealousy imposes don't bother me."

"Friend," answered the Portuguese, "you seem to be a gallant sort, a lover from the 10th century. I discern in you a fearless knight of chivalrous antiquity — a charming virtue, though I don't share it. Today we won't see His Majesty again; it's late, you must be hungry. Come to my home for refreshment, I'll complete your instruction tomorrow."

Following my guide, he bade me enter a residence built in the same style as that of the King's palace, though considerably less spacious. Two young Negroes served supper on woven rush mats, and we seated ourselves in the African manner, for the Portuguese was wholly naturalized and had completely assimilated the native habits and customs.

A slab of roasted meat was brought and after saying grace (such superstitions never desert the Portuguese), the saintly fellow offered me a filet from the platter just laid before us.

Suddenly I was seized by an involuntary impulse.

"Tell me the truth, as a fellow European," I said, unable to hide my apprehension, "the meal you're serving me would not by chance be a portion of the hip or buttocks from one of those demoiselles whose blood earlier flooded the altar of your master's idol?"

"What of it!" replied the Portuguese phlegmatically. "Would such details stop you? Do you imagine you're going to live here without accepting the local diet?"

"Scoundrel!" I screamed, pulling away from the table, ready to heave the gorge. "Your delight makes me tremble. I'd die rather than touch it. How dare you ask heaven's blessing for this dreadful meal? Abominable fellow! Your mishmash of crime and superstition already tells me where you're from. I should've known."

Horrified, I rose to leave. But Sarmiento stopped me.

"Wait," he said. "I forgive your disgust in consideration of the customs and the prejudices of your country. But not to indulge them. Stop being difficult and learn to adapt. Disgust

is only a weakness, my friend; a minor disorder of organization   o
that if not cured while young becomes our master if we let it.
'Tis the same for many other things. Imagination seduced by
prejudice creates repugnance. But if we try it, we like it. Prox-
imity determines our taste more powerfully than the force of
repulsion. I arrived here as you did, with my mind filled with   5
stupid ideas from my country; I disapproved of everything
and found it all absurd: the people's customs frightened me as
much as their morality; yet today I do just like them. We owe
more to habit than to Nature, my friend. The latter creates us;
the other shapes us. It's foolish to believe there exists a moral   10
good covering all manner of conduct, which is absolutely neutral in itself and becomes right or wrong depending upon the
country in which it's judged. The wise man, if he wants to live
happily, must adapt where taste and climate lead. In Lisbon I
might have done like you but here in Butua I behave like the   15
Negroes. So then! What in damnation do you want for your
supper since you don't want what everybody else is having?
I've got an old monkey but it will be tough; I shall order it
grilled."

"All right then. I should certainly eat the rump or saddle   20
of your monkey with less disgust than the fleshy parts of your
king's sultanas."

"Not *that*, by Christ! We don't eat women's flesh; it's too
stringy and tasteless, and you shan't see it served anywhere.*

---

* The most delicate, so we hear, is the flesh of young boys. A shepherd in German
constrained by necessity to devour such an awful repast, acquired a taste for it and
certified it to be the best. An old woman in Brazil told Pinto, the Portuguese governor,
the very same thing. Saint Jerome attested to the fact and added that during his voyage in Ireland, he had observed that, among shepherds, eating male children was an
established custom; they preferred the fleshy parts, he said. See also James Cook's
A Second Voyage Round the World.

0   The succulent meat you disdain is the thigh of a Jagas, killed yesterday in combat — fresh, young, and oven-cooked in its own juices. Take a look. But never mind. Whilst you feast on your monkey, let me nibble a few morsels."

   "Never mind your monkey," I said, perceiving a plate of

5   fruits and cakes manifestly prepared for our dessert. "Take your abominable supper by yourself. Let me eat some of this — in a corner as far from you as possible. It will more than suffice."

   "My dear compatriot," said the *man-eating* European as

10   he devoured his Jagas, "you'll overcome your illusions: I've already seen you denouncing many things hereabouts that one day you will turn to as delicacies; nothing can prevent habit from shaping our tastes, there is none we cannot acquire."

   "Listening to you, my brother, your master's depraved

15   pleasures must have quickly become your own."

   "Many of them, my friend. Look about at these young Negroes; as with him, they taught me to do without women and I can tell you that consequently I fear no privation. Were you less scrupulous, I'd offer you a sample, just as I would this —"

20   and he held up the disgusting piece of meat he was devouring — "but you'd turn me down."

   "Doubt not, old sinner. Rest assured I'd flee your infamous country no matter the risk of being eaten by its inhabitants, rather than stay a minute longer if it meant corruption

25   of my morals."

   "The custom of eating human flesh ought not to be considered an aspect of moral corruption. It is as simple to nourish oneself with human flesh as to eat beef.* You might

---

* Cannibalism is certainly not a crime, which it can surely induce, but remains itself morally neutral. To discover its original cause is impossible, Messieurs Meunier, Pauw, and Cook have written extensively on the subject but have never resolved it; ☞

say that war, which destroys members of the human species, is   o
a plague; but after such destruction, whether of the entrails of
the earth or of a human being, either one, may serve as sepulcher for the disorganized elements; it's absolutely all the same."

"Very well. But if flesh arouses gourmandism," I replied,
"as you and those who eat it claim, the impulse to destroy   5
can induce fulfillment of this delight, at which point crimes
conceived soon become crimes committed. Travelers relate
that savages eat human flesh but forgive the practice by as-
serting that they only eat their enemies; yet who can say with
assurance that those savages who today devour those killed   10
in battle didn't start by making war for the pleasure of eating
people? In that case, would there be any taste more dangerous
or more to be condemned? It would become the first among
motives for men to fight and destroy one another."

"Believe none of that, my friend," said Sarmiento. "Ambi-   15
tion, revenge, greed, and tyranny: those are the passions that
bring men to take up arms and force them to destroy one other.
It remains to decide if such destruction is as evil as we think
and if, in resembling a plague that propagates by the same

---

the second of these authors analyzed it best in his *Study of American Indians* (Vol. 1).
And yet we can read and reread the passage in question but gain nothing in the way
of erudition. What is certain is that the custom was once common on our planet and
is as old as the earth. But the cause and original motivation by which some portion
of a human body was placed before a human being to dine upon is completely unknown. Just four possible motives may be adduced that might have legitimized the
custom: superstition and religion, two which may count as one, disordered appetite
arising from the same cause as the hysterical vapors in women; and revenge. Several
features of historical fact sustain these motives, and need or depraved refinements of
debauchery may also be adduced. But it is impossible to know which of them gave rise
to the custom. In the beginning it was surely not a country but an individual, led to it
by one of these four motives, who gave an account of his experience: he praised the
food, and the nation progressively followed his example. It would not be unworthy,
it seems to me, for the various academies to offer a prize to the one that discovers the
indisputable origin of this custom.

o   principles, whether it's not equally useful. But all this would lead us too far astray: first we'd have to analyze how you, frail and vile creature without the power to create, can conceive the power to destroy. How could we come to your view that death is destruction, for Nature by its laws concedes nothing
5   of the sort; her acts are only a form of metempsychosis and perpetual reproduction. Then we'd have to demonstrate how such changes of form, which only serve to facilitate her creations, can become crimes against these laws, and how helping or serving them can at one and the same time outrage them.
10   You can see that such discussions would take too much time and rob you of sleep. Go to bed, my friend. If you like, take one of my Negrœs with you, or a few women if you prefer."

    "None of that would please me. Only a place to rest," I said to my respectable predecessor. "*Adieu*, I shall go to sleep dis-
15   liking your opinions and abhorring your customs while thanking heaven for the opportunity I've had to meet you."

The next morning Sarmiento came to wake me and told me, "I must finish your instruction regarding the master you'll be serving. Come with me. We'll have our talk during a walk in the country."

    He continued his explanations: "It is impossible to describe, my friend, the subjugation of women in this country. To possess many of them is a luxury but made little use of. Whether rich or poor, men think as one on the matter. Females are worked here like our beasts of burden in Europe. They sow and plow the fields and harvest the crops; in the house they clean and serve and, in addition, they are offered up to the gods and immolated. They are perpetually faced with the men's ferocity and barbarism and become victims of their ugly moods, intemperance and tyranny. Cast your eyes across

this corn field and you can see poor naked women cowering   o
as they plough the furrows, trembling beneath their husband's
whip as he drives them forward. Returning home, they will
cook and serve dinner, and receive a merciless hundred lashes
for the slightest negligence."

"The population must suffer awfully from these odious   5
customs."

"Indeed, it's nearly extinct. Two peculiar things have done
much to cause its downfall. One is the belief that a woman
is impure one week before and one week after the time of
month when Nature purges her. That leaves less than a week   10
when her husband believes her worthy to be used. The second,
equally destructive to the population, is strict abstinence, to
which a woman is condemned after giving birth. For the next
three years her husband has nothing to do with her. To these
causes of depopulation, we can add the ignominy to which the   15
same woman is subjected once she becomes pregnant. From
that moment she dares not appear in public; people laugh at
her and point fingers; even the temples reject her.* A population once overly dense must have authorized these ancient
customs: a people too numerous, constrained from expand-   20
ing or forming colonies, must necessarily destroy itself; today
these criminal practices are senseless in a kingdom that would
prosper from a surplus of subjects if it wanted to communicate with us Europeans. I suggested as much but they didn't
like it at all; I told them their nation will perish within a cen-   25
tury but they couldn't care less.

"If horror of propagation is imprinted upon the minds of
the subjects of this empire, it is all but engraved in stone in the

---

* Curiously enough, the debasement of pregnant women was reported in the South
  Seas Canary Islands by Captain Cook, and several countries in Asia and America
  observe the same custom.

o soul of the monarch. Not only do his tastes oppose what Nature wants, but even were he to abandon himself and succeed
in arousing a woman, she would be put to death for showing
too much ardor. She brings about life only to lose her own;
thus, these women take all precautions either to avoid procre-
5 ation or to destroy its fruits. Yesterday you were surprised by
how many women there were yet among that number barely
400 can be used. Banished without exception in a special
house during their time of infirmity, punished, or condemned
to death for the slightest infraction, or else sacrificed to the
10 gods, their numbers are in constant decline. Are even enough
women left to work in the gardens, care for the palace, and
service the monarch?"

"What are you saying!" I cried. "A woman who obeys
Nature's law becomes unfit to tend her master's gardens? It
15 seems cruel enough to make her work without judging her
unworthy of such tiring labor because she submits to the fate
heaven attaches to her humanity."

"Nevertheless. The King would not want the hands of a
woman in such a condition to touch a single leaf on his trees."

20 "Shame on a nation so enslaved by prejudice that it thinks
like this. It must be very close to its ruin."

"So it is, and although the kingdom is vast, today it counts
less than 30,000 souls. Weakened everywhere by vice and corruption, it will soon collapse and be taken over by the Jagas,
25 who submit today but will be victorious tomorrow. They only
need a chief to pursue revolution."

"Doesn't that show that vice is dangerous and moral corruption pernicious?"

"Not generally, no. I admit it might be so, relatively, for
30 an individual or nation but I deny it as a general rule. Such
difficulties mean nothing in Nature's greater scheme of things.
What difference to her the power of an empire, more or less,

whether it expands owing to its virtues or destroys itself by
corruption — a vicissitude that is one of the first laws of the
hand that governs us, in that the vices she occasions are necessary; Nature creates only to corrupt. Put another way, if vice
corrupts, then vice must be one of her laws. Crimes of the
Roman tyrants, which people find so dreadful, were Nature's
means for provoking the fall of empire. Society's conventions
are, therefore, opposed to those of Nature. Man punishes what
is useful to these all-encompassing laws and essential to those
of the universe itself. Don't shrink your ideas but let them be
writ large; remember that everything serves Nature, and no
change on earth does not fit with her purpose."

"So you're saying the most reprehensible conduct serves
Nature as well as the best?"

"Certainly. The gaze of the really wise man must be con-
sistent. He needs to be convinced of the nullity of difference
between actions and so choose the one better suited to self-
preservation or his own interests; such is the fundamental
difference between Nature's designs and those of man. The
former almost always profits from what harms the latter; vice
becomes useful to Nature while it often ruins a man. Thus a
man does wrong, if you like, by surrendering to his depraved
morals and perverse inclinations; but the evil he does is merely relative to the climate in which he lives. If you judge him
based on the general order of things, he's merely complied
with the laws; judge him on his own terms, you'll be able to
see his delight."

"Such a system annihilates all virtue."

"But once again, virtue is only relative, a truth of which
we must be convinced before passing through the porticoes of
the Academy. That's why I told you yesterday I wouldn't act in
Lisbon the way I do here. It's false that virtues exist except by
dint of convention; they're all local and the only ones worth-

while, the only ones that can make men happy, are those of the country in which he lives. Do you believe that an inhabitant of Peking could be happy in his own country with French virtues or, inversely, that Chinese vice could induce remorse in a German?"

"A virtue that's not universal has an unstable existence."

"What does it matter — solidity? Why do you need universal virtues when what's national can suffice?"

"And heaven? You yourself invoked it yesterday."

"My friend," said Sarmiento, "you confound custom born of habit with spiritual principles. Yesterday I might have followed a custom of my country but without believing that one kind of virtue pleases the Eternal One more than another. Recall the situation. We went out for a political talk and you made me a moralist whilst I was only a teacher.

"The Portuguese," continued Sarmiento, "once hoped to become the masters of this kingdom in order to extend their colonies from coast to coast, with nothing from Mozambique to Benguela to hinder their traders. But the people here refused to allow such a scheme."

"Why weren't you put in charge of the negotiations?" I asked.

"Me? You must understand me. Couldn't you guess from my principles that I've always worked solely for my own interests? When like you I was first brought to the empire, I was in exile on the African coast after an embezzlement scheme in the diamond mines of Rio de Janeiro, where I was employed as an intendant. As is common in Europe, I preferred to make a fortune for myself rather than for the king. I was wealthy and spent millions in the name of luxury and abundance. I was discovered because I didn't steal enough; a little more boldness and everything would have been kept quiet. Only second-rate criminals break their necks; the best most often

succeed. I should have been politically astute and pretended   o
to reform. Instead of flaunting my wealth like your ministers in France, I should have sold off my assets and declared
bankruptcy.* I didn't do it and so I lost. Ever since I began to
study men I noted that with their wise laws and superb maxims they've succeeded only in showing that the guiltiest are   5
always the happiest; he is unhappy who wrongly thinks he
must compensate by doing some little good to atone for the
wrongs he was fated to commit. Yet had I remained in exile,
I would have been unhappier still. Here at least I still enjoy
some authority and I play a kind of role. I choose to be a low   10
and slavish intriguer given to flattery, like all ruined rascals.
It's brought me success; I quickly learned the language and,
despite their awful customs, I conformed to them. I've told
you already, my dear friend, that true wisdom requires a man
adapt to the country in which he lives. With you destined to   15
replace me, my sincerest wish for your tranquility is that you
become capable of thinking the same way."

"Do you imagine that like you I plan to spend my life here?"

"If not, don't say a word. They won't suffer your departure
kindly once they come to know you. They'd fear your convey-   20
ing information to the Portuguese concerning their weaknesses. They'd rather eat you than let you go."

---

* Poor Sarmiento did not know to what extent the imbecilic expedient he mentions
worked in France — only poorly, for those who tried. Monsieur Sartine was dismissed
after resorting to this foolish idea. Few people in high positions, true, have stolen so
clumsily and with such impunity. Coming to Paris from Spain after 30 years as clerk
to become the public prosecutor with an income of 600,000 *livres*, Sartine dared
claim that he no longer could be useful to the king because he had impoverished
himself in His Majesty's service — a rare impudence well-suited to that despicable
adventurer; and while such insolent rascals were never deprived of their lives much
less their freedom or their assets, unfortunate servants were hanged for stealing five
cents. Such are the fine-tuned contradictions that make one despise any government
that tolerates them.

"Finish explaining to me, my friend, why your compatriots want to control the poor lands."

"Don't you know? We're the European brokers who furnish Negrœs to all merchant peoples on earth?"

"Execrable — the idea that you grow rich and happy from the despair and enslavement of your fellow man."

"O Sainville! You'll never be a philosopher! What makes you think men are all equal? The force differential between strength and weakness established by Nature clearly proves that she had to subjugate one group of men to another, and animals are essentially enslaved to all. No nation is without its inferior castes. Negroes are regarded in Europe as the Ilotes were in Lacedaemonia and pariahs by the people of the Ganges. A chain of universal morality is a chimera, my friend, possible among equals, but not between superior and inferior; diversity of interest necessarily destroys relational affinity. What do you expect there to be in common between one who can do everything and another who dares do nothing? It doesn't matter who's right; it's only a question of being convinced that the weakest is always wrong. In brief, so long as gold is reckoned sovereign wealth, and Nature buries it in the entrails of the earth, we shall need strong backs to extract it. To that problem owes the necessity of slavery. Whites subjugate blacks who themselves might have enslaved others; but one of the two had inevitably had to fall under the yoke of the other. 'Twas in the nature of things that the weakest be enslaved, and so it was with blacks, owing both to custom and climate. Finally, whatever your objection, it's no more surprising to find Europe putting Africa in chains than to see a butcher slaughtering the steer that will feed you. Might makes right everywhere. Can you think of anything more eloquent?"

"Surely there must be some greater wisdom," I replied. "We were created by the same hand; all men are brothers.

As such we owe each other mutual aid; and if Nature cre- | o
ated some who are weaker, it was to make available to the
others the charms of benevolence and humanity. But let's
get to the bottom of things. You made one continent supply
the other three with gold. Does gold really measure a state's
true wealth? Consider your country alone. Tell me, Sarmiento, | 5
do you believe that Portugal flourishes today with its mines?
Start from 1754, by which time it had received more than two
billion from Brazilian mines; and yet by then your nation possessed less than five million écus and was in debt to England
fifty million more — that is, you owed thirty-five times more | 10
than you owned. If gold impoverishes you to such an extent,
why do you sacrifice so much for the sake of extracting it from
the earth? And if I'm wrong, if it makes you rich, why do you
remain dependent on England?"

"'Twas the expansion of your French monarchy," returned | 15
Sarmiento, "that propelled us into England's embrace. Though
we endure it for other less clear reasons, that's essentially what
happened. No sooner did the House of Bourbon occupy the
throne of Spain than, instead of seeing your country as an ally,
we feared it as a powerful enemy. We hoped to find in England | 20
what Spain found in you; we didn't expect they would become
despotic protectors who took advantage of our weakness. We
blindly forged our own fetters. We allowed the importation
of English fabrics without reflecting on how such tolerance
would harm our own industry, without seeing that the Eng- | 25
lish were giving us only what they'd already established was
in their own interest. It was their profit and our loss. Such
was the time of our ruin: not only did our manufactures decline and English industry cannibalize our own, but the food-
stuffs we sold them were far from bringing revenues equiv- | 30
alent to the fabrics they imported, such that we had to pay
for them with gold from Brazilian mines. Our galleons were

compelled to moor in their harbors while rarely dropping anchor in our own."

"And so it was that England took over your commerce," I said. "You found it easier to be led than to lead. England thrived on your ruination and the dynamism of your ancient industry which, run to ground in your hands, she soon dominated. Meanwhile, luxury continued to undermine your country: you possessed gold but wanted it manufactured and so sent it to London to be crafted, which cost you twice because one part went to be molded for your luxury and another to payment for the labor. Even your crucifixes, reliquaries, rosaries, and ciboria were made by the English — all such instruments of idolatry by which superstition degrades the true cult of the Eternal One. Finally, they succeeded in subjugating you to such an extent that they took charge of your navigation in the Old World and sold you the vessels and ammunition for your colonies in the New World. While increasing their domination, they even took over your own domestic trade; only English stores were to be found in Lisbon, from which you made not the slightest profit because everything went to the principals. In all this you had only the vain honor of lending your name. They went further. Not only did they ruin your commerce; they also tarnished your credit by forcing you to deal with them alone. And they made of you, through such shameful servitude, the playthings of all Europe. A nation so demeaned would soon vanish and you saw it happen: arts, literature, sciences, all sunk under the wreckage of your commerce; everything deteriorates when it languishes; it is to a nation what nutrient juices are to the various parts of the body; it does not melt away without damage to the entire organism.

"To emerge from such torpor," I concluded, "would take a century and nothing on the horizon announces a new dawn.

You'd need a Peter the Great — but geniuses are not born   o
among people degraded by superstition. You must first shake
off the yoke of religious tyranny that weakens and dishonors;
then, little by little, activity will be restored, foreign merchants
will reappear in your harbors, and you'll sell them the products of your colonies from which the English have stripped   5
out only the gold. In this way you won't notice what has been
taken from you; you will still have as much left, your credit
will improve, and you will be free of their control."

"And so it is. We're reviving our factories."

"But first cultivate your land. Your factories will be sourc-   10
es of real wealth only when you plant your own soil with the
necessary raw materials. What profit can you make from the
fabrics you manufacture if you have to import the wool? What
benefit would you derive from your silk if you don't know how
to tend your blackberry bushes and silkworm cocoons? How   15
can your oils turn a profit if you don't take care of your olive
trees? Who will buy your wines if imbecilic regulations make
you tear out your wine stocks to grow wheat? Such idiocy
advances in ignorance of the fact that wheat never grows well
in soil proper to vineyards!"   20

"The Inquisition deprived us of those to whom we en-
trusted such detailed knowledge," said Sarmiento. "Brave
agriculturists whom it condemned and exiled taught us that
by tilling the earth, instead of delving into its bowels to mine
all the gold it might provide, we could render the colony more   25
useful to the country. The harsh and bloody tribunal is a major
cause of our decline."

"What keeps you from abolishing it? Why don't you do
with it what you did to the Jesuits, who never did you harm?
Destroy and annihilate without pity the gnawing worm that's   30
slowly undermining you; shackle with their own chains those
dangerous enemies of liberty and commerce; let's see no

more of the *auto-da-fe* in Lisbon; let the victims consumed by flames be the bodies of the evildoers themselves. If you had such courage, something quite good might happen. The English, rightfully opposed to that awful tribunal, would nonetheless become its defenders; they'd protect it because it serves their interests; they'd support it because it enslaves you in a way that suits them — just as the Turks long ago supported the Pope against the Venetians. For superstition is a truly powerful tool in the hands of despotism, and our own interests incite us to make others respect what we ourselves despise. Believe me, neither puerile respect nor any secondary consideration should make you neglect your agriculture. A nation is only truly rich by virtue of its surplus of necessities, yet you don't have even the essentials. Don't blame the slighter population, which is numerous enough to work your land. Your workers aren't weak but your administration lacks intelligence. Free yourself of withering inertia. Impoverished, sitting on your pile of gold, you remind me of the sort of plants that, lacking sustenance, briefly rise above the soil only to wilt moments later. Above all, restore your navy, which in the past provided such prestige; bring back those glorious times when the Portuguese flag opened onto the golden gates of the East; when it was the first to courageously round the unknown Cape of Storms and teach nations the routes to the precious Indies, from which they brought back such riches. Did you need the English then? Did they pilot your ships? Did their weapons chase the Moors from Portugal? Did they help you in your past struggles? Did they establish you in Africa? In a word, did they support you before your decline? Are you not the same people? In the end, you ought to have allies but never protectors."

"For that," said Sarmiento, "not only must the Inquisition be taken to task but the entire clergy, *en masse*. They must be

removed from the counsels and debates. Solely occupied with
turning us into bigots, they prevent us from becoming merchants, soldiers, or farmers. How can we destroy the power
that thrives on our weaknesses?"

"You can do it just the way England's Henry VIII eliminated constraints on his people. Today the Inquisition makes
you tremble — but did you fear it as much when you condemned to death the Grand Inquisitor of Lisbon for having
joined the conspiracy against the House of Braganza? What
did you do then? Why not dare do it now? Don't those who
conspire against the nation deserve a fate more frightful than
those who plot against kings?"

"We mustn't hope for such change. It would be risky to
stir up the nation by taking away the trinkets they've played
with for centuries. The Portuguese love the chains that oppress them far too much to break them. In addition, the English impose themselves upon us. Our first fault was to accept
the yoke. Inescapable. We're like children who stumble when
the apron strings are removed. Perhaps it would be best if
we stay as we are. When exhausted, change is harmful."

Just at that moment in our conversation, 10 or 12 savages
arrived, together with some 20 black women, on the way to
the palace.

"Ah!" said Sarmiento, "Now comes the tribute from one of
the provinces. Let's return promptly, for the King will surely
want you to take up your duties."

"But at least tell me: how do I deduce the kind of beauty
he desires? Unless I know, how can I possibly meet his
expectations?"

"First, you will never see their faces; they'll always be concealed. As I said, two Negroes, clubs at the ready, will stand
nearby during your examination to keep you from temptation.

However, later you'll see some of them with impunity; once delivered, he shields us only from those he covets the most. But as he does not know which among them he'll want when they arrive, all are veiled. As for their bodies, your eyes being unaccustomed to the charms of these Negresses, I understand your difficulty in discerning those who will please him. But color means nothing to beauty in terms of form. As to their shapes, let them be regular, lovely, well-proportioned. Reject without exception all imperfections that could undermine delicacy — their flesh must be firm and fresh. Verify virginity — a most essential point. Sublimity in voluptuous forms made a masterpiece of the Grecian Venus who was deemed worthy of a temple for that most sensitive and enlightened people. In any event I shall be present at first. Look into my eyes and you'll see the right choice reflected therein."

Informed of the detachment just arrived, the monarch had already asked about us and gave the order, as Sarmiento expected, for me to begin immediately. After a few hours of rest and refreshment, the women were brought to a remote apartment in the palace. Soon I found myself standing between two Negroes, their clubs high over my head, with Sarmiento at my side. There I started to exercise my so important and respected function. The youngest among them embarrassed me. Half were under 12 years old. How find *beauty* in shapes barely sketched? But on a sign from Sarmiento, I unhesitatingly admitted them if I discovered no essential flaws. The other half offered more fully developed charms and I had less difficulty in choosing. I turned back those of sizes and proportions so coarse that I could scarce dare present them. With the monarch waiting impatiently, Sarmiento delivered the results of my first operation. He immediately took the women into his secret apartments and the emissaries were sent away together with the females I hadn't chosen.

An order came for me to be settled in a residence close to   o
that of the Portuguese.

"We can leave," said my predecessor. "The monarch, occupied in examining his recent acquisitions, won't be seen for
the rest of the day."

"But can you conceive," I said to Sarmiento as we walked   5
back, "how a human being could require for his debauches
seven or eight hundred women?"

"It all seems normal to me."

"Dissolute man!"

"You're wrong to insult me. Isn't it natural to seek to mul-   10
tiply our pleasures? However beautiful a woman, however
passionate you are, after a fortnight it's impossible not to tire
of the monotony of her features. How can one whom we know
inside and out inflame desire? Isn't arousal more certain when
the exciting objects are in constant flux? Whereas you've only   15
one sensation, the man who changes and multiplies experiences a thousand of them. Inasmuch as desire is only the effect of irritation caused by the collision of atoms of beauty
upon the animal spirits,* the vibrations of which give rise to
the force and multitude of such collisions, isn't it clear that the   20
more you multiply what causes the shocks, the more violent
the irritation? Moreover, who would doubt that 10 women before us at the same time will produce, from the emanation of
the multitude of shocks of their atoms upon the animal spirits,
an inflammation more violent than could be produced by a   25
single one?"

---

* By "animal spirits" we refer to the electrical fluid that circulates in the cavities of our
nerves. All our sensations owe to the irritation of this fluid; it is the basis of pain and
pleasure — in a word, the only kind of soul admitted by modern philosophers. Lucretius would have reasoned still more acutely had he known of it, given the principles
around which he came close to this truth without yet seizing upon it.

o "In such debauchery I see neither principles nor sensitivity. To me it's nothing but revolting brutishness."

"Why worry about principles when it comes to a pleasure
we're sure to obtain only when we break down barriers? As
to sensitivity, forget the idea that it enhances sensual plea-
5 sure. Perhaps good for love and useful to the metaphysics of
it, but for the rest, it adds nothing. Do you believe that Turks,
or Asians more generally, who commonly take pleasure de-
tached, are not as happy as you — and where do you see sensitivity? A Sultan indulges in pleasures unconcerned about
10 sharing them.* Who even knows but that certain individuals,
capriciously organized, don't view such vaunted sensitivity
as harmful to their pleasures? All those maxims that seem
wrong to you may have their reasons. Ask Ben Mâacoro why
he severely punishes the women who dare share in his plea-
15 sure. He will respond — as will three-quarters of the world's
inhabitants (badly organized, you say) — that a woman who
experiences as much pleasure as a man is concerned with
something besides the man's pleasure; and such distraction
compels her to take care of herself and neglect her duties to
20 the man; he who wants a full measure of pleasure must draw
it all unto himself. What a woman subtracts from the sum of

---

* "Nothing is simpler to imagine," said Fontenelle (surely the most sensitive of our
poets), "than that one might be happy in love thanks to a person whom one does not
make happy. There exist solitary pleasures that need not be communicated; it is only
the pure effect of self-love or vanity, not the desire to do good unto others, which
owes to intolerable pride: one accepts being happy only on the conditions that the
same is rendered to the other. Is not the sultan in his seraglio far more modest? He
receives pleasures without number and does not pretend to render any in return. If
we study the heart of man, we will find that sensitivity is so overestimated that it is
nothing but the debt one pays to pride; it's nothing we want." *Dialogues of the Dead:
Soliman and Julietta de Gonzaga.*

This sentiment is found in Montesquieu, Helvetius, La Mettrie, etc., and will
always be the expression of true philosophers.

sensual enjoyment always comes at the expense of the man's   o
pleasure. The objective in those moments is not to give but
to receive. The sentiment one gets from the benefit *granted*
is merely moral and therefore suitable only for a certain kind
of person; by contrast, *received* gratification is physical and
necessarily suitable for all, a quality that makes it preferable   5
to that which can be only apperceived by some. In a word, the
pleasure tasted with an inert being cannot help being complete, because only one agent experiences it, and, thus, it's
far livelier."

   "In that case," I replied, "we might as well say that a statue   10
provides sweeter satisfaction than a woman of flesh and blood."

    "You don't understand me at all. The voluptuous plea-
sure that people imagine consists in what the succubus *can*
but does *not* do, in faculties it must possess but employs only
in *doubling* the sensation of the incubus, not trying to feel its   15
effects."

   "In all that, my friend, I see only tyranny and sophisms."

   "Sophisms — not at all. As to tyranny, so be it. Indeed, how
do you know it doesn't enhance sensual pleasure? Sensations
reinforce each other: pride, which is of the mind, adds to sen-   20
sation; despotism, pride's child, may likewise make pleasure
more intense. Look at the animals. See how they retain such
superiority and the kind of sensual despotism you stupidly
reject; see the imperious ways they have with females, caring
little to share what they feel, and indifferent once their need is   25
extinguished. Does not Nature teach it is always thus? Let us
sort out our ideas as to how she operates. If she wanted equality of feeling as regards pleasure, she would have built it into
the constitution of the creatures themselves; yet we observe
the opposite. As one of the two sexes has decided superior-   30
ity, how not be convinced of it as proof of Nature's intention?
Or that this force and authority, constantly manifested by the

one who possesses it, would not be found equally in acts plea-
surable and otherwise?"

"I see all this very differently. Sensual pleasures must be a
very sorry affair when not shared. *Isolism* frightens me. I consider it a plague, punishment for a cruel or villainous human
being, abandoned by the whole world and therefore, too, by
his companion. He who can't spread happiness ought not to
feel it."

"By such pusillanimous principles we are forever stuck in
childhood and go nowhere. See how we live and die amidst the
fog of prejudice, lacking the strength and energy to attack it."

"What need for that, from the moment it outrages virtue?"

"Virtue, always more useful to others than to us, is not the
essential thing; truth alone serves us and if we find it only by
moving away from virtue, is it not better to reach the light by
such diversion than remain in the dark and be a good-hearted
dupe?"

"I'd prefer being weak and virtuous rather than bold and
corrupt. Your soul has been degraded at the dangerous school
of the awful monster whose court you inhabit."

"No, it's Nature's fault. She endowed me with a vigorous
organization that seems to swell with age and cannot agree
with common prejudices. What you call my depravity is only
the story of my life; I've found happiness in my systems and
never known remorse. By this tranquility, borne along the evil
path, I convinced myself of the insignificance of the actions of
men. In lighting the torch of philosophy at the ardent hearth
of passions, I saw from its glow that one of Nature's first laws
was to vary her works and only in their opposition could be
found the equilibrium that maintains general order. Why is it
necessary to be virtuous, I told myself, when it's just as well to
be evil? Everything Nature creates is necessary but not useful
as regards ourselves; so it's easy to be malicious, relative to

my fellows, while still seeming to be good in their eyes. Why
should I care?"

"But aren't there men who'll punish you for having outraged them?"

"He who fears them hath no pleasure."

"He who defies them is sure to irritate and, as the interest   5
of the many is always at odds with that of the individual, one
who sacrifices everything for himself and disregards what he
owes others, heeding only what gratifies him, will meet with
pitfalls and must ineluctably succumb."

"The prudent man avoids them and the wise man learns   10
not to fear. Place your hand upon this heart, my friend. Though
vice has reigned here fifty years, observe how calm."

"Perverted tranquility is the fruit of habit and owes to
false principles. Don't lay them at Nature's door; sooner or
later she'll punish you for outraging her."   15

"So be it. I raise my eyes to heaven and await the bolt of
lightning. I do not hold forth the arm that launches it — but
glory to me that I brave it."

And we entered the abode that was to be mine.

It was a simple place, partitioned by screens into three   20
or four rooms, in which I found several Negro servants, provided by the King. They had been ordered to ask if I wanted
any women; I declined and dismissed them as well as the Portuguese, assuring him that I only needed to rest.

Once alone, I seriously reflected on my unfortunate fate.   25
The villainous soul of the only European in my company made
him seem just as dangerous as the murderous cannibals upon
whom I depended. And this awful role I was to play — the infamous work I had to do or die. It didn't diminish my feelings
for Léonore — I'd carried it out with such disgust and hor-   30
ror that nothing of what I owed that charming young woman
could be in any way compromised. But I did it, and the awful

duty conferred such bitterness on my situation that I would have fled immediately but, as I've told you, there was my hope that Léonore might be brought here and I would come upon her — or so I might imagine — and it eased my distress.

I had not lost her portrait, which by precaution I'd kept secure in my wallet with my letters of credit. You cannot imagine what a portrait means to a sensitive soul. One must be in love to understand the comfort it can provide, the great charm of contemplating at leisure the divine features that enchant you, of gazing upon the eyes that follow yours, to address this beloved image just as if the tender object it depicts were in your arms — sometimes, wet with your tears, warmed by your sighs, brought to life by your kisses — art that is sublime and delicious and inspired only by the love that guided the painter's brush. So it was that I took up this captivating token of my love. On my knees, I invoked her thus: *O, you whom I idolize, I sincerely swear that amidst horrors my heart will remain forever pure. Fear not that the temple in which you reign will ever be soiled by crime. Beloved wife, console me in my torments; fortify me against defeat. Ah! Crime, if it approached, would soon be rebuffed by a simple kiss plucked from your rose red lips.*

It was late. I fell asleep and awakened the next day when Sarmiento came to invite me to for a second walk together in a place I'd not yet visited.

"Do you know," I asked, "if my work satisfied the monarch?"

"Yes. He asked me to tell you so," said the Portuguese as we started out. "You are now as knowledgeable as I. You shan't need any more of my lessons. I was told he spent the whole night in debauchery. This morning he will purify himself by a sacrifice of six victims. Do you want to witness it?"

"Oh! Great heavens!" I answered fearfully. "Protect me as you can from such frightful spectacles!"

"I well understand. You wouldn't like it, all the more be-   o
cause you'd see some of the very objects you chose go under
the sword."

"And therein lies my torment. I thought about it all night.
It shall make the work unbearable. When one I choose becomes victim, I will die from cruel remorse. Knowing as much   5
will give rise in my mind to the frightful idea I could have
saved her had I found some flaw — yet did not."

"Again a childish chimera from which you should free
yourself. If fate did not befall this one, it would take another.
For the sake of tranquility, you have to get beyond all such   10
petty nonsense. Does the general who blasts to kingdom
come the enemy's left flank feel remorse because he might
have saved it by crushing the right? If the fruit must fall, why
not shake the tree?"

"Enough of your cruel consolations. Let us take up once   15
more the details of what I must learn of the despicable country which I'm unfortunately compelled to inhabit."

"One must be born, like me, in a hot climate," continued
the Portuguese, "to become used to the burning heat; the air
is tolerable only from April to September. The rest of the year   20
is so cruelly hot that it's common to see animals in the countryside expired under the blazing sun. To the extreme heat we
can surely attribute the moral corruption of the people; we can
scarcely realize the extent to which the air works upon a man's
constitution, how he may be honest or vicious depending on   25
the weight of the air upon his lungs and its quality — more or
less healthy, more or less scorching.* Those who believe like
you that laws apply to all men despite the atmospheric varia-

---

* The difference comes to 3,982 livres of air pressure to which we are subject, depending on variations in the weather. Is it at all astonishing that we are capable of noticing
a clear difference between one season and another?

tions dare say so in the face of those fundamental truths! But you must admit: here corruption could not be more extreme. Every kind is common, and all go unpunished. A father does not distinguish between daughter, son, slave, or wife — all serve his lascivious debaucheries. The despotism he enjoys at home, his absolute power over life and death, makes it truly hard on those who would oppose him. Whatever their need for women, the men treat the ones they possess no better. I've already described the way they're treated in general; at home they have it just as bad. Only on her knees may a spouse address her husband; she is never allowed to sit at the table and for food receives only scraps tossed to her in a corner, as we do with animals. Does it matter if she succeeds in giving him an heir? Where we are from, it's a distinction that elevates her. Here extreme contempt and abandonment and disgust, as I said, are the rewards she receives from her cruel husband. Often, still more ferocious, he does not let her give birth but destroys his own offspring. What happens if despite his efforts the unfortunate fruit of the womb comes into the world? If the father doesn't like it, he kills it straightaway. The mother has no rights to the young child and won't acquire any when he attains the age of reason; then he will join his father in mistreating the one who gave him life.* Women of the common folk are not the only ones to be treated this way; those of the powerful share the ignominy. The fate of wild animals is preferable. We conceive with difficulty the level of submission and humiliation to which they are reduced — constantly trembling, expecting to die any moment at their tyrant's merest whim.

---

* It is possible that the people hold to this execrable custom of their Hottentot neighbors, where it is everywhere established. Of singular interest is the fact that Captain Cook discusses it on several of his voyages, particularly the one which took him to New Zealand.

"Think of the old feudal government of Poland to have
some notion of what goes on here. The kingdom is divided
into 18 small provinces, similar to those vast seigniorial lands
in Europe. The Chief of each lives in the district and enjoys
almost the same authority as the King. His subjects answer
directly to him; he may dispose of them as he likes. There
are laws — perhaps even too many — but all tend to make
the weak submit to the strong and maintain the despotism
that renders men unhappier still. Yet, although they might
in turn exercise the same despotism in their own homes, in
fact they're masters of nothing. From the soil he harrows by
sweat and toil, a man has only food enough for himself and his
family. Everything else belongs to his Chief, who is sole and
absolute owner on condition that he deliver an annual tax to
the King, punctually and four times yearly, in currency of girls,
boys, and food. As his vassals provide the tribute, he has only
the burden of passing it on to them and, because he is taxed
proportionately by what he can pay, he is never overcharged.

"Crimes of thievery and murder, completely overlooked
among the high and mighty, are punished with the most extreme rigor if committed by an ordinary man anywhere outside his home. If he is the head of a family, its members are
considered his subjects and he is exempt from punishment
for offenses he commits on them. In other circumstance he
is sentenced to death. The guilty party, once arrested, is immediately brought before the Chief, who cuts him down with
his own hand; such executions create entertainments, like our
European hunting parties. Chiefs commonly detain criminals
until they have a certain number; then, gathering six or seven
together, they spend a few days mistreating them before fin-
ishing them off. These manhunts provide occasions for feasts
and debauchery that conclude with their wives, whom they
bring along to share out for pleasure. Within his own district,

the King exercises the same prerogative but it's larger so he has more opportunities to multiply these horrors.

"All Chiefs, no matter their authority, report directly to the King, who has the power to condemn and execute them on the spot and without trial for rebellion or crimes of *lèse majesté*. But the offence must be real for otherwise all would revolt and side with the condemned; they would overthrow a king whose despotism was unstable.

"The monarch of Butua is indifferent to posterity because the reign will not continue. It's not the same for his 18 grand vassals, whose children succeed their fathers in their fiefdoms. When a Chief dies, the elder son takes over the government and household. He reduces his mother and sisters to utter servitude. They are henceforth without standing, ranked beneath his wife's slaves unless he wishes to marry one of them. In that case, she is saved from abject servility; yet custom makes it just as hard to be a wife. If a woman is pregnant when the father dies, she must kill the offspring or herself be killed by the successor.

"With respect to the King, upon his death the Chiefs gather, and these barbarians, like their neighbors the Jagas, confuse cruelty with bravery by electing, as their new monarch, the most savage among them.* Over 9 days they perform feats with either prisoners of war or criminals, or else amongst themselves; they engage in extreme hand-to-hand combat. The most valorous — he who seems boldest and commits

---

* Bravery and ferocity may be confounded. What is bravery but the stifling of natural feelings to help us preserve ourselves? Ferocity involves protecting others but again requires suppressing Nature's laws. One is thus wrong to say that a ferocious man is never brave. Courage, that is to say, is only a type of ferocity and, philosophically speaking, it must be classified among the vices. Only our prejudices, which are far from Nature, make it a virtue.

the greatest atrocity — is chosen to be the commander; he   0
is carried triumphantly to his palace where further excesses
follow upon his election for nine days more. Intemperance
and debauchery may go so far that the new king himself suc-
cumbs and the ceremony starts anew. Rarely are these feasts
celebrated without costing many lives.   5

"When the nation goes to war with its neighbors, each
Chief provides the King with a contingent of men armed with
picks and arrows, and their number is proportional to the need.
If the enemy is powerful, a considerable number of troops are
deployed; fewer for a simple dispute. The cause is always some   10
land that's been ravaged, or the abduction of women or slaves;
combat ensues after a few days of preliminary hostility, then
all is resolved and the opponents return home.

"Despite the low morality of these people and the numerous crimes they commit, they are devout, credulous, and su-   15
perstitious; the power of religion over them is almost as great
and violent as it is in Spain and Portugal. The theocratic government is feudal. A religious potentate resides in the same
city as the King. Subordinate to him are religious headmen
assigned to each province, each of whom commands a college   20
of secondary priests and lives with them in a vast building
next to the temple. The idol is everywhere the same as the one
found in the palace of the monarch, who alone is privileged
to have a private chapel separate from the temple where he
makes his sacrifices. The serpent, which is revered here, is the   25
most ancient of venerated reptiles; its temples may be found
in Egypt and Phoenicia, and also Greece, from which the cult
spread everywhere in Asia and Africa.* For the people here,

---

* The serpent is an emblem of God's rival. From the Jews we know the story of the
bronze serpent. The cult of the serpent is. in a word, universal. The instrument in the
form employed in our churches is a retention of this idolatry.

the idol is the image of the Creator of the world; and to justify
the representation as half human and half animal, they say, is
to show that He created both.

"The governor of every province must provide 16 victims
each year, of both sexes, to the religious headman who, together with his college of priests, immolates them at specific
dates as prescribed by ritual law. The idea of human sacrifice,
considered the purest that one can offer to the divinity, is the
result of pride. Man viewed himself as the utterly perfect being
on earth, imagining nothing could better appease the gods
than to sacrifice his fellow man. This explains why the custom
proliferated and multiplied to such an extent and people all
over the world adopted it. Celts and Germans immolated old
persons and prisoners of war; the Phœnicians, Carthaginians,
Persians, and Illyrians sacrificed their own children; the Thra-
cians and Egyptians, virgins, etc.

"In Butua, the priests are entirely in charge of educating
the young; they raise the sexes in separate schools over which
they exercise exclusive control. The major and almost only
virtue they inspire in women is complete resignation and the
profoundest submission to men's will; the priests persuade
them that they are uniquely created to depend upon men, and,
following Mohammed, are mercilessly damned when they die."

"Like Mohammed?" I interrupted Sarmiento. "You're
quite wrong, my friend. Your unfairness with respect to women
makes you embrace a notion both false and baseless. Mohammed does not damn women; I'm surprised that you, with your
vaunted erudition, are not more familiar with the Koran. The
prophet clearly states in his 60th chapter: 'Anyone of faith and
good morals will enter heaven'; and in several other places he
positively establishes that we will find in heaven not only the
women whom we most cherished on earth but also beautiful virgins — all of which proves that, apart from these latter

celestials, he would admit terrestrial women. It never entered
his mind to exclude them from eternal beatitude. Forgive this
digression in favor of the sex that you despise but I idolize —
and go on with your interesting stories."

"Whether Mohammed damns women or saves them,"
said the Portuguese, "they certainly won't make me yearn
for heaven — even if I believed the tale. Indeed, were they
wiped off the face of the earth, may Lucifer skin me alive if I'd
complain. Damnation to him who cannot forego, in his own
pleasures and in society, the inferior sex — false and deceptive,
ever harmful and dissembling, perfidious and convoluted, yet
able like a snake in the grass to lift its head in the instant it
takes to spit venom! But interrupt me no more if you want me
to continue.

"As for men," my instructor went on, "they submit, first
to the priests, then to the King, and most assuredly to their
Chiefs; they're always prepared to shed their blood for one or
the other.

"While debauchery in European schools is often a danger, here it is the rule. A husband would look down upon his
wife were she to give up her virginity to him.* That right belongs to the priests. Only they can pluck the illusory flower we
foolishly overvalue. Exempt from the rule are those women
destined for the King. Carefully locked away in the provin-
cial governors' houses, they attend no schools and the right
to take them, which priests dare not dispute, belongs to the
monarch, as chief of temporal and spiritual affairs. All such
depucelations take place on specific holidays in their calendar.
The temples are closed to all but the priests; the most impres-
sive silence reigns and anyone who disturbs it is unmercifully
put to death.

---

* These people are not alone in their view of the matter; we advise the reader, a character soon to appear will describe this custom in greater detail.

"The deflowering takes place at the feet of the idol. The chief starts and the whole college follows. Girls are offered twice, boys once; the sacrifices occur after the ceremony. At 13 or 14 years old, when students return to their families, they are asked whether they have been sanctified; if not, boys are horribly despised and girls find no husband. The practice takes place in the provinces just as in the capital, the only difference consisting in the monarch's right to perform, if he wishes, in front of the priests. Here, as in the kingdom of Juida, if somebody refused to send his children to school, the priests would kidnap them."

"What infamy!" I exclaimed. "All such turpitude scandalizes me to no end. I won't stand for pederasty in religious initiation. To what extent must a people be corrupted as to make a custom of the most disgusting vice, destructive to humanity, scandalous and wholly contrary to Nature?"

"Such invective!" answered the Portuguese, himself an unfortunate adept of this intolerable depravity. "Listen, my friend: allow me to digress a moment. I should like to convince you of your mistake at the risk of contradicting some of my principles, the better to prove the unfairness of your own.

"You shouldn't think," he continued, "that this sort of misbehavior, of which so much is made in Europe, is as consequential as some think. Howsoever you might envisage it, it would be dangerous for one reason only: *harm to the population as a whole.* But is this the case? Let's examine the situation. What happens when it's tolerated? We may suppose it results in a small reduction in the number of births. Is that so harmful? And what government is so weak as to be concerned by it? Must a state have more citizens than it can feed? Once some such number is exceeded, aren't all men fairly able to decide if they want to procreate or not? I know nothing more laughable than the endless protestations in favor of increasing

the population. Especially your fellow citizens, those dear   o
French who don't realize that their government treats them
with such indifference that emigration and death are of no
concern to it, that if the law sacrifices them daily and inhumanely, it's only due to overpopulation. A smaller population
would make people mean something to the state while sparing   5
them the atrocious blade of Themis.

"Let fools protest as loudly as they like; let them compile
their disgusting accumulation of sumptuous projects to increase the population, the excess of which already represents
one of their nation's greatest vices; and let's see if what they   10
want is good. I daresay it's not and declare that wherever you
have a middling population and limited wealth, the equality you seem to so favor will be more complete and consequently afford individuals greater happiness. A large population and more luxury produce inequality that results in much   15
unhappiness.

"In a small or middling populace, by contrast, all men are
brothers; but when covered in luxury and demeaned by sheer
number, they no longer know one another. As one and the
other increase, the rights of the stronger are born and grow   20
and gradually subjugate the weakest, despotism becomes established, and the people are degraded, soon finding themselves crushed beneath the weight of chains forged by overabundance.* What diminishes the population actually serves
the state instead of harming it. From a political standpoint, for   25
the nation's philosophers, therefore, the worst vice of all is in
fact a virtue, not a crime.

---

* Here Sarmiento contradicted his own principles, for we have seen and will see again
that he is far from a partisan of equality. It often happens that, in support of a system
under discussion with an informed person, one is obliged to distort some principle,
in terms of morality or opinions held, to better convince his adversary. That clearly
happened here with the Portuguese.

"Shall we consider it from Nature's point of view? Well, if Nature intended all grains to sprout, she would have made the soil of better quality so it needn't long remain fallow. Always fertile, it would await only planting and we could harvest all we sowed. Cast a glance upon the physiology of women and what do we see? One who lives 70 years, let us suppose, is of no use for the first 14, nor for about the last 20; that leaves 36 from which we must deduct 3 months of every year when indisposition prevents her from fulfilling Nature's plan, assuming she is sensible and wants the fruit to be good. Thus, Nature permits her at most 27 of 70 years. I must wonder if it's reasonable to think Nature intends nothing to be wasted when she allows so much to be lost.* And if her own laws establish as much, can we rightfully punish what she herself demands? Propagation is surely not a law of Nature but something she tolerates. Did she need us to create the first humans? You mustn't think we'd be any more necessary to her to preserve them; beliefs we adopt to the contrary are only the result of pride.

"Were not a man left on earth, everything would go on as before. We enjoy what we find here but nothing is created for us. Poor creatures, we're subject to the same contingencies as other animals; we're born and die like them yet can't live and multiply like them. We dare have pride. We dare believe ourselves to be a precious species for which the sun shines and the plants grow. What deplorable blindness! You can be sure that Nature would do as well without us as she would without ants and flies; and as a consequence we're not obliged to serve her by propagation and expansion of a species to which she is

---

* How few years of fertility would remain if we supposed a woman is pregnant every year, which subtracts nine months during which any seed goes wasted and can bring forth nothing. Women's fertility would not be more than 81 months in 70 years. What more proof do you want?

indifferent and whose total extinction would violate none of
her laws. Thus, we can be fewer without offending Nature in
any way — and indeed, I'm only saying that we serve her by
not increasing the numbers of a sort of creature whose complete ruination, in returning to her the honor of first creation,
would grant her a right that only her tolerance confers upon
us. That is the way of it with that so called terrible and dangerous vice, against which society stupidly passes laws to protect
itself; that is how, in fact, it shows its usefulness to the state
and to Nature, lending energy to the first by reducing the excess, and augmenting the power of the second, by allowing it
to exercise its principal function.

"And were this penchant not a natural one, would we receive its impressions from childhood? Would it not give way
before efforts of those who would guide the early years? Let
us examine the human beings branded by it, for it makes its
stamp felt despite all efforts to oppose it; it strengthens with
passing years; it resists advice, solicitation, terrors of the life
to come, punishments, contempt, and the tartest traits of the
opposite sex. Is that the way of depravity, the way of such a
proclivity? How do we want to explain it if not as clearly owing
to Nature? And if that's the case, what is there to be offended
about? Would Nature inspire something that outrages her?
Would she permit something that disrupts her laws? Would
she bestow the same gifts on those who serve her as on those
who degrade her? Let us better study this indulgent Nature
before daring to fix her limits. Analyze her laws, scrutinize
her intentions, and never venture to make her speak without
listening.

"Let there be no doubt in the end: our wise mother has
no intention of extinguishing this proclivity. To the contrary,
it forms part of her plan that some men do not procreate at

all and women older than 40 cannot; propagation is not one of her laws. Nature does not esteem it and it does not serve her; we can use it as it seems good to us without displeasing Nature, or in any way attenuating her power.

"So cease inveighing against the simplest deviation, a fancy to which man is propelled by a thousand physical causes that nothing can change or destroy, a habit that serves both Nature and the state itself yet commits no wrong upon society, and which finds antagonists only among the abjured sex — little reason, all in all, to raise the gallows. You may not want to imitate the Greek philosophers, but at least respect their views. Did not Lycurgus and Solon bring the goddess Themis to defend these unfortunates? They adroitly turned the reigning vice they found there to the advantage and glory of the nation. They profited from it to stir patriotism in the souls of their compatriots. In the famous battalion of lovers and beloved — men and boys — resided the value of the state.* Understand that what makes one people flourish can never degrade another. Efforts to cure these infidels involve braided flowers and the sex they reject — yet, if these chains be broke or resist love's yoke, do you imagine that sarcasm or invective any more than iron chains or the promise of execution could convert them? One must deal with fools and cowards on one side, fanatics on the other. We can be guilty of stupidity and cruelty, and come out with not one vice less.†

"But we digress. Let's move on. What will you gain from my presentation if you're continually interrupting me?

---

* See Plutarch's *Life of Solon and Lycurgus.*

† "As to the penalties inflicted upon the enemy of the pure and chaste pleasures of Nature, they must depend on the character of the nation that governs the legislator, without which the law that protects morals may become as dangerous as the infractions themselves." Jean Sales, *De la philosophie de la Nature.*

"Crimes against religion," continued the Portuguese, "exist here as they do in Europe, and they're even more severely punished.* The high priest becomes sovereign judge and executioner. One word against the idol or the clergy, negligence in public service to the temple, failure to observe certain celebrations, refusal to send children to school — all these are punished by death. One might say that this unfortunate people, pressed to imagine its end, diligently does all it can to accelerate it.

"Completely ignorant concerning the transmission of facts, whether through written language or hieroglyphics, the people preserve no memorial that might advance their knowledge of genealogy or history. They nevertheless believe themselves to be the most ancient people on earth. They are certain their country dominated the entire continent and the ocean all around, but today they know nothing about it. Its inland location and perpetual troubles with peoples to the east and west prevent it from expanding to the coasts and deprive it of knowledge thereof. Its sole commerce consists in the export of rice, cassava, and corn to the Jagas who, inhabiting a sandy country, often lack these basic necessities; they import fish that the people like and consume as avidly as human flesh. Quarrels over these exchanges are a frequent cause of war, and so they do combat instead of commerce; their trading posts become battlefields.

---

* The logic of theocracy always supports the aristocracy. For tyranny, religion is only a means to an end; it props it up and lends it force. The first duty of a free government, or one recovering its freedom, must incontestably be to completely smash all religious constraints. To banish the king without destroying the cult of religion is to lop off only one head of the hydra. Despotism retreats to the steps of the church; persecuted, there it goes into exile and would regain its forces in order to re-shackle men when they they're so clumsy and ham-fisted as not to pursue and destroy it in its perfidious place of refuge, together with the rascals who provide it.

o   "Politics, which teaches one how to deceive everybody
but oneself, a science born of falsity and ambition, of which
the statesman makes a virtue, the citizen a duty, and the honest man a vice — politics, I say, is entirely unknown to these
people. Although some among them are both ambitious and
5   false, they're artless in this regard and those with whom they
deal do no better; the result is that both sides manage to deceive each other awkwardly but with much industry. The people of Butua also aim to be strongest in combat and to win as
much as they can at every exchange; and here we see the limit
10   of their ruses. Insouciant, they don't concern themselves with
tomorrow, taking what pleasure they can in the present, never
looking back and never to the future. They don't know how
old they are; they have some idea of their children's ages until
they're 15 or 20; then they lose track and speak of it no more.
15   "These Africans have some limited knowledge of astronomy but intermixed are so many errors and superstitions that
it is difficult to understand anything about it. They know the
course of the heavenly bodies as nicely predicting variations
in the atmosphere, and they demarcate time by the phases of
20   the moon. When we ask what is the hand that moves the stars
in space, what is the most powerful being, they respond that it
is their idol, that it created everything we see and may destroy
all if it so chooses; and to prevent such destruction they constantly spill blood upon their altars.
25   "Their daily fare consists of corn, fish when commerce
allows, and human flesh that they have from public butcher-
ies, always available; sometimes they also have monkey meat,
which is highly prized in these parts. From corn they make a
liqueur that is highly inebriating and superior to our *eau de*
30   *vie*; sometimes they drink it alone but often they mix it with
brackish bad water. They also have a way of preserving and
storing yams that makes them delicate and flavorful.

"They have no money or even a sign representing it; each   o
lives on what he has; and those who want foreign goods procure them from merchants by barter, or by lending slaves or
women and children to perform work or provide pleasure.
The King's table receives first fruits of everything, whether
grown in the country or imported from abroad. There are men   5
charged with collecting the various tributes; and so, wanting for nothing, the nation is self-sufficient in all ways. The
same may be said of the chiefs' and priests' tables. Nothing
is sold to the people that is not furnished to the high houses.
Once those tributes are imposed, the merchant takes what   10
he can get.

"The houses are as mediocre as the people, scarcely visible except in the most highly cultivated areas. One might see a
dozen houses together, under the authority of the eldest head
of family; and seven or eight of such small villages constitute a   15
district, the governor of which oversees the individual chiefs
and reports to the King. Governors' individual needs, desires
and caprices are explained to the village lieutenants, who
promptly execute the orders of those little despots; the governor can otherwise, and under no threat of blame from on   20
high, burn down the village and exterminate its inhabitants.
The village lieutenant or individual chief has no authority in
his district; he oversees only his family. He is in such fashion
only the despot's emissary. It is not at all astonishing to see
some little sovereign pass the order to a village in his depart-   25
ment to send him such and such goods, or a young woman or
boy, and refusal to honor the summons costs the entire village
its existence. Still more commonly, two or three of the important chiefs unite — simply for amusement — to sack, destroy,
and burn down a village and massacre the inhabitants without   30
distinction as to age and sex. These unfortunates emerge from
their huts with their wives and children, to kneel before the

blows to come, devout victims, heads bowed, without even
an idea of the spirit of vengeance or self-defense. The effect is
powerful: abasement and humiliation of the people and, clear
and singular proof of the excesses of despotism and authority on high — an example that gives rise to much reflection!
Might one part of humanity really be, as I suppose, subordinate to the other by decrees from the hand of Nature? Must we
not believe as much when we find these behaviors in the early
stages of our civilized societies, such as among this people living in incomprehensible Nature's midst? If she makes animals
far more powerful than man submit to him, might she not
also have granted him rights over the enfeebled portion of his
own kind? And if so, what would then become of our systems
of humanity, charity, and well-meaning assistance?"

"Scold me again for interrupting," I said to the Portuguese. "But I can't accept your principles. No conclusion can
be drawn in favor of tyranny in consequence of all the horrors
shown among these people. Man corrupts himself even in the
bosom of Nature because he is born with passions, the effects
of which make us tremble should civilization not rein them
in. But to conclude that we must choose our models from
amongst wild and savage people, or recognize them as true
because inspired by Nature, would be to advance something
quite false. Just because he can be corrupted by his passions,
man's distance from Nature may be counted as the same within the cradle of civilization or at the furthest distance from
it. Thus, one must calmly judge mankind behind the wall of
tranquility that separates him from his passions, erected by
the legislator that civilizes him."

"I intend to move on," replied Sarmiento, "for it would
be necessary to decide whether the hand that breaks down
those walls has the right to build them, whether that be a good
thing; and if the passions it wishes to subjugate be good or

bad; and if, in some way, in either case, whether opposition
to their effects does not contribute more to the happiness of
man than does the civilization that degrades him. However,
such a dissertation would take far too much time and neither
of us would convince the other. So let me resume:

"When the priests desire a victim, they announce that
their God has appeared and told them He desires this or that
person, who must be straightaway brought to the temple.
Cruel to be sure, but a law dictated only by the passions, all of
which it favors.

"Without the intimate union of spiritual and temporal
chiefs, the people would perhaps be less servile. But the equiv-
alence of their powers proves to them that they must unite to
better satisfy themselves, as a result of which the weight of
the despotic authority presses the unfortunate people from all
sides, crushing and destroying them.*

"Inhabitants of the Kingdom of Butua view with sovereign distrust all those who can't earn a living. They say that
every individual in each district is to be fed, but only if he
doesn't fail in his duties. If he does fail, he is abandoned and
receives no help whatever and so soon becomes the victim of
the rich, who immolate him, saying that a dead man is less
unhappy than one who suffers.

"As to medicine, the secondary priests of the temples are
the practitioners; they have botanical tinctures that sometimes allow them to prescribe appropriate remedies. They
never perform work for free and require payment from the
family in the form of women, boys, or slaves; they do not accept food — why would they? — because idol worship brings
in more than enough.

---

* I repeat: it will always be the same with despotic governments, and never will a wise
people succeed in undoing the yoke of one without the other.

"A man marries as many women as he can feed. The Chief of each district, following the King's example, keeps a large seraglio, generally proportionate to the extent of his domain. The seraglio, made up as noted of tributes exacted, is under the direction of slaves who, though not eunuchs, live wholly dependent and in such fear for their lives that malfeasance is rare. Within the seraglio a privileged sultana, although she may be displaced, is regarded as mistress of the house; the infants she bears during her reign are considered legitimate. The eldest child born during the father's lifetime, with whichever of his wives, inherits all the property. So long as the first sultana is favored, she wields authority over the others, though not spared the cruel subordination imposed upon her sex. Once she has children, she's relegated to some corner of the house and no one knows what happened to her. The surest way she can retain her status is to never become pregnant; and in this the women are remarkably skilled.

"Besides lions and tigers in the northern part of the kingdom, which is all forest, one can find here quadrupeds absolutely unknown in Europe. Among them there's one animal a little smaller than a steer, like a cross between a goat and a deer. One also sees giraffes.* There are many unusual birds though they alight but seldom and, having never been hunted, remain little known.

"Nature is also extremely varied as to plants and reptiles, and both orders include many which are poisonous. The people, singularly refined in all manner of cruelty, use one such plant, unique to this climate, to make a poison so potent that

---

* An animal seventeen feet high, found also among the neighboring Hottentots. See Bougainville, *Voyage autour du monde,* vol. II, p. 402.

it kills in a moment's time.* Sometimes they dip the points of   o
their arrows in it so that the slightest wound can cause the victim to fall into convulsions that end in a quick death; but they
refrain from eating the flesh of those killed in this manner.

"Let me describe the people in a few brief strokes. They   5
are short, extremely black, nervous, with tight curly hair,
naturally healthy, well proportioned, with fine teeth, and they
live to be quite old. They are given to committing all sorts of
crimes, principally those of lust, cruelty, vengeance, and superstition; they are also quick-tempered, perfidious, wrathful,
and ignorant. Their women are physically better made, with   10
superb figures, nearly all fresh of face with beautiful eyes and
gleaming teeth. But they are so cruelly treated and worn down
by the tyranny of their spouses that their charms are gone by
age 30 and they rarely live much past 50.

"As to arts and ornamentation, there is little more than   15
you see around you: some pottery nicely glazed with the juice
of a plant indigenous to these parts; screens and mats and
wicker baskets, finely detailed, made only by women.

"The King, who knows of white women and has had several of them after they were found stranded upon the shores   20
of the Jagas, owns few items he deems more precious, and
you may see them in his palace. The little he knows of these
women has made him very fond of them, and he would give
up a portion of his kingdom if more could be procured.

"Completely insensitive, yet perhaps just for that, hap-   25
pier than we are, these savages can't imagine one could be
affected by the death of a relative or friend. They will watch
someone expire, wholly unmoved. Without a thought they'll
often even help it come about in the aged, or if they see no

* Pauw states that this same plant is indigenous to America.

hope of recovery. It is a thousand times better, they say, to be rid of those who are useless or suffer than to allow them to live in a world in which they know nothing but horrors.

"The way they bury their dead is simply to place the corpse at the foot of a tree, without the slightest sign of respect, without ceremony and no more attention than one would pay a dead animal. After all, of what use are our own customs? A dead man is no longer good for anything; he feels nothing, and it's mad to imagine we owe him anything beyond leaving him somewhere on a spot of earth. Sometimes, when death is not due to disease, they eat the body. In any event, the priests play no role; whatever other humiliations they inflict, they don't expect to be paid for the right to return a corpse to the elements that comprised it.

"Their notions concerning the fate of souls in the afterlife are quite confused. First of all, they don't believe the soul is distinct from the body; they say it's only the result of the way we are organized by Nature. Each type of organization necessitates a different soul and that is all that separates us from the animals. Their system seems to me quite philosophical.

"But pathetic outlandishness soon extinguishes this spark of reason. They say that death is only a kind of sleep, at the end of which they will emerge along the banks of a charming river, whole and just as they were when alive, and all their desires will be met and they will have white women and fish in abundance. This fabulous place welcomes the good and bad alike, because it is the same, according to them, to be one or the other, that nothing depends upon them, that they don't make themselves, that the Being which created everything cannot punish them for having acted according to His plans. That men cannot do without the absurd idea of an afterlife is a peculiar mania of mankind. So much so that they require powerful help from study and reflection in order to succeed

in absorbing a chimeric idea born of pride, as ridiculous   o
to admit as it is cruelly destructive to all felicity on earth."

"My friend," said I, "it seems to me that these systems —"

"— are invariable on this matter," responded Sarmiento.
"One must be willfully blind to imagine that we survive in any
way. That would entail rejecting all demonstrations based on   5
reason and good sense and contrary to all the lessons Nature provides. To distinguish in ourselves something besides
matter is to misunderstand its properties, not to see that it
is susceptible to all possible modification. If the sublime soul
must survive our death, if it were some immaterial substance,   10
would it deteriorate like our organs? Would it grow? Would
it degenerate with the decline of old age? Would it be vigorous and healthy when we suffer? Would it become sad, beaten
down, and languish once our health went sour? A soul able
to put up with the constant physical changes could scarcely   15
be of an ethical sort. You must be mad, my friend, to think
for even a moment that we owe our existence to anything besides the particular combination of elements that constitute
us. Change these elements and you alter the soul. Separate
them out, everything is annihilated. The soul subsists in these   20
elements; it is only the result but in no way distinct. The soul
is to the body as the flame is to the elements consumed. Can
one exist without the other? Would the flame exist without
the elements that feed it? And the reverse — would they be
consumed without the flame? Rest easy, my friend, as to the   25
fate of your soul after this life is done. It shall be no unhappier
than when it suffused your body. And you won't be pitied for
having vegetated a few moments on earth any more than you
were pitied before you appeared there."

Without giving me time to demolish or refute a view so   30
at odds with reason and the intricate views of a sensitive man,
so injurious to the power of the Great Being who has endowed

o us with an immortal soul by which we could arrive at the sublime idea of His existence, from which flows so naturally the
   necessity of our duties — as much in regards to the Holy and
   all-powerful God as to the earthly creatures among which he
   places us — the Portuguese, permitting not a word of reply, I
5 say, he who quite disliked being crossed, resumed his account:
       "Your knowledge of the mores, customs, and laws of the
   people of the kingdom of Butua should make it easy to guess
   their morality. They consider none of their acts of tyranny
   and cruelty to be crimes, not their excesses of debauchery
10 nor their hostilities. To legitimize the first of these, they say
   that Nature, in creating individuals who are unequal, proves
   that some should submit to others; else she would have put
   no distance between them. That is the argument they use to
   mistreat their women who, according to their thinking, are
15 only animals and inferior, and over which Nature gives them
   all manner of rights. As to debauchery, they say that men are
   formed in such a manner that one thing can please some while
   displeasing others; and as Nature offers other beings which,
   by being weak, have no choice but to satisfy a man's wants and
20 needs, these cannot be crimes. Men are endowed with tastes
   for certain things and also have what they need for satisfaction. Why would Nature unite the two if she were offended by
   the way they were used?
       "All that I've just told you," concluded the Portuguese,
25 "will greatly increase your horror of the people. Given your
   obligation to live here, perhaps it was wrong of me to provide
   so many details."
       "Rest assured," I replied, "that there is not a single principle
   of these monsters that I don't rank with the most awful lapses of
30 human reason. I'm not more scrupulous than need be, as I believe you must know. But to favor, follow, or believe in such revolting customs is well beyond the forces of my head and heart."

Sarmiento wanted to reply but I no longer wished to re- 0
spond, sure I would never convert this hardened individual.
He was the sort whose perversity is all but impossible to cure
because he suffers not a whit nor desires a better way of life.
We'd stopped in front of a dwelling. To put an end to our dialogue I indicated that I wished to go inside — the home of a 5
common man whom we found seated on a straw mat eating
boiled corn. His wife, on her knees in front of him, was serving him with every possible sign of respect.

As the Portuguese was known to be favored by the King,
the peasant immediately rose and kneeled before him. Shortly 10
after, he introduced his daughter, a child 13 or 14 years old.

"You find courtesy in these parts," said Sarmiento. "Tell
me in which of your European countries would a stranger be
welcomed like this. Something good comes from the despotism you find frightening and, here at least, quite in accord 15
with Nature."

"Such a practice belongs among the aberrations and
anomalies!" I cried. "And as it inspires in me only aversion
and disgust, it cannot accord with Nature."

"Custom, rather. Don't confuse the way things are done, 20
owing to education, with the laws of Nature."

Sarmiento, meanwhile, having harshly repulsed the little
girl, demanded fire, lit his pipe, and went out.

We returned to the city.

Three months passed in this sorry state. I cursed my 25
misfortune, in despair of any prospect of coming upon
Léonore, yet loving and thinking only of her. Then fate, as if to
soothe my pain, at last gave me the opportunity to perform a
good deed.

One morning I went out alone so that I might dream at 30
will of my love; such solitary walks were preferable to those
with Sarmiento, in which he was always pestering me with his

moral misinterpretations and exegetics, ever seeking to attack
and pervert my principles. On this morning it so happened
that I came upon a spectacle that would bring tears to the
eyes of any but this ferocious people, of anybody inclined to
experience the tender pleasure of being moved to pity by the
pain endured by the sweet delicate sex that heaven created to
share our misfortunes and mingle with roses all the thorns
scattered upon life's path — and not, instead, to be despised
and treated like a beast of burden.

One of those unfortunate women was harrowing a
field where her husband intended to plant corn, and she was
yoked to a heavy plough. With all her strength she dragged it
through the thick spongy earth. In addition to this painful and
overwhelming labor, the woman had two infants bound to her,
each suckling one of her breasts. She bent under the weight
of it and she wept, sweat and tears streaming down the heads
of her children. A misstep caused her to trip and fall — and I
thought she must have died. Her barbarous husband assailed
her, armed with a whip, and overwhelmed her with lashes to
force her to get up. I listened only to Nature and my heart.
I rushed upon the villain and plunged him into the furrows.
I broke the straps that bound his half-dead companion to the
tiller of the plough. I raised her up, pressed her to my breast,
and set her beside me beneath a tree. She fainted and would
have died without my help. On my knees I held one of her
infants, bruised from the fall. At last the poor woman opened
her eyes and gazed at me, unable to conceive there existed
anyone anywhere who would help and avenge her. She stared
at me, astonished. Soon her tears of gratitude anointed the
hands of her benefactor.

She took up her children, kissed them, and handed them
to me. She seemed to be asking me to save their lives as well
as her own. Though the delightful scene gratified me, I saw

her husband coming at me with one of his comrades. I stood
up and decided to give them both what they deserved. My appearance made them afraid. I took charge of the woman and
her children and brought them to my home. I installed them
there, this unhappy family, and barred the husband from visiting. That evening I made a request to the monarch, as if I
were planning to make the woman an object of pleasure. The
monarch, who had already much reproached me for living a
celibate life, acceded to my demand without question and enjoined the husband from coming near me. When I proposed
to her that she be my slave, you cannot imagine her joy. I put
her in charge of taking care of the house and made her life
so pleasant that when she learned I dreamt of leaving the
country she wanted to kill herself out of despair. As you see,
this soul, like any other, was sensitive, grateful, and delicate.
Women, so cruelly treated in these harsh climes, have everything needed to make their men happy. If only their masters
would renounce the hideous right to be tyrants, they'd come
to prefer the gentler right to cultivate virtues that would ease
their lives.

No sooner had Sarmiento learned of what I'd done than
he condemned it; not only did it shock him and run completely counter to his disgraceful maxims, but he claimed it was
even against the law, for it robbed her husband of his rights
over his wife.

"And how with all your intelligence," continued the cruel
sophist, "do you imagine you're doing a good deed when,
with respect to both parties, one of them remains unhappy?"

"The one left suffering is the criminal."

"Not so, since he only acted according to the customs of
his country. What matter? Crime made him happy; your opposition made him unhappy."

"It is right to demand that the guilty party suffer."

"What is really right is that only the weak suffer; they're created to vegetate in servitude. You disturbed the natural order by helping a feeble human being over against the master, who had all rights over her. Blinded by false pity, with its misleading impulses and selfish principles, you disturb and pervert Nature's plan. Furthermore, even supposing them equal, I maintain that if the action of this one you call human impacts both but leaves one unhappy, that action is not virtuous but at best indifferent. A good action doesn't come at the expense of human happiness; thus, an action resulting in something disagreeable for one of the two individuals, in putting things to rights, cannot be virtuous. At best it's neutral because all you've done is reverse things."

"The action is good if it avenges the crime."

"Not if it leaves someone unhappy. For an action to have the quality of goodness you imagine, we'd have to know more about what is and isn't a crime. So long as ideas of vice and virtue are not well developed but full of variation and uncertainty, whoever goes to avenge some evil against someone in a way that leaves the other party unhappy would surely have done nothing virtuous."

"Your reasoning means nothing to me." To the execrable fellow I angrily added: "So sweet is it to do such actions that even if equivocal there remains at the bottom of one's heart the delicious pleasure of having done them."

"Fine," replied Sarmiento. "Say you acted because it flatters you and that in doing so you gave yourself pleasure that conforms to your organization; also, you surrendered to a weakness in commending your own so very sensitive soul. Don't say you've done a good deed. And if you see me do the opposite, don't say I did anything wrong. Say rather that I wanted pleasure just like you, and each of us sought what was best for the way we see and feel."

Heaven's vengeance would come, at long last, to the sorry   0
Portuguese.

Although the swindler told me about his *modus operandi*
(details of which I conceal from you for they would surely   5
make you tremble), Sarmiento didn't reveal the atrocious
crime he was planning. Soulless and devoid of gratitude (like
all those of overweening ambition), the man forgot that he
owed his life to the King, and hatched a daring plot against
him, planning to overthrow him. Supported only by crown   10
troops, he thought he could compel the most important vassals to recognize him or else reduce them to servitude. I feared
I myself would be swept up in the storm. Fortunately, the King,
in need of my services and sure I was innocent, spared me and
punished only the guilty.   15
      I was to remain unaware of either the rascal's plot or dis-
covery of it until one day we went out together for our usual
stroll. Six Negros lay in wait and fell upon him. In a trice he lay
dying at my feet. He was still breathing.
      "I know the hand that strikes," he said, "and well it should,   20
because in two days I would have seized power. Let him who
betrayed perish one day like me. My friend, I leave you in
peace; I'd change nothing even at this cruel hour when truth
pierces and the veil falls away; and if I take any regret to the
grave, 'tis only to have not done more and given full measure.   25
Men like me die in peace. Only those with hope die unhappy.
He who trembles still believes, but he in whom faith is extinct
has nothing to fear. Die like me if you can."
      His eyes closed and his atrocious soul went to appear be-
fore his Judge, soiled by all his crimes — the greatest among   30
them, his final impiety.

I lost not a moment but hurried to the King and explained myself. He recounted to me the odious designs of the Portuguese, assured me I had nothing to fear, that he understood I was innocent and could continue to serve him in all tranquility. Relieved, I returned home. Alone to reflect, I convinced myself how true it is that no crime goes unpunished and the equitable hand of Providence knows, sooner or later, how to deal with those who cross or outrage Him. Nevertheless, I felt both sorrow and pity for the Portuguese and regretted his death. The more a man is led to commit evil, the more he's trapped by the causal chain of circumstance and deserves pity. Yet regret, too, because he was the only human being with whom I could reason; isolated amidst these barbarians, I could only grow weak and still more unhappy.

In the exercise of my duties not a single white woman appeared in the first five groups I examined. I could no longer entertain hopes of coming upon my darling Léonore in these parts, and while finding her and bringing her back to Europe still constituted my sole purpose, I'd already taken serious steps toward making my secret departure when the monarch sent word that he had something to tell me. He thoroughly understood the Portuguese language, which I'd learned with Sarmiento; so I was altogether capable of conversing with His Majesty.

A contingent of white women, he informed me, was being held in a small Portuguese fort located on the border of Monomotapa, where they might easily be captured. But to go there would require crossing nearly impassable mountains while the surrounding gorges were under constant surveillance by the Bororès, a people still more warlike and crueler than his own. But the time was right because those proud and intractable neighbors were at present occupied with the Cimbas, their greatest enemies, and there was consequently no danger in undertaking the mission.

"As for the Portuguese, I do not fear them," continued the   o
monarch, "They are few in number at the fort; nothing should
threaten my plans."

I need not tell you how eagerly I seized upon the idea
— my hopes rekindled, for Léonore just might be among the
women — and I sought permission to accompany the detach-   5
ment, or even command it myself. Once at the Portuguese
fort, were I lucky enough to find her there, we could return to
Europe. If she weren't there, the expedition would still give me
an opening to European settlements that would let me quit
these barbarians and find myself once again among Christians.   10

But Ben Mâacoro was quite as clever as me. He feared my
desertion. Attached to the services I rendered, he determined
to do everything to keep me with him, no matter the price,
and consequently I would not be allowed to accompany the
troops or take any part whatever in the expedition. He told   15
me about it only to express his pleasure while warning me, at
the same time, to be less exigent in my choices concerning the
women, for their color alone would satisfy him.

My sad sorry hope, no sooner formulated than repulsed,
made my situation seem still more frightful. I could only fear   20
the hope I'd just cherished. If Léonore were indeed one of these
women, how could I keep her from the King? To me would fall
the painful task of delivering her to him myself without even
realizing it. At the time I'd always supposed that love's flame
would insure I couldn't do such a thing; but that idea was only   25
the fruit of intoxication that reason crushed straightway. From
that moment, the only way I could find peace was by convincing myself that Léonore could not possibly be among them. I
came to regard the notion as a chimera that had briefly made
me happy. I asked myself: How could she possibly be found   30
along the east coast of Africa since, when I was in Morocco, she
was believed to be on the western coast? Either she had to have

been taken by land across the continent, which seemed nearly incredible, or by sea around the Horn of Africa, more difficult still. Thus I barred the idea from my mind. When a seductive illusion serves only to torture, the simplest solution is to banish it.

Thus I now became so completely convinced my fears were groundless that I no longer paid more attention to arrivals of white women than black, and my firm resolve to flee as soon as possible only grew stronger. From the moment I decided it was impossible that Léonore might appear in the kingdom, I had to do everything possible to continue my search elsewhere.

So the detachment went forth. Thirty warriors departed quietly, crossed the mountains without incident, and put to flight the Portuguese at Fort de Tete on the northern frontier of Monomotapa. With little trouble they captured and brought back four white women, veiled, to put before the King.

Once alerted, as before I placed myself between the two Negroes armed with clubs, ready to crack open my skull at the least word or slightest misstep. Nothing frightened me more than this formality, for if I harbored the least suspicion that Léonore was among these women, death a thousand times would not have stopped me from seizing her and fleeing to the ends of the earth. But so certain was I that nothing could happen that I examined them with the same indifference as all the others. Two seemed to me to be from 25 to 30 years old, one of whom appeared ungainly, with very dark tawny skin, far from what the king demanded. The third was quite prettily turned out but not so young as the king preferred. The last of them drew my greater attention; I suspected she was much younger than the first two. Her skin dazzled, and every part of her body was formed by the hand of the gods. She evinced loathing at the examination and when it was necessary to observe and judge her virtue, she recoiled horribly in self-defense.

fig. 6

The manner in which these women were veiled for presentation contributed much to the terror that the ceremony inflicted upon the souls of those from another country. Not only
was it impossible to view them but they themselves, with their
eyes wrapped tight beneath their veils, could discern neither
the company around them nor what was being done to them.

The youngest woman's repeated efforts to defend herself
considerably embarrassed me; the force to constrain her was
at odds with tact and accommodation. Nevertheless, I had to
provide a report and so found myself obliged to ask the king
what he wanted me to do. He sent along two women from
his personal guard, furnished with an order to hold the young
woman and prevent her from interfering with my duties. They
seized her and I continued my examination, which became
very discomfiting. Not the best anatomist to decide about
something that, in the end, seemed to me quite uncertain, with
her I contented myself with stating in my report that I guessed
she possessed what was necessary to please her new master
and that if things were not completely in order and *intact* as
he desired, the illusion would be sufficient. As to the other, I
deemed her unfit as an older woman like the first two; but
the king, so enthusiastic about white women, was only to be
satisfied with all four; not a single one was to be rejected. My
duty completed, the women entered the seraglio and I retired.

No sooner was I alone than the resistance displayed by
the young woman, her charms, and the cruelty by which I
had to request help, agitated my heart in a thousand ways.
I wanted only a little rest but my own charming creature
offered herself unabated to my imagination.

You whom I worship! I cried, *Am I guilty? No, adored
spouse. No charms of another could compare with yours, the
temple built upon the soul. But you inflame me, and you're
beautiful, Léonore — you and only you!*

My senses, calm until now, I confess, erupted impetu-
ously. Unable to contain myself any longer, it seemed to me
that love itself could be glimpsed through the gauze that concealed the unfortunate captive, revealing to me the cherished
features of my beloved. Seduced by such sweet but cruel illusion, for a moment I dared, for the first time ever, to be happy
without Léonore. I slept and the chimeras vanished with the
shadows of the night.

The next day I asked Ben Mâacoro if he was pleased with his
prisoners. But I was quite astonished to find him in a state
of mind I'd never seen before. He was bothered and distract-
ed, hardly answered me, and I even suspected he viewed me
with distemper. I retired without daring to repeat my question, frightened by the sudden change in His Majesty. Fearing
someone had warned him against me so that I would sooner
or later become the victim of his injustice and barbarity, from
now on I could think of nothing but how to escape.

The fate of my unhappy Negress disturbed me. I did not
want to give her back to her spouse, who would undoubtedly
have killed her. Nor did I want to take her with me, no matter
what she wanted. Affecting disgust, although I never had rela-
tions with her, I asked one of the King's old chieftains — one
of the more honest — to be good enough to accept her among
his slaves and treat her well.

Then I quietly took my leave, early on the third night after
the arrival of the European women in the Kingdom of Butua.
How long would I be misfortune's sorry victim, a miserable
toy buffeted by her caprices? I fled, continuing to search the
ends of the earth for the very same woman whom — in fact —
I'd just delivered into the hands of an unalloyed and brutal
libertine, the most odious of men!

"Lord, but you make me tremble," said President de Blamont, interrupting Sainville. "Was that Léonore? And you, Madame — was that you? And you were not — not then eaten?"

None could contain laughter at Madame de Blamont's naïve vivacity.

"Madame, I beg you," said the Count de Beaulé, "Let us not further interrupt Monsieur de Sainville. First, we're all eager to learn how his adventures ended. Secondly, we hope to learn from this charming young woman herself just how she came to be here and how she could have escaped all the dangers that beset her."

Sainville continued: I fled and walked south, far closer than I imagined to the frontier bordering the land of the Hottentots. The next day I sighted the Berg River, and two or three Dutch villages along its banks that were part of a chain of settlements from the Cape that reached some 50 leagues into the African interior. I found the people in these colonies so well adapted to the country that it was difficult to distinguish them from the indigenous peoples. Some among them were the grand-children of Dutch from the Cape but had spent their whole lives there; they were sons of Europeans and Hottentots, and could be neither told apart nor understood. In those hamlets I was nevertheless welcomed with every sort of kindness and recognized as European. But only through sign language could I make out their ideas or make myself understood. There was never any way we could talk with one another.

My plan at first was to follow the course of the Berg while never losing sight of the Lupata Mountains at the foot of which sits the Cape. But later I thought it better to keep along the coast, hoping to find more Dutch villages and in consequence more help — and this proved successful. Those villages, extremely common in those parts, offered sanctuary nearly every night. I encountered groups of savages, several of which seemed to me to belong to the newly discovered yellow nation; and the 18th day after leaving Butua, having traveled nearly 150 leagues along the coast, I arrived in Cape Town, where I quickly found as much assistance as might be had in the best city in Holland. My letters of credit were accepted and I could draw advances of whatever sums I wished, even the whole amount, if I thought it useful.

With these issues resolved, taking care to dress appropriately, I went to see the Dutch governor. No sooner did he learn the object of my travels and view the portrait of Léonore than he told me confidently: a woman, the spitting image of the miniature before his eyes, was on board *Discovery*, the companion ship on the voyage of Captain Cook. It was under the command of Captain Clarke and had lately dropped anchor off the Cape. The woman, he added, was singularly amiable and sweet, quite attached to the lieutenant of the vessel, and said she was his wife; and with that status she was quartered with him and the other officers, gaining everyone's esteem.

Recalling immediately that in Morocco I'd been assured the same woman had been sighted on an English vessel, I showed the portrait to the governor a second time.

"Monsieur!" I cried, frightened and bewildered, "are you sure you're not mistaken? Was it really her? Was this woman really married to another?"

"You may be sure of it," he responded. When he showed the portrait to his own wife and several officers, the response was unanimous. The image could belong to none other but the wife of the lieutenant aboard *The Discovery*.

Thus it was I believed myself lost and without recourse. Afflicted by so many facets of terrible pain, I could see nothing that might staunch the horror. Because I'd been afraid that Heaven would restore Léonore to me in Butua, in the hands

of the monarch, I'd blinded myself to what passed right before my eyes. And now I refused to see as I might have, had I
examined things more closely, that my fears were groundless.
Yet with no news of Léonore since Salé, I somehow believed
that either she'd left from there for some English colony or,
instead of going to Africa, as was believed, to London. From
Salé, she might have gone to either of these places. In view of
which, nothing seemed simpler than to admit the inconstancy
of she whom I adored and suppose she'd married the lieutenant of *The Discovery* and accompanied him to the South Seas
on Cook's third voyage.

My mind teeming with these ideas, and knowing not
more than six weeks had passed since the British ship had
left the Cape, I resolved to follow and catch up with the vessel, to board it and snatch Léonore from the hands of the one
who dared take her from me. To the perfidious woman herself I'd recall our solemn oaths before heaven and force her to
fulfill them or else throw both her and myself into the ocean
and drown.

Once resolved, though without informing the governor
of my intent other than follow my unfaithful wife, I begged
him to sell me a small but agile vessel that would enable me
to promptly catch up with the British ship. At first he laughed
at the plan, thought it a youthful folly, and tried in every way
to dissuade me. But when he saw my violent tenacity and that
despair would befall me if I was forced to renounce my plan,
and having no reason to refuse once I proposed to pay for it
all, he accommodated me with a light Dutch ship that he assured me would meet my needs. He gave all orders necessary
for the cargo and equipment, with enough provisions to last 6
months; he also provided 6 small iron cannon to use against
the savages, expressly forbidding me to fire on any European
except in self-defense. For crew he gave me 10 armed marines,

30 sailors, two good commerce officers, and an excellent pilot. I paid for it all in cash and also left with him the balance owed my crew for 6 months.

Once all was made ready, and after overwhelming the governor with marks of my gratitude, I put to sail toward mid-December, in the direction of Tahiti, where I knew Captain Cook must be headed.

Hardly had we rounded the Cape than we encountered a considerable storm, an event common in those parts, after which we lost sight of land. Unused to the open seas, having only made trips along the coast on small boats where the roiling ocean is less severe, I suffered in every possible way. But bodily torments are nothing when the soul is powerfully afflicted. Moral sensations completely absorb physical woes and all activity concentrated in the soul shows it to be the source of all pain.

On the 38th day we sighted land — the point of New Holland, known as the Land of Van Diemen. There we learned from the natives that the English had been and gone not long before; but we were without interpreters and could obtain no further clarification. We learned only that the direction was northerly and so we followed, intending to put into port at Tahiti.

Permit me if you will, *continued Sainville*, to suppress nautical details and descriptions of the islands we touched upon, for what may be said of the route we followed is well described in Cook's voyages and you'd learn nothing new. Let me dwell instead for some longer while upon my discovery of a singular island that we came upon when harsh winds by chance took charge of our vessel. It is entirely unknown to navigators. Altogether interesting in itself, it differs in essential ways from

the descriptions of Captain Cook. My encounters there were   o
so extraordinary that you must forgive me for drawing your
attention to them.

The wind was up and the sea calm when we rounded New
Zealand by way of Queen Charlotte's Sound. We advanced
full sail toward the Tropic of Capricorn and, suspecting the   5
group known as the Society Islands were only a little distant
to portside, the pilot steered us toward the Cape. But suddenly a western wind of frightful impetuosity propelled us
away from those islands. The tempest grew fearsome, accompanied by hailstones so large that huge ice pellets wounded   10
several of our sailors. Immediately we brailed our sails, our
top-gallant yard, and soon were obliged to work the ship differently and go by bare poles. In this fashion we risked being
carried to ground, which might save us or kill us. Next dawn
we at last sighted land — as much desired as feared. If the   15
violent wind did not die down by sunrise, we'd surely break
apart. It did calm, however, and we were able to steer. But our
vessel had clearly been damaged during the storm and was
taking on water by the hour. We were constrained at all events
to sail toward the island we'd sighted, with a view to repairs.   20

Even with rocks on all sides, the island appeared charming. In our terrible state, we had at least the prospect of
making repairs in appealing surroundings.

I sent out the lieutenant in a small boat to find anchorage
and sound out the disposition of the inhabitants. Three hours   25
later he returned with two natives who greeted me in the European manner. I spoke to them using languages of the continent but of these they understood nary a word. Yet I perceived
that with French, they redoubled their attention and their ears
picked up. Whatever the case, from their highly intelligible   30
signs, nothing savage about them, I understood that their
chief sorely wished to receive us, provided we came in peace;

and if that were the case, we would find all the help we needed. Assuring them of my pacific intentions, I offered several gifts which with noble gestures they refused, and we went forth. We found ourselves at 12 to 15 fathoms, near enough to the coast, which was lined with pretty red sand, and we set down anchor. Before leaving ship I noted that we were situated above the Tropic of Capricorn at between 260 and 263 degrees latitude, and between 25 and 26 degrees southern latitude, not far from land once sighted by Davis.

Islanders of both sexes and in endless numbers lined the coast when we arrived. They received us with signs of joy, the sincerity of which we could not doubt. So taken were some of our sailors by the appearance of the women that they made to beguile them but were quickly reproved for the sake of decency and pride, and we continued on peacefully without allowing that signal error, common enough among Europeans, and so we lost nothing of the good will of the people. Hardly had I set a foot on land than two inhabitants advanced toward me with great demonstrations of friendship. They made me to understand that if I wished they would conduct me to their chief. I accepted the offer, gave the necessary orders to my crew — I demanded complete discretion — and went off with just my two officers. After a quick tour of the fine European-style fortifications that defended the port, and to which we would soon return, our guides brought us onto a superb avenue with palm trees, arranged in rows of four and lining the whole way from the harbor to the city.

Constructed along geometric lines, the city offered a charming impression. It was circular in shape and two leagues in circumference. The streets, all aligned, were promenades rather than passages, bordered by trees on both sides, with soft sandy footpaths by the houses, and they made for pleasant walking. The houses were uniform; none was larger or

higher than another. Each had a ground floor, first floor, and
an Italian-style terrace above; a nicely proportioned entrance
was set between two windows, each surmounted by a case-
ment that brought daylight to the first floor. The facades,
neatly painted, were symmetrically arranged pink and green
squares, lending each street a decorative touch. Walking by
several, they seemed all the more pleasant and gay because
islanders gathered outside them to watch us pass, contribut-
ing to the liveliness and diversity of the scene. We arrived at
a plaza, rather large and perfectly round, with trees all about.
Two circular buildings filled the space; painted like the houses,
only slightly larger and elevated. One of these served as the
Chief's palace; the other consisted of two public spaces, the
use of which I will presently explain.

To us, nothing special indicated the Chief's residence;
we saw no insulting guards who, by show of arms and other
precautions to allay his fear lest some unfortunate impoverished wretch appear on bended knee before him and so reveal
the tyrant to the people. Rather, the man himself received
us himself at his palace door. All those who had guided and
accompanied us hurried to address him; everyone rejoiced
in seeing him and he made gestures of friendship to all.

Great by virtue alone, so respected for his singular wisdom and protected by the undivided heart of the people, that
in seeing him I believed myself transported back in time to a
Golden Age. It was as if I saw Sesotris in Thebes, when kings
were friends to their subjects and subjects, children to their
monarch.

Zamé — such was the name of this extraordinary individual. He was apparently about 70 years old though he looked at
most 50. Zamé was tall with a pleasant face and lively gaze, yet
of noble bearing, a gracious smile and shock of lovely white hair.
His appearance united maturity with the majesty of old age.

He immediately recognized us as Europeans; aware that French is the continental idiom, he used that language to ask me to what nation I belonged.

"From the one whose language you speak."

"I know it well," responded Zamé. "I lived three years in your country. We will talk of it. But those with you are not from France."

"No, they're Dutch."

To them he addressed several flattering words in their own language.

"It must astonish you to meet a savage as knowledgeable as I," he continued. "Come, follow me, I'll enlighten you and tell you my story."

We followed him into the palace. The furniture was simple and clean, more Asian than European, though some pieces were typical of our country. Six women, very beautiful, surrounded another woman, about 60 years old. All stood when we entered.

"Here is my wife," Zamé told me, introducing the older woman. "These three are my daughters; the other three, their friends. I also have two boys; had they known you were coming they would already be here. I'm sure you'd like them."

Perceiving my surprise at such candor, Zamé added:

"You're amazed. I see that. You've been told I'm the chief of the country and you are thoroughly surprised that, unlike your sovereigns in Europe, I don't make my greatness consist of arrogance wedded to silence. And do you know why? It's because they learned only to be kings while I learned to be a man. Come, put yourself at ease, we will talk, I'll explain everything. Let us start by your telling me what you need and want. I'm anxious to know, in order to give orders to provide for you at once."

Touched by such great kindness, when I could not re-   o
frain from expressing my gratitude, Zamé turned to his wife
and, still in our tongue, said: "I am pleased that you see here
a European but angry that he is teaching you his country's
custom of thanking the benefactor as if it were not the latter
who owed thanks."   5

I went on to tell him what we needed.

"You will have all that," said Zamé, "and even some good
workers to help; but you say nothing of provisions you must
lack. Perhaps you believe I'd give them to you? Not at all, I will
sell them to you — for nothing except the certitude of spend-   10
ing two weeks with me. Notice how I can be as indiscreet as
you."

Still more touched by this frankness, so rare these days in
a sovereign, I prostrated myself before him.

"Well, then," he said, raising me up and addressing his   15
wife: "Zoraï, here is how they act with their chiefs, respecting
instead of loving them." To me he said: "Send your men back
to the ship. They'll find there already a portion of what they
want and can request what else they need; they may stay in
the city if they prefer, but you and your officers shall have no   20
other lodging than my home. It is as commodious as it is vast.

ⓖ *fig.* 7   Sometimes I receive friends; courtesans, never."

Zamé gave his orders as I gave mine; I made him see that
my officers' presence was required aboard ship.

"Well, then, I will keep only you, but tomorrow they must   25
return to dine."

They saluted and left.

Soon after, two citizens of the same sort we'd seen in the
city, dressed the same way (as were all, and all in the same
color), came to notify Zamé that dinner was served; and   30
we passed into a large room where the meal was laid out in
European style.

"Here is my only concession to ceremony for you," said the amiable host. "You won't eat so comfortably as we; I've ordered chairs to be brought. We sometimes serve ourselves, to us it means nothing."

Without waiting for my thanks, he sat down beside his wife, placed me next to him, and the six young ladies took their seats.

"These lovely persons," said Zamé, indicating the three friends of the family, "will make you think I love the female sex. You wouldn't be wrong; I do. Though perhaps not as you understand. The laws of my country permit divorce; and nevertheless" — he continued, taking the hand of Zoraï, his wife — "I've known only her and will surely never have another. But I'm old and it is a pleasure for me to see young women; their sex has so much to recommend it. My friend, I've always believed that one who doesn't love women is not fit to be put in charge of men."

"Oh, what an excellent man!" *cried Madame de Blamont.* "Already I love him passionately. I hope this time at dinner you weren't afraid of eating human flesh as you were with the vile Portuguese."

"Far from it, Madame," said Sainville. "There was no meat whatever. The entire meal consisted of a dozen dishes served on superb Japanese blue porcelain, each platter overflowing with vegetables, jellies, fruits, and pastries."

"The pettiest prince in Germany eats better than I. Is it not so, my friend?" said Zamé. "Do you want to know why? He feeds his pride more than he fills his stomach and imagines grandeur and magnificence in bringing down twenty beasts to

nourish one — himself. My vanity has other aims. To be held   o
dear by my country's citizens, to be loved by those around me,
to do good and prevent wickedness, to make everybody happy
— here, my friend, are all the things required to flatter vanity
in someone whom chance has for a time raised above others.
We don't abstain from meat by religious principle but for rea-   5
sons of diet and humanity. Why sacrifice our fellow creatures
when Nature offers another way? Besides, can you believe
it a good thing to devour and put into our bowels the flesh
and putrefied blood of a thousand different animals? Nothing comes of that but a bitter chyle that can only damage our   10
organs, weaken them, and precipitate infirmities that hasten
death. The food I offer you has none of these inconveniences.
The fumes returned to the brain by digestion are light and
never damage the fibers. Drink our water, my dear guest, and
note its clarity, savor its freshness. You cannot imagine the   15
care I take in making it good. What liquor rivals it? Is anything
healthier? Now you needn't ask me why I look so young for
my age. I never abused myself physically although I traveled
widely. I always avoided intemperance and never tasted meat.

   "You're going to take me for a disciple of Crotone* and   20
it will surprise you to learn that I have nothing to do with all
that. I've a single principle: to try to surround myself with the
greatest possible aggregation of happiness, and begin by making others happy. I owe you still more apologies concerning
the bourgeois manner in which I received you. A sovereign   25
who eats with his wife and children! Who doesn't bribe 4,000
scoundrels at one table for monsieur, another for madam?
Such triviality and bad form! Isn't that what they'd say in
French? You see I know the language. How onerous and cruel

* The city in Italy where Pythagoras taught.

for a sensitive soul, my friend, is this intolerable luxury which owes uniquely to the blood and sweat of the people. Do you believe I'd dine on these plates of gold were they served to me at the expense of the happiness of my subjects? Or while rickets-ridden children of those who brace such luxury sustain their own sorry existence with a few pieces of brown bread kneaded in the bosom of poverty and moistened with tears of pain and despair? No, the idea makes me tremble; I could never stand it. What you see today on my table, all inhabitants of this island may have on theirs; and thus I eat with pleasure. Well, now, my dear Frenchman, have you nothing to say?"

"You're a great man," I responded with enthusiasm. "More than that I cannot say, but you delight me and I admire you."

"Now listen," said Zamé. "You use an expression that shocks me. Let us leave the word 'great' to the despots who demand respect. Their certitude that they can inspire no other sentiment makes them renounce all those they cannot incite and lay beyond their reach, while requiring instead only what owes to wealth and the power of the throne. No man alive is greater than another, with respect to the state in which Nature created him; let those who claim inequality do so by dint of virtue. The inhabitants of this country call me their father and I want you to call me your friend. Did you not tell me that I'd done you a favor? Well, then, I have the right to be a friend — and demand the same of you."

The conversation turned general. The women, most of whom spoke French, joined in with as much wit as equal parts grace and naiveté. I'd already noticed that they were all dressed in absolutely the same manner as the women in the city, a costume both simple and elegant. A tight-fitting and cleanly tailored *juste-au-corps* outlined their figures; they were svelte with extremely high waists; their veils appeared to be made of material finer and suppler than our gauze, warm

yellow in color, which nicely matched their hair, falling in soft
undulations around their hips, ending in a large knot at the
left thigh. The men were all dressed in Asian garb, their heads
covered by a type of turban, light and agreeable in form, and
the same color as their garments.

Gray, pink, and green are the only three colors for their
clothing. The first, for old people, green for maturity, and the
last, for youth. The material they use is soft and light, the same
for all seasons, as might be expected given the warm climate;
it rather resembles the taffeta of Florence. That of the women
is the same. These materials and that of their veils are woven
by their own manufactures from the third layer of the bark of
a tree that he showed me, which resembles a mulberry. Zamé
told me that this species of plant is unique to his island.

The two citizens who announced dinner were the only
ones to serve it. All took place in good order and the meal
lasted under an hour.

"My dear guest," said Zamé, rising, "you're tired. We will
conduct you to your bedroom; tomorrow we'll wake early and
talk. I'll explain my people's form of government and convince
you that the man you took to be a sovereign is merely a legislator and friend. I will tell my story and at the same time see to it
that your needs are met. It is not enough to talk about oneself
to friends; the essential thing is to take care of them. I leave
you in the hands of one of my faithful servants" — he pointed
to one of the citizens who had served us — "he will settle you
in. You will find everything quite simple, I expect. Were you
at the home of a financier, you would have two valets turned
out in gilt to accompany you; here you'll have only one of my
friends, as I call my domestics. Mendacity, pride, and egoism
would be the ceremonial price you would pay with one whilst
all you see here is only the work of my heart. I leave you now
— goodnight."

The apartment to which I was taken proved to be simple but clean and comfortable, just as everything else I'd observed in this charming house. Three mattresses, filled with dried palm leaves made tender and soft as feathers, comprised my bed. They were laid out on mats on the ground. Hanging from the walls was a light netting of the same material as the women's veils, to protect one from the bites of a small fly, bothersome in one season of the year. In this bedroom I passed one of the best nights I had enjoyed since my misfortunes began. I believed myself to be in the temple of virtue and slept tranquil at the foot of its altar.

The next morning Zamé sent someone to inquire if I was awake; and as I was up and about, I was told he awaited me. I found him in the same room in which I'd been received the day before.

"As a young foreigner," he said, "I believe you would like to know about the man who welcomes you and take pleasure in learning how you've found, at the end of the world, one who speaks your language and is familiar with your country. Be seated and listen."

The Story of Zamé

At the end of the reign of Louis XIV — *so began Zamé* — a French warship seeking passage from China to America discovered this island, unknown to any navigator then or since. For nearly a month officers and crew took advantage of the state of weakness and innocence in which they found the people, and they caused much trouble and disorder. As they sailed off, one of the ship's young officers, hopelessly in love with a woman of the island, hid away and let his shipmates leave without him. As soon as they were gone he gathered

the nation's chiefs, and with the woman he loved (with whom   o
he'd made himself understood) speaking on his behalf, he declared that he remained on the island only because of his great
attachment to the people. He wanted to protect them from
certain misfortunes presaged by the discovery of the island,
and he showed the assembled chiefs a place on the island that   5
was, sadly enough, a gold mine.

"My friends," he told them, "here is what arouses the rapacity of men from my country. This cursed metal, the uses of
which you are wholly ignorant, that on this island you trample
underfoot, is the most cherished object of their desires. To   10
claw gold from the bowels of the earth, they will return in
force. They will subjugate you and put you in chains; they will
exterminate you or perhaps, what's worse, enslave you as their
neighbors the Spanish do every day on a continent hundreds
of leagues distant, about which you know nothing, and which   15
abounds in these sorts of riches. I believe I might save you
from their rapacity by living amongst you. Knowing how they
invade and take hold of an island, I might be able to prevent it;
knowing how they do battle, I could teach you how to defend
yourselves. Perhaps at least I can save you from their greed.   20
Furnish me the means to act and, as my only compensation,
let me have the woman I love."

The response was unanimous. Accorded his mistress, he
was also provided all the help he might need to carry out his
plans.   25

Exploring the island on foot, he found it to be circular in
shape, about 50 leagues in circumference, entirely surrounded by rocks, except along the coast where you managed to
land. He therefore judged that to be the only part requiring
fortification. Perhaps you've not observed how he made the   30
port inaccessible. We will visit it this afternoon. There I will
convince you that, had we not judged you were weak and your

difficulty was the sole cause of your arrival on our island, you wouldn't have landed so easily. This part of the island, the only gateway to Tamoé, he thus fortified in the European style. He brought batteries that I alone keep furnished and maintained. He also raised a militia and established a garrison constructed at the entrance to the bay.

So pleased was the nation by the wisdom of his care and superiority of his ideas that, after the death of his father-in-law, one of the main chiefs, he was unanimously elected sovereign of the island. He thereafter changed the constitution because, he explained, the perfection of his enterprise required that the government become hereditary in order that he could pass on his designs to his successor, who could be made to follow and improve them. To this the people consented.

About this time I was born, the fruit of the marriage of this man, so dear to the nation; and it was to me that he confided his plans. I am happy to have fulfilled them.

I shall say nothing about his administration; he could only make a start to what I finished. In detailing my operations, you will become familiar with his. Let us return to what preceded them.

After I turned 15, my father spent five years teaching me history, geography, mathematics, astronomy, drawing, and the art of navigation. At last he brought me to the gold mine he feared so attractive to his European compatriots.

"We will take from here all we need," he told me, "for you to travel with both pomp and practicality. You cannot leave here, unfortunately, without this metal. But regard it with mistrust, for debasement would follow if our simple and happy nation began to set store by it. Don't suppose that gold has any but a fictive value. It means nothing in the eyes of people wise enough to reject its extravagance."

After filling several chests with the metal, he had the site closed and the land cultivated in order to obliterate any trace of it. Aboard a large ship constructed according to his own specifications and with my journey as its sole aim, he embraced me with tears in his eyes:

"You, my son, whom I perhaps shall never see again and sacrifice to the happiness of the nation that has adopted me — go out and discover the universe. Learn from the world over everything that seems most advantageous to the happiness of your people. Buzz among the flowers and return home with the honey. You'll find among men much foolishness and little wisdom, a few good principles mixed with frightful absurdities. Grow learned, come to know your fellows before attempting to govern them. Don't be dazzled by the royal crimson of kings, and disdain the pomp concealing their mediocrity, despotism, and indolence. I've always detested kings and your destiny is not to occupy a throne. I wish you to become father and friend to our adoptive nation. I want you to be its legislator and guide. The people need, in a word, not chains but virtues.

"Distrust entirely the tyrants that Europe will set before your eyes. You'll find them everywhere surrounded by slavish sorts who keep the truth from them, for those in favor have too much to lose in revealing it. Kings do not like it; they nearly always make themselves feared. The only way not to be afraid of the truth is to be virtuous; he who hides nothing, whose conscience is pure, is unafraid. But as for the one whose heart is soiled, he listens only to his passions and likes illusion and flattery because they conceal from him his wrongdoings and make light of the yoke with which he afflicts his subjects, showing them to be filled with joy whilst they're drowning in their own tears. In trying to understand why courtiers engage in flattery that makes them veil the eyes of their master, you'll discover the vices of government. Study them to avoid them. The obligation to make the people happy is essential and it is quite as sweet to succeed as it is terrible to fail. Legislators must live for moments when their efforts bear fruit.

"The diversity of cults will surprise you. Everywhere you'll see men infatuated by their own religion, imagining this one to be good or that one alone to come from God — who never uttered a word about one or the other. Examining them all philosophically, you'll see that religion is useful to man only inasmuch as it lends force to morality and curbs perversity. For this it must be pure and simple. If a cult offers your eyes nothing but empty ceremonies, monstrous dogmas, and imbecilic mysteries, flee from it, for it is false and dangerous, and for your nation it would prove to be nothing but an endless source of crime and murder. You would be just as guilty for bringing it to this corner of the world as the vile charlatans who spread it across the earth. Flee all such, my son; detest the deceitful handiwork of some and the stupidity of others. It will not improve the people. But if one presents itself, simple in doctrine, virtuous in morality, distrustful of pomp, rejecting puerile fairy tales, and that has as its sole objective the worship of a single God — seize upon it. For it is good. Not by antics — here revered, there despised — may we please the Eternal One, but by goodness and purity of heart. If there be a God, here are the virtues that shaped Him, the only ones that men ought to imitate.

"You will be also astonished at the diversity of laws. Examine them all with equal attention just as with religion. Consider that their only useful purpose is to make men happy and regard as false and atrocious all that deviate from this principle.

"The life of one man is too short to reach my stated aim. I can only prepare your way; it will be up to you to finish what

I started. Bequeath our principles to your children and two   o
or three generations will bring our good people the greatest
happiness. Go then, be off."

So saying, he embraced me once more and I set out
across the waves. I traveled the world over. Twenty years I was
gone from my native land. Those years I spent learning about   5
my fellows, mingling with them in vesture of every kind, betimes like the famous emperor of Russia. Companion to art-
ists and artisans, I learned both to build ships and to transmit
cherished features to canvas, to model stone and marble, to
erect a palace, to direct manufactures. At the side of a farmer   10
I acquired knowledge of the soil and learned to sow seeds and
cultivate plants, to graft and trim them, to tend to striplings
and make them strong, to harvest the grain and use it to nourish my fellow man. On a still higher plane the poet embellished
my ideas, gave them color and intensity, and taught me the art   15
of portraying them; the historian showed me how to transmit
facts to posterity and make known the customs of all nations.
With help from a minister of the altar, I learned about the unintelligible science of the gods while law's henchmen showed
me a science still more imaginary, by which a man is put in   20
chains to improve him. The financier instructed me in raising
taxes and explained the atrocious system of fattening oneself
at the expense of the unfortunate and reducing people to poverty yet not allowing the state to flourish. The merchant, still
more costly to the state, taught me how to valuate products all   25
over the world in the denominated currencies of nations, to
exchange them based upon the indestructible bond that links
all peoples of the world, to become friend and brother to the
Christian as well as the Arab, to those who worship Fo-Hi and
the adepts of Ali alike; he doubles his money by rendering   30
himself useful to compatriots, and enriches himself and his
people with all the gifts of art and Nature, resplendent with

the luxury of all the earth's inhabitants, content with their great joys without having ventured beyond the walls of his own offices. More adaptable, the negotiator initiated me into the affairs of kings. His eye pierced the thick veil and looked centuries into the future, and he calculated and appreciated with me, in consequence of their present state, customs and doctrines, and the revolutions to come. Introducing me to the offices of kings, he brought tears to my eyes. He showed me how, in all of them, pride and greed sacrificed the people at altars of wealth; the throne of graspers was everywhere raised on rivers of blood. Finally, the courtier, lighter and more deceitful, taught me to how to beguile monarchs, for they alone showed me the despair of being born to become a king.

Everywhere I saw much vice and little virtue; everywhere I found the vanity, envy, avarice, and intemperance that enslaved the weak to the whims of the strong; everywhere I could divide man into two classes, to be pitied equally. In one, the rich man was a slave to his pleasures; in the other, the poor man a victim of fate — yet I never perceived in one the urge to do better nor in the other the possibility of becoming better, as if both cultivated their common unhappiness and sought only to add shackles to shackles. The wealthiest among them invariably tightened his chains by doubling his desires while the poorest, insulted and mistrusted by the other, received not the slightest encouragement necessary to bear his burden.

I asked for equality and was called a dreamer. Soon I perceived that those who rejected it ought to lose it and — what am I saying? — from that very moment I believed equality alone could make people happy.* From the hands of Nature all men are born equal. To view them as not of the same kind is

---

* Let us never forget that this work was written a year before the French Revolution.

false. Wherever equal they can also be happy whilst that is im-   o
possible where distinctions exist. Such differences can render
at most one part of the nation happy but the legislator must
work to make all so equally. Don't object to the difficulties in
bridging the gap; it is only a question of silencing certain doctrines and equalizing fortunes, operations no more difficult   5
than establishing a new tax.

In truth it was not as hard for me as for others. I worked
to build a nation that remained too close to the state of Nature
to be corrupted by that false system of distinctions. Success
came to me more easily.   10

Convinced of the need to plan for equality, I studied the
second cause of man's unhappiness, which I located in his
passions. Forever torn between the latter and the law, I convinced myself that the only way to make him less unhappy in
this respect was for there to be less passion and fewer laws.   15

Another operation proved simpler than might be imagined. By abolishing luxury and introducing equality, I annihilated pride, cupidity, avarice, and ambition. On what can one
pride oneself when, except for talents and virtues, everything
is equal? What is there to covet, what riches to conceal, what   20
rank to aspire to, when every fortune is like every other and
when everyone possesses more than enough to satisfy his
wants? Men's needs are all the same. Although Apicius* did
not have a larger stomach than Diogenes, the former nevertheless required 20 cooks while the latter dined on a single   25
nut. Both occupy the same level. Diogenes would not lose,
for he had nothing but the simple things to make him happy,

---

* The most gluttonous and debauched of Romans; intemperate in everything, he long
kept Sejanus as a mistress. He wasted 15 million in debauchery alone at table and in
bed; in the end he was ruined. When his accounts were done and he had not more
than 100,000 livres in rents, he poisoned himself in despair.

while Apicius, who would never have put up with the necessities alone, would suffer in his imagination.

If you wish to live according to Nature, said Epicurus, *you will never be poor. If you wish to live by following public opinion, you will never be rich. Nature demands little; public opinion, much.*

From the first, I told myself, I shall have fewer vices; and in this way a great number of laws will become unnecessary. For crime necessitates laws: diminish their number, provided what you regard as criminal is simple, and the law is rendered useless. How many follies and how many foolish actions entail no injury to society and therefore, justly appreciated by a legislator-philosopher, might no longer be viewed as dangerous and still less as criminal? Suppress the laws made by tyrants that only prove their authority and more fully subjugate man to their whims; you will find, when all is said and done, that with the number of restraints reduced to a few, the man who suffers their weight is vastly relieved. The great art would be to combine law and crime in such a way that any crime would but lightly offend the law while the law, less rigid, would weigh heavily only on a very few crimes. Again, it is not difficult, and here is where I believe I succeeded. To this we shall return.

By establishing divorce, I destroyed nearly all the vices of intemperance; there would no longer remain anything of the sort were I to tolerate incest, as is done among the Brahmins, or pederasty, as in Japan; but I saw they could be troublesome, not so much concerning the acts themselves, and not to say that alliances within families do not provide an infinity of good results whilst pederasty poses no danger, aside from decreasing the population and that by itself it is a wrong of little importance.

Real happiness for a nation clearly consists not so much in the size of the population as in the perfect balance between

the people and its resources.* If I believed those vices harm- 0
ful, it was only relative to my plan of governance inasmuch
as the firſt deſtroys equality, which I wanted to eſtablish, by
enlarging but insulating families; and the second, by forming a separate class of men self-sufficient unto itself, which
would necessarily deſtabilize the equilibrium I deemed es- 5
sential. But juſt because I wished to annihilate these devia-
tions, I was wary of punishing them. The Spanish Inquisition
with its auto-da-fé and the Place de Grève with its gibbets
were proof enough that the beſt way to propagate aberrations
is to erect a gallows. I made use of public opinion which, as 10
you know, rules the world. I ſpread disguſt concerning the
firſt of these vices; the second I covered with ridicule. Twenty
years have put an end to them. I would be saddled with them
forever were I to make use of prisons or call on the executioner.

Religion gives birth to a multitude of new crimes — that 15
much I knew. As I traveled through France, I came across the
ſtill-smoldering massacres at Mérindol and Cabrières. I saw
the gallows raised at the Chateau d'Amboise; in the capital
I could ſtill hear the frightful bells of Saint Bartholomew's.
Points of doctrine drenched Ireland in blood and, in Eng- 20
land there were the terrible conflicts between Puritans and
Nonconformiſts. In Spain the unfortunate anceſtors of your
religion, the Jews, were burned alive while reciting the same
prayers as the people who tore them to pieces. In Italy they
talked to me of the Crusades of Innocent VI and, as I passed 25
through Scotland, Bohemia, and Germany, I was daily shown
battlefields on which men had charitably slit their brothers'
throats to teach them to love the Lord.†

---

* Large empires and large populations (so says Monsieur Raynal) have two great
problems. Rather, few people, but happy; small but well-governed.

*Great God! I cried. Don't such frenzies serve the furies
of hell? What barbarous hand moves them to slaughter each
other for their primitive beliefs? Is a religion holy if it requires
bodies heaped on high and stigmatizes its catechumens with
blood? What can they mean to you, O just and holy God, our
systems and our judgments! What difference to your grandeur
the way men invoke your name? What you want is that he be
just; what pleases you is to be humane. You don't need genu-
flection or ceremony, or dogma and mystery. You want only our
hearts and expect only our love and gratitude.*

In religion let us dispense with cult, I told myself, and
all fodder for argument. Let there be such simplicity that it
can give rise to no sect. I'll show you the good people as they
worship and you will judge if they err. We believe in an Eternal
One on high, good enough to listen to us without a mediator.
As sacrifice we offer only our souls. We stand on no ceremony
for it is from God alone we ask forgiveness for our faults and
help in avoiding them; to Him alone we confess what troubles
our conscience. Priests are superfluous. We have banished
them forever; we no longer suffer that sort of individual who is
useless to the state, to Nature, and always harmful to society;
no longer do we fear the sight of our fellow man massacred
for pride.

I told myself: Give laws to this excellent people, yes — but
will you punish offenders with death? Heaven forbid! Only the
Sovereign Being may dispose of a man's life; I should believe
myself a criminal the moment I'd dare usurp such a right.

---

† Twenty years' battle in Bohemia cost the lives of more than two million men in order
to decide if it was necessary to make communion under the two species, or simply
under one. Animals that do battle with one another over females have at least the
excuse of being in the wild; but what can be the excuse of men who cut each other's
throats for a little flour and a few drops of wine?

You Europeans, accustomed to forge the image of a barbarous   o
and bloodthirsty God, imagine a place of torments to send all
whom God condemns; you believe you imitate His justice by
fomenting the same kinds of murders and mortifications. You
don't see that you've established the basis for committing the
greatest of crimes — killing a fellow human being — only out   5
of a dream born of your imagination.

The idea, my friend, that evil can ever bring forth good
is one of the most stupefying products of foolish minds. Man
is feeble, he was created so by the hand of God; it's not for
me to either sound out the reasoning of the Supreme Being   10
or punish a man for being what he is. I must use every means
possible to make him as good as he can be, but none to punish
him for not being what he ought to make of himself. I must
enlighten him, as is every man's duty, but the right to regulate
another's actions belongs to no one. The people's happiness is   15
the first duty the Eternal One imposes upon me; and my work
is not to slaughter them. Willingly I shed my own blood to
spare theirs, but I do not want the people to spill a single drop
owing to their weaknesses or rapacity. If they're attacked, let
them defend themselves; if their blood flows, it will be in their   20
own defense, not to further my own ambitions. Nature afflicts
the people with pain enough and I've no right to impose it
upon them.

From the honest and upstanding citizens I received the
power to be useful. I did not have it to impose it upon them. I   25
shall be their ally not their persecutor; I shall be their father
not their assassin. Men of the sword who lay claim to the sorry
honor of massacring their brothers, these bloodthirsty vultures whom I compare to cannibals — I shall not allow them
on this island. Instead of rendering service, they cause harm;   30
where the people allow it, the suffering they cause shows on
history's every page. I see these men as atrocious, whether

they're disrupting the legislator' wise projects or refusing to unite the nation when glory is at stake, whether putting the country in chains if it's weak or, if it has energy, leaving it to decay. Such monsters, for a nation state, are nothing if not dangerous.

With these considerations in mind, I turned to commerce. That of your colonies I found frightening. What need, I asked myself, to create such far-flung settlements? Does genuine happiness, as one of your fine writers has said, require taking pleasure in things sought so far away? Must we be eternally in thrall to such contrived tastes? Sugar, tobacco, spices, coffee, et cetera — is it worth sacrificing men for such wretched things?

Foreign commerce, as I see it, is useful only insofar as a nation has too much or too little. If a surfeit, it can exchange its superabundance for objects of pleasure and frivolity; luxury and opulence may be permitted. If it has not enough, a nation must clearly seek what it needs. Neither case applies to France, where you have little in excess yet lack for nothing. You can make people happy with what they have, rich on your own soil with no need of acquisitions nor exchange to be better off.

Won't your abundant country produce more than you need without obliging you to establish colonies or send ships to the four corners of the world? More advantageously situated than any European empire, you need few of the products found around the world. The Midi in Provence, Corsica, and the land neighboring Spain could provide you with sugar, tobacco, and coffee. You can see in this class of superfluous products some are a little useful; and if we look to spices, what seems like privation is actually good for your health, so what there to regret? Have you not everything you need to provide comfort for the ordinary citizen and luxury for the rich?

Your cloth rivals that of England, and Abbeville once furnished   o
Rome, the most magnificent city in the world. Your painted
linens are superb, your silk the softest in all Europe; you send
marvelous and quality furniture all over the world. Tapestries
by the Gobelins are better than those of Brussels, your wines
are drunk everywhere and have the supreme advantage of im-   5
proving with age. Your wheat is so abundant that often you
must export it.* Your oils are more excellent still than those
of Italy, your fruits tasty and healthful; perhaps with work you
could grow some of those that are found in America. Your
woods for heating and construction will always be abundant   10
if you learn how to care for them. So what need have you of
foreign commerce? Oblige foreign nations to come to your
ports and simply accept their currency or fancy goods in exchange for your overabundance, but stop equipping vessels
to go seek their own; don't put one-sixth of the population   15
at risk on the dangerous high seas just to satisfy the caprices
of the rest, a fatal arrangement you will regret when you see
what your pleasures cost in lives of your brothers. Forgive me,
my friend, but such considerations always enter into my calculations. We'll bring you everything in order to obtain from   20
you what you can provide in return — but keep no colonies.
Not just useless, they're ruinous and pose a great danger. It's
impossible for a mother to require full obedience from her
children at great distance.

25

Here I took the liberty of interrupting Zamé to explain to him
what had happened to the British colonies in America.

* France, with a population of 23 million, annually harvests 50 million setiers of wheat;
that is to say enough to nourish all its inhabitants; and yet even with such wealth the
nation, without natural disasters, is sometimes on the brink of famine!

"What you're telling me," he replied, "I predicted. The same will happen to the Spanish and, more likely still, the Republic of Washington will gradually grow, like that of Romulus. First it will subjugate America and then make the whole world tremble. Except you, the French, who will end by casting off the yoke of despotism and in your turn become Republicans, for that is the only kind of government suitable for a nation as frank and full of energy and pride as yours.*

Come what may, I repeat: a nation lucky enough to meet all its own needs must consume what it has and not permit export of the surplus except on condition that others come seek it. "One day soon, as we travel across this fortunate island, we'll take up that topic. For now, let's return to take up the thread of my story."

The decision I made, after study, was to bring back to my island, with a view to augmenting its own natural production, a considerable number of European plants that seemed beneficial. I planned to teach myself the art of directing manufactures that might be employed to put an end to the use of all objects of luxury, to enjoy our own improved and better products, and to break off entirely all but internal lines of commerce, restricting them to exchange by barter.

We have few neighbors, just two or three islands to the south, still uncivilized, from which the inhabitants occasionally come to visit; we give them our surplus without receiving anything in return. They have nothing more valuable than we do ourselves. Commerce otherwise established would not

---

* The reader ought to understand that it required the state of mind of a man imprisoned in the Bastille in 1788 to make such a prediction!

be long in drawing us into war; they don't know the extent
of our power; we would crush them. But my first rule is to
avoid bloodshed. So we live in peace with our neighboring
isles; I am happy to have made them esteem and appreciate
our government: they would come to our aid without fail if
we needed help — but they would be useless. If attacked by an
enemy, all our citizens become soldiers; not even one would
not prefer death to a change of government. Here again you
see the fruits of my policies. By being beloved, I turn them
into soldiers; from their love and my forging indissoluble
bonds comes promise of a happy life, flourishing agriculture,
an abundance of all they desire. In opposing usurpers they
protect their households, their wives and children, and the
unique happiness they enjoy in life — for these things they
would indeed do battle. If ever I had need of this militia, a
single word from me would suffice: "My children," I would say:
"These are your homes, your properties, and now come those
who would take them from you. Let us march!"

Do your sovereigns of Europe have anything similar to
offer their mercenaries, who know nothing of the motivating
cause for which they're ready to go forth and stupidly spill their
blood and die in a dispute the substance of which they are not
only indifferent to but wholly ignorant? You should have in
your country a strong and solid administration; it should not
change at the whim of your sovereigns or the flimsiest fantasies of their mistresses. A man who knows how to govern,
one who knows the secret of the machine, must be respected
and retained. It is imprudent to confer such knowledge upon
many at the same time. What would happen if they were certain of being in power for only a short while? They'd look only
to their interests and entirely neglect your own. Strengthen
your borders, make your neighbors respect you. Renounce
the spirit of conquest and never have enemies. Take care to

guarantee your borders and you won't need to forever sustain an army but rather will free 100,000 hands to work the plough, far more useful than a rifle that's used not four times in a century — not even once by the plan I've developed. You will no longer take children from families who need them nor introduce license and debauchery among the elite* — all for the imbecilic luxury of a substantial standing army. Nothing so amusing as to hear your writers constantly laud "the people" while everything the government does shows that there are too many of them. If it weren't, would the government be hobbled on one hand by the celibacy required of the flower of the nation that's plucked for military duty? Equally denied liberty and constrained by the absurd chains of abstinence is that multitude of priests and religious folk. With all this, since there are still *too many* despite such powerful impediments to population growth, is it not ridiculous to continue fuming about it? Am I mistaken? Do you want a larger population? Is that essential? Very well, but don't seek to enlarge it beyond your means. Open your cloisters, keep no useless military, and the number of your subjects will quadruple.

One day in Paris, I stopped by the arena of Themis where priestlings of the temple, decked out in elegant morning coats over black skirts, were coming from supper with their harlots to condemn to death some unfortunate fellow worth more than any of them. Those butchers of human flesh provided us with a spectacle.

I asked: "What crime did this poor man commit?"

"Pederasty," came the reply. "As you well know, a frightful crime. It galls, harms, and destroys the population. The scoundrel deserves to be destroyed."

---

* This truth is all the more important in that there are few schools worse than the garrisons, where young men's morals and demeanor are soon corrupted.

"Well considered," I replied to this philosopher. "Monsieur is quite the genius."

Following a crowd into a nearby monastery, I saw a poor young woman of 16 or 17, fresh and beautiful, who had just renounced the world and swore to bury herself alive, in solitude.

"Friend," said I to someone next to me, "what is this young woman doing?'"

"She is a saint," I was told. "She renounces the world to confine in the depths of a cloister the source of 20 children that she might have brought into the world for the pleasure of the state."

"What a sacrifice!"

"Oh, yes, monsieur. She is an angel, with a place made for her in Heaven."

"What nonsense!" said I to my companion, unable to accept the foolishness of it. "You execute an unfortunate man whom you say was wrong to interfere with propagation, yet here you crown a young woman who shall commit the same crime. Think again, Frenchman — think and don't be angry if a reasonable stranger traveling through your nation often finds it a center of madness and absurdity."

I've a single enemy to fear: the inconstant European, the vagabond who renounces his own comforts to go interfere with those of foreigners, imagining that riches to be found elsewhere are more precious, always demanding better government because he never knows how to temper his own. He is turbulent, ferocious, ever apprehensive, and born to foment unhappiness worldwide, bringing the catechism to all Asia, putting Africa in chains, exterminating the inhabitants of the New World, and searching the high seas for vulnerable isles to subjugate. Yes, he's the only enemy I fear, the only one against whom I will do battle if he comes; the one we shall destroy and who shall never set foot upon this isle. He can reach us

only along one coastline, as I told you; it is thoroughly fortified. There you'll see the batteries I've put in place, an ac-
complishment which was the final objective of my voyage. In
Cadiz I had three warships built. I loaded them with cannons,
mortars, bombs, rifles, ammunition, gunpowder — all the
frightening munitions of Europe. It was the last use to which
I put the gold from my father and I stocked it all in the port
stores he'd constructed. The cannons were fitted to their em-
brasures. Twice a month one hundred young men perform
the various maneuvers necessary for such artillery; my fellow
citizens know that these precautions are taken only against
would-be invading enemies. They don't worry about it or seek
to learn more about the effects of these infernal munitions,
experiments about which I've always concealed. The young
men conduct their operations without firing; were the situation serious, they know what would result, and that suffices.
With my gentle neighbors hereabouts I wouldn't need to take
such precautions. Your barbarous compatriots force them
upon me. I'd never employ them without being sorry to do so.

Such was the formidable armamentarium with which,
after 20 years, I returned to my country. I had the good fortune to reunite with my father and receive still further counsel.
He scuttled the ships I returned on, fearing that the ability
to make distant voyages might incite avarice among his own
good people and that the example of the Europeans, with
their hopes of enriching themselves elsewhere, might destroy
their tranquility. He wanted this friendly and peaceful people,
happy in their clime, to live on what they produced, with few
laws and a simple cult, to retain their innocence forever, never
touched by foreign nations that would inculcate not a single
virtue but, rather, many vices. I followed the plans laid down
by the respectable and dear author of my existence, improving
upon them where I thought possible. We've turned this most

agrarian of nations into one that is civilized but gentle; and it   o
confers happiness on natural man, far from the barbarous and
dangerous excesses with which your countries are cursed for
their domination, and hated and detested for the submission
they require, cruelly depriving people of happy independence.

    Savage life is the natural state of man; he was born in   5
the deep forest like the bear and the tiger. Only in refining his
needs could he see it was useful to come together to better
find means to satisfy them. In taking him to civilize him, think
of this primitive state, of that state of liberty by which Nature
shaped him, and add only what might improve that happy   10
condition in which he then found himself; make him capable
but forge no chains; let him more easily fulfill his desires but
not subjugate him to them; establish limits for his own happiness but don't crush him with a jumble of absurd laws. Let
your work tend to magnify his pleasure by leading him to the   15
powerful and sustained art of enjoyment; provide him with
a religion as gentle as the God it serves, unharnessed from
anything based only on faith; make it consist in works, not religious belief. Don't let your people suppose they must blindly
believe this or that group of men who in the end know no   20
more than they do themselves. To be convinced of what they
must do, what will please the Eternal One, is to always keep
souls as pure as when they first came forth from His hands.
Thus will the people rush to worship the good Lord who requires only the virtues necessary for the happiness of the indi-   25
viduals who practice them. That way people will cherish your
administration and subject themselves to it; and here, too,
you'll find them to be faithful friends who would rather perish
than abandon you, and who will work with you to preserve
the country.   30

0   "We shall resume our conversation tomorrow," Zamé told me.
"Now that I've told my story, young man, it remains for me
to convince you of what I've done. Let us dine. The women
are waiting."

     All transpired as the night before. The same frugality, ca-
5   sual ambiance, care taken, and amiability on the part of my
hosts. With us in addition were his two sons, difficult not to
like as soon as we met and talked with them. One was 22, the
other 18; both physiognomies showed the same kindness and
friendliness as their parents. They overwhelmed me with po-
10   litesse and marks of respect; they entirely lacked the insulting
curiosity or distrust so often apparent in youth the first time
they encounter a stranger. They observed and talked with me
only to shower compliments, interrogated only to take from
my responses occasions to commend me.*

---

* A French *philosophe* who ventures abroad will find among the individuals of his own
country subjects for study just as interesting as the foreigners he meets in his travels.
One may point to the fatuousness and impertinence of our debonair travelers, their
tone of denigration when they talk of everything about which they know nothing
and of everything they don't find at home. They bring an insulting attitude full of
contempt to anything that does not smack of foolish cleverness; in a word, they uni-
versally cover themselves with ridicule, surely one reason other peoples view them
with antipathy. Our ministers, it seems to me, should pay more attention and not
accord the privilege of travel to people who can only degrade the nation in the eyes of
Europe, the better not to extend beyond its frontiers these sorts of vices with which
we are all too familiar.

     In Italy the inn is full when the coach arrives late. The door is shut but from a win-
dow the proprietor asks the traveler his nation. "France" comes the servant's insolent
response. "Begone," responds the other. "I have no room." "My people are mistaken,"
says the traveler smartly. "These are hired servants who only met me yesterday. If you
please, Monsieur, I am English." And in a trice it's settled with an eager reception. Is
it not frightening that the discredit of the nation is such that one must conceal it to
enter not only high society but even a tavern? And why not be liked when success
costs nothing beyond foreswearing the wrongs that dishonor us even at home in the
eyes of wise people who coolly examine the situation? The Revolution now changing
our mores may yet prune the feathers of the fools among us. For our own happiness,
let's at least hope so.

In the afternoon Zamé wanted us to go and see whether
or not my crew needed anything; it would have been difficult
to improve on his orders and impossible they could have been
better carried out. It was then he showed me the difficulty of
entering the port and how well it was defended. Two embank-
ments surrounded and protected it, dominating it to the point
that no ship could avoid being bombarded by numerous artil-
leries mounted on these redoubts; a boat entering the harbor
would come under fire from the fort. Even if these defenses
were breached, two vast arteries defending the approach to
the city would be occupied by the nation's youth, making inva-
sion impossible.

"Up to the present I have had no need of any of this," said
Zamé. "Thank heavens. And I hope the people never will. You
see the enormous cliffs that dominate left and right. More
than 300 feet high, they form the mouth of the port but make
it inapproachable from any side. So surrounding us, they
serve as ramparts. The people rejoice that they'll long enjoy
the happiness we've brought them. Such certainty is my pride
and joy. I shall die happy."

We went back.

"You are young," Zamé told me shortly before we entered
the palace, "I must make amends for tedium I've caused you
this morning. Here is a spectacle you will appreciate."

As the doors opened I saw a hundred women surrounding the wife of the legislator, all dressed identically in pink,
because this was the color of youth.

"Here are the prettiest people of the capital," Zamé told
me, "I wanted to bring them together before your eyes, so you
might decide for yourself between them and the women of
France."

Perhaps if I were less occupied by my heart's own goddess,
I might better have discerned the astonishing assemblage of

pretty features before me; but I ever only saw that tender object of my affection. Each time beauty appeared before me in
whatever form, I saw only Léonore.

Nevertheless, one would be hard put to bring together
that many pretty faces in any city in Europe. In general, the
bloodline on Tamoé is superb. Zilia, whom I shall attempt to
describe, will give you an impression of the female sex, accorded a host of unique charms, it seems to me, as Nature
intended for the happiest country on earth.

Slender and lissome, Zilia had skin of the purest white
and features the very emblem of candor and modesty; her
large dark blue eyes, more tender than lively, seemed to express love at the height of delicacy, sentiment at its most
voluptuous. Her mouth was deliciously formed, her teeth
white and beautiful; she seemed a little pale until one's gaze
fell upon her and then she burst to life, fresh as a rose. Her
brow was noble, her hair, so nicely patterned, ashen blonde
in great quantity, elegantly matched by the gracious contours
of her veil, streaming across alabaster breasts, always exposed
in accord with the fashion of the country — all finally lent
this pretty woman the air of a goddess of youth. She had just
reached her 16th year, still growing despite all, her arms lithe
and fingers to our eyes so very supple and slender.

"Do not think me insipid, Mademoiselle," *said Sainville, addressing Aline,* "but in a single word I might have described
this charming young woman by doing nothing more than
pointing to you."

"In truth, Monsieur," said Madame de Blamont, "is that really the case? Do you not flatter us? My daughter as lovely as Zilia?"

"I dare say, Madame," replied Sainville, "that to more
closely resemble her would be impossible."

"Continue, Monsieur, go on," said Count Beaulé to Sainville, "We don't want to spoil our dear Aline."

Aline blushed. Her mother kissed her and *our young adventurer continued*:

"My son's wife," Zamé told me, introducing Zilia, "She can say only three words in French, the first ones her husband taught her." As he found her disposed, the charming father continued: "Say them, daughter"

Soft and delicious Zilia lay a hand to her heart and looked to her husband with grace and modesty. She blushed and said, "*Voilà votre bien.*" The women began to laugh and I saw what gaiety, candor, and touching felicity reigned among this happy people.

I asked Zamé why husbands were not with their wives.

"So that you might judge the sexes separately," he replied. "Tomorrow you'll meet the young men, and the day after we'll all be together. I have but few pleasures to provide, so I offer them sparingly."

These interesting women, animated by the presence of their leader's adorable wife, gave themselves over to a thousand innocent pleasures the rest of the day, with all manner of comportment that showed off their natural graces. In the end they convinced me of their sweet and friendly character. They played several of their country's games, as well as European ones, and in all of them they were gay, polite and honest, ever modest and decent, if you excepted their habit of leaving their breasts exposed. But custom is everything and I saw that the way they dressed, quite their own, never produced the least impropriety; the men are made to see their women thus; in the past they were used to seeing them naked. Thus were the laws of Zamé used to reestablish instead of destroy.

"We do not become excited by what we see on a daily basis," said my amiable host when he perceived my surprise at this custom. "Modesty is only a virtue by convention. Nature created us naked, so it pleases her. In addition, in becoming leader of the people, in their state of nudity, had I wished to encase the women in whalebone in the European fashion, they would have been in despair. When one changes the customs of a nation, provided they are not harmful, it is necessary to conserve as much of the old as possible. That way everyone can become used to things and no one is revolted."

A collation, simple and frugal, was served to these lovely women; the same politesse, discretion, and restraint followed them everywhere, and then they withdrew.

The next day there was a meeting and I could not see Zamé until the afternoon; I spent the morning busy with the ship.

"Come along," said my host as soon as he was free. "There remain many things to tell you that will give you fuller knowledge of our land and our customs. I told you that divorce is permitted in my country. Here are the details:

"Nature, by according women only a few years for reproduction of the species, seems to indicate that she permits a man to have two companions. When his spouse stops providing children, he still has 15 to 20 years to desire and enjoy the prospect of having more. The law that permits him a second wife can only help him fulfill his legitimate desires. Any law that opposes this arrangement goes contrary to Nature, both in terms of rigor and injustice. Divorce has nevertheless two inconveniences: for one thing, the children of the older wife can be mistreated by the younger; for another, fathers always prefer the last begotten.

"To eliminate these difficulties, children here leave the paternal home as soon as they no longer need the mother's breast. The education they receive is *national*; they are no longer the sons of so-and-so, they are children of the state.

The parents may see them in the houses where they grow up,   o
but they do not return to the paternal home; by this means,
there is no family spirit or focus on any individual child,
which is always fatal to equality and sometimes dangerous to
the state. Nor is there any fear of parents having more children than their inheritance can provide. Only one family to a   5
house on a loan basis, and there are often vacancies; once a
home goes empty, it is returned to the state. The state is the
sole owner of all assets; the citizens are only usufructuaries.
As soon as a male child reaches his 15th year, he is brought
into the house where the young women are raised. There he   10
chooses a spouse the same age as himself. If she consents,
the marriage takes place; if not, the young man seeks until
he finds acceptance; at that moment, he is provided a vacant
house and the land on which it stands. No matter whether it
belongs to his family, it suffices that the estate be available for   15
him to take possession. If the young couple have parents, they
attend the wedding. The ceremony is simple, with the spouses
simply affirming their mutual love in the name of the Eternal
One and swearing they will work together to have children
and that the husband shall not repudiate his wife, nor the wife   20
the husband, except for legitimate reasons. This done, the parents attending as witnesses shall leave, and the young people
will become their own masters under the supervision and direction of their neighbors, who are obliged to help and give
counsel, and to aid them over the next two years, at the end   25
of which such tutelage will end. If parents wish to help, they
may take charge and provide daily counsel to the newlyweds
during the two prescribed years.

"The causes for which a spouse may ask for divorce are
three in number. A man may repudiate his wife if she is un-   30
wholesome or if she does not want or can no longer have children, and if he proves that she is of a shrewish temperament

and she refuses her husband what he may legitimately ask of her. For her part, the woman may ask to leave her husband if he is unwholesome, if he does not want or cannot give her children when she can still have them, and if he mistreats her for any reason whatever.

"On the outskirts of every city you can find a whole street with houses that are smaller than those meant for the usual households; these the state provides to the unmarried and repudiated members of both sexes; to them are annexed, as with the others, small plots so that these individuals of either sex need ask nothing, either of family in the case of the unmarried, or of one's partner, if a spouse.

"A husband who has repudiated his wife and desires another, may choose her either from among the repudiated, if he happens to find one who pleases him, or he can seek her in the young women's house of education. The wife who repudiates her husband does the same; she can choose from among the repudiated and find one who accepts her, or she may choose among the young men if one will have her. But if a repudiated spouse desires to live apart in a small habitation provided by the state without wishing to assume new constraints, the decision is up to him. One is not forced to do these things; they are all done in good faith. Children can never be obstacles; the state relieves parents of that burden, for they are scarcely born before they are taken away. Beyond the two choices, repudiation is not possible; both must have patience, each to mutually suffer the other. One cannot imagine the extent to which a law that disencumbers fathers and mothers of their children is able to avoid family division and discord. Here marriage partners need only smell the roses, never feel their thorns. Nothing in all this breaks the bonds of Nature: parents can see and cherish their children all the same. We allow everything related to sweet sentiments of the soul; we only take away what can spoil or destroy. Children, for their part, cherish their parents no ₀ less; accustomed to view their nation as a second mother, they become not less loving but also better citizens.

"It has been said and written that only a republic is suited to provide a national education. That is a mistake. Such a system is appropriate for any government that would have the nation itself beloved. I adapted republican education for the island of Tamoé and will explain why. The ease of repudiation, as I have just detailed, avoids adultery to such an extent that this crime, so common among you, is here most rare. But if proved, it becomes a fourth category by which married couples may separate. Often two households undergo reciprocal exchange. In fashioning the bonds of marriage we make the shackles so light that amorous gallantry seldom soils the knots.

"The funds to sustain the couple being always the same amount, the only consideration concerns choice of spouse. Women being all equally rich, and all men provided with the same fortune, they have only to listen to their hearts. Thus, once we have what we mutually desire, why change? Yet if we do wish to change, what grounds will we have to trouble the happiness of others? There are nonetheless intrigues; wrongs are inevitable but also rare and secret, and those who engage in them suffer such shame that no trouble results for society. No recklessness, no complaints, very few misdeeds. On such matters, is that not the best you can hope for? In Europe, with all the means you employ, with your houses of ill repute and their unfortunate victims indecently devoted to lack of public restraint — with all that, I say, do you obtain even half of what I do with the means I've just described?*

---

* Let us not tolerate such establishments with the excuse that they prevent greater harm and that the intemperate man, rather than seduce his neighbor's wife, will find satisfaction in these cesspits. Is it not quite a singular thing that a government is ☞

o "As concerns personal possessions, everything is just as
we have shown. The subject owns nothing and possesses only
what the state gives him; and at his death everything returns
to it. But as he made use of it during a whole lifetime passed in
peace, he has the greatest interest in not leaving a wasteland
5 behind. His comfort depends on how he cares for his domain;
he is in this way compelled to maintain it. When spouses grow
old, or after one of them passes away, the elderly and widowed
who once helped the young are now themselves to be taken
care of, and it is up to the latter to help them and for all to be
10 managed with the same order as before. These young people
have no direct interest in maintaining their elders' domains,
already having everything they need and with nothing to in-
herit; but they do so by way of thanks, by fealty to the nation
and because, in addition, when decrepit they themselves will
15 need the same kind of help and it will be refused them if they
haven't given to others.

"I need not have you observe to what extent equality of
fortune absolutely does away with luxury. Nowhere is there
better or more efficient sumptuary law. The impossibility of
20 possessing more than one's neighbor thoroughly annihilates
the destructive vice found in all the nations of Europe. Among
delicate comestibles you may desire better fruits than someone else — yet this is not splendor, only the result of care and

---

without shame in making the same grave error for 1500 years, imagining it would be
better to tolerate the most despicable excesses than to change the law? But who are
the victims of these horrible places? Are they not girls and young women originally
seduced by greed and intemperance? Thus the state permits one group of the nation's
girls and young women to be corrupted in order to better preserve the other — such a
singularly wise calculus and just take a look at the fine result! A thoughtful and philosophical reader must admit that Zamé reasons better in wanting no side to lose, and
by the fine disposition of his laws — by which no party is to be sacrificed for another
and that all keep themselves equally pure.

pains taken to succeed. It is emulation and, as it works to   o
improve the well-being of citizens, the government should
encourage it.

"Consider now, my friend," continued this respectable
man, "the multitude of crimes that such institutions can
forestall. If I prove that I diminish their number without cost,   5
without causing citizens any pain, will you admit that I've
done a better job than those brutal inventors and partisans
of your atrocious laws which, like those of Draco, are never
pronounced without sword in hand? Will you agree that I've
fulfilled the wise and grand principle of Persian law, which   10
enjoins the magistrate to prevent crime and not to punish it;
it takes but a fool and an executioner to send a man to his
death while it requires much care and cleverness to prevent
him from deserving it.

"With equality of goods and possessions, no thievery; the   15
thief only desires to appropriate what he has not, and what he is
jealous of, seeing that it belongs to another; but when everyone
possesses the same, such criminal desire can no longer exist.

"Equality of goods maintains union, with the kindness of
the government bringing all subjects to equally cherish their   20
regime. When the state does not commit crime, neither is
there revolution.

"Children raised outside the father's house — no incest;
brought up with care and always under the eyes of honest &
dependable teachers — no rape.   25

"Little adultery, thanks to divorce.

"With equality of rank and possession forestalling intestinal divisions, all sources of murder are extinguished.

"With equality, no more avarice or ambition — and
how many crimes owe to those two causes alone! No more   30
impatient successors waiting in the wings, for now not the
death of one's parents but coming-of-age confers possession.

No more patricide, fratricide, and other crimes too atrocious to mention.

"Suicides are few and only among the unhappiest. Here, everybody being equal and content, why would one wish to destroy oneself?

"No infanticide. Why get rid of children when they're never at one's charge and one can only expect them to help? Impossible for them to be troublesome as they only enter the world to grow up and be married; and the daughter is not exposed to dishonor or crime — as she is with your people, to be left weak, seduced, and unhappy. She no longer must choose between stigmatization and destruction of the unlucky fruits of love.

"Nevertheless, I confess, not all infractions can be done away with; one would need be God and work with something besides man to wipe crime off the face of the earth. But compare crimes found here with those to which the citizen is inevitably led to commit by the vicious organization of your governments. Don't punish him when he does wrong because you then make it impossible for him to do right. Change the form of your government and don't vex the man who, when that government is bad, cannot help but conduct himself badly. For not he but you are guilty — able to prevent wrongdoing by changing your laws, yet you nevertheless allow them to continue, odious as they are, simply for the pleasure of punishing the wrongdoer. When an unfortunate fellow is punished by the same hand that has brought him to the precipice — would you not call savage the one who puts him to death? Be fair and tolerate crime because your government's own vices entail it; and if crime harms you, change the constitution that brings it about, as I've done. Make it impossible for the citizen to commit crime but don't sacrifice him to the ineptitude of your laws and your stubborn unwillingness to change."

"So be it," I said. "But it seems to me that if you have few   o
vices you must also have hardly any virtues. Does not such a
government, in which virtues are lacking, want for energy?"

"First of all," Zamé replied, "were that so, I'd prefer it. A
thousand times I'd rather annihilate man's every vice rather
than engender virtues; for we know that vice is far more   5
harmful than virtue is useful, and that especially in your governments, vice unpunished is far more essential than virtue
unrewarded. And if you think that getting rid of vice makes
virtue impossible, you're wrong. Virtue does not consist in
avoiding the commission of vice but, here as in your country,   10
in doing what's best under the circumstances. Charity is not
the same as in your land, however, I quite agree. Pious be-
quests serve only to fatten monks and alms only encourage the
do-nothings. But there is helping one's neighbor, aiding the
infirm, caring for the sick and elderly, using good principles to   15
educate children, and preventing quarrels and intestinal divisions. Courage is on display in patiently accepting the ills that
Nature sends our way. But does it not come at a higher price
when it leads us to destroy our human kin? Yet even that may
be exercised with sublimity of intent when it is a question of   20
defending the nation. Cannot friendship also be placed in the
ranks of virtue, and extend the gentlest and most agreeable
influence? We like hospitality, we make an effort to exercise
it upon friends and neighbors. Despite equality, rivalry is not
extinguished. I'll take you to see our carpenters and masons   25
so you may judge for yourself their zeal to surpass one another,
whether by suppleness of action or by the way they square the
stone, fashion it and artfully compose, from the ground up,
the simple form of our houses."

I continued to object: "Say what you like but there exists   30
in your nation a second class. The worker is only a hireling,
considered lower and hence different from the citizen who
does no work."

"Wrong," said Zamé. "There's no difference between the man you will soon see building a house, and the one you encountered yesterday seated at my table. Their situations are the same and so are their fortunes — absolutely the same. Nothing distinguishes one from the other, and elevating one by demeaning the other is not allowed. Zilia, my daughter-in-law whom you admired, is the daughter of one of our most skillful manufacturers; and it was to recognize his worthiness that I allied myself with him.

"Aptitude alone qualifies our young people for the various occupations. One with a talent for farming, who finds himself constitutionally unsuited or disgusted by all other work, is happy to cultivate that portion of earth conferred upon him by the state, to help others in the same situation, and to provide counsel as appropriate. Yet another capably handles a spokeshave, so we make him a woodworker. We don't lack for tools, for I brought back several trunksful from Europe. When the iron wears out we make repairs with gold from our mines, so that lowly metal for once serves a useful end. Another student shows an affinity for architecture and becomes a mason. But none of them are mercenary; one pays for the services they render with other services; they work for the good of the state. What a despicable prejudice, the idea that this would debase them. Why would they be demeaned in the eyes of their compatriots? They have the same goods and status at birth; they are perforce equal. If I admitted distinctions, they'd surely rank above the idle rich. The most esteemed citizen must not be the one who does nothing but he who makes himself the most useful."

"But in according compensation by merit," I said to Zamé, "you must distinguish those who obtain it, producing jealousies and perforce differences in spite of all."

"Wrong again. These distinctions excite emulation but not jealousy. We warn against this vice from childhood by accustoming students to desire to equal those who do well, and do better if possible; but in no wise should they be envious. That can only bring about painful and afflicted souls instead of encouraging efforts to surpass those who deserve reward. That will engender the interior pleasure we obtain from praise. These principles, inculcated from birth, destroy seeds of hatred. We prefer to imitate or surpass rather than to hate; and thus all come, little by little, to virtue."

"And as to punishment?"

"Light and proportionate to the only offenses possible in our nation; they never humiliate or destroy. One loses a man by blackening his reputation and from the moment society rejects him there's nothing left besides despair or capitulation, a dire result that produces nothing good but leads ineluctably to suicide or the gallows. With gentleness and less prejudice, one brings him around to virtue and perhaps one day to heroism. Our punishments consist in confrontation with established opinion. I've studied the minds of my people and found them sensitive and proud, with a liking for renown. I humiliate them when they do wrong. When a citizen commits a grave affront, he walks through the street between two public criers who announce in a loud voice the misdemeanor with which he has despoiled himself. It is remarkable how much anger this ceremony incites and how deeply people are wounded. I thus reserve it for the gravest of errors.* Lighter crimes are treated less harshly. Consider a negligent household, for example, which is careless with the goods provided by the state. I move them to uncultivated ground where they must redouble their effort and pain to feed themselves; should they become more active, I return the household to its original place.

---

* Excepting murder, which is more severely punished and which Zamé discusses below.

"With regards to crimes of morality, if the guilty parties live in another village, not mine, they are punished by a mark upon their clothing; if they inhabit the capital, I punish them by barring them from my home. I receive neither libertines nor adulteresses, and such debasement brings them to despair for they love me and know my house is open only to those who cherish virtue, which they must practice or never see me. They change and adopt correct behavior; uncounted many have responded to my simple solution. Honor constrains. One brings them to the place one desired in knowing how to handle them. Humiliate them birch in hand and you discourage them, lose them. We'll talk more about this. I told you I want to communicate my ideas on the law and I hope you'll approve all the more, for it is in their execution that I've made my people happy.

"As to rewards," continued Zamé, "I employ a system of military ranks. Although everyone is a soldier born to the defense of the country, and all are equals in their homes, yet they need leaders in battle and higher ranks compensate merit and talent. A good mason I might make an infantry lieutenant; a citizen recognized for intelligence and virtue will become captain; a celebrated agriculturalist will be a major; and so on. Chimeric but flattering. While punishment must not be too severe, neither must we overvalue rewards. For the former it's only a question of choosing what is the most humiliating and, in the latter, what bears best on self-esteem. The way to make men do whatever is wanted depends solely upon these two methods; but to find the means you must know the man, which is why I always say that such knowledge constitutes the chief art of the legislator. It's quite convenient, as you've done in Europe, to make punishments and rewards the same for everyone. Major and minor infractors alike must cross a *pons asinorum* — by this way or not at all. But does expedience

make it the best? In your country punishment corrects nothing and reward counts for little. What happens when for
centuries you've the same number of vices without acquiring a single virtue? You've in no way altered man's natural
perversity."

"But at least you have prisons," I said. "In all your wisdom,
you've not forgotten that deterrent, essential to government?"

"Young man," responded the law-giver, "I'm astonished
that with all your wit and intelligence you can ask such a
question. Don't you know that prison, the worst and most
dangerous of punishments, is nothing but an ancient abuse
of justice, and that despotism and tyranny follow in its wake?
The necessity to keep in custody one who shall be judged led
naturally first to the invention of irons, maintained under bar-
barism. That atrocity, like any act of severe rigor, was born
of ignorance and blindness. Inept judges, daring neither to
condemn nor absolve, would often prefer to keep the accused
in prison, conscience clear because they don't take the life of
the man but neither do they return him to society. Is that any
less absurd? A guilty man must submit to judgment; if innocent, he must be absolved. All operations between these two
poles can be but vicious and false. The lone excuse to justify
the inventors of this abominable institution would be hope
of reform, but one must know very little about men to imagine that prison can ever produce such an effect. It is not by
isolating the wrongdoer that one corrects him but rather by
delivering him to the society that he outraged; from society
he must receive his daily punishment — this is the school that
can make him better. Reduced to fatal solitude, to dangerous
stagnation, to deadly abandonment — his vices take root, his
blood boils, his head ferments. The impossibility to satisfy his
desires fortifies him, nurturing crime, and he'll emerge still
more cunning and dangerous. These are the ferocious beasts

destined for barred cages and chains. The image of God who created the universe is not made for such baseness. For any citizen who does wrong you must have but one objective. If you wish to be fair, let his punishment be useful to him and others; anything that deviates from that aim is infamy.

"Moreover, prison is assuredly useless for those who are incarcerated because numberless dangers from this sort of vexation only make things worse. Secret detention, so common in France, cannot be held up as a good example, for the public is kept in the dark. It is an unpardonable abuse everywhere condemned and never justified — a poisonous weapon in the hands of a liar or a tyrant, an unsavory monopoly between the distributor of those shackles and the worthless rascal who, nourishing the unfortunate prisoners, lies and spreads calumny to prolong their pain; a dangerous means accorded without discretion for families to wreak vengeance upon one of their members (guilty or not) owing to hatred, hostility, and jealousy. Every such case in the end is finally a gratuitous horror contrary to the constitution of every government, and a right that kings usurped only because the country itself was weak.

"When a man has done something wrong, make him repair it and serve the society he's disrupted. Let him compensate for his wrong and use every means in his power to do so; but don't isolate or sequester him, for a man locked away is no longer any good to himself or to others. A nation in which the unhappy man counts for nothing while rascals take all — that's a country ruled by money and harlots, a place where despotism and prevarication trample humanity and justice underfoot, and a place that permits those kinds of indignities. If your prisons, where so many left to suffer are worth more than those who put them there or keep them there — if, I say, stupid incarcerations ever resulted in not twenty, not even

half a dozen, but a single conversion, I'd advise they continue   o
and fault the subject who doesn't reform himself, not the prison. But it is absolutely impossible to provide a single example
of a man reformed by his chains. Could it happen? Can one
become better amidst baseness and degradation? Might one
gain something surrounded by the most contagious examples   5
of avarice, cunning and cruelty? Your character is degraded
and morals corrupted; you become a low liar and perjurer, ferocious and sordid, traitorous and malicious, as underhanded
as everyone around you; you exchange, in a word, your virtues
for vices. Leaving prison, filled with horror for all men, you've   10
no aim henceforth but to avenge yourself by injuring them.*

"But what I have yet to tell you tomorrow, relative to the
law, will more fully develop my systems concerning all that.
For now, follow me. Yesterday I showed you my most beautiful
women; today I want you to see a few of the troops I'd bring to   15
bear against any enemy that wished to invade."

"First allow me, benefactor," I said to Zamé, "to learn the
extent of your arts."

"We banish those of luxury," responded the philosopher.
"We tolerate only the citizen's useful arts: agriculture, dress,   20
architecture, and the military. I proscribe all others excepting
several pastimes which I'll perhaps have occasion to show you.
I like them all and cultivate them privately, but only in moments of relaxation. Wait" — he said, revealing, in a nearby
room —: "A painting of my own composition. Do you like it?   25
It is titled *Calumny Dragging Innocence by the Hair to the
Tribunal of Justice.*"

"Ah! That's an idea of Apelles of Kos; you must have painted it after him."

---

* The French happily felt this way in pulverizing those monuments of horror, those
infamous bastions where shackled philosophy cried out, even before suspecting they
would have the energy to break free of their chains.

"Yes," replied Zamé. *"Ancient Greece provided the idea &
France furnished the subject."* *

"Let's be off, my friend. Infantry awaits. I want you to see it."

Armed like European soldiers, some 3,000 young men
were filling the public square. They separated into platoons,
each of which was headed by several officers.

"Here you see my dukes, barons, counts, masons, weav-
ers, carpenters, bourgeois — in a word, my good and faithful
friends, ready to spill their blood for the nation. From 15 cities across this island, none as big as the capital, we could call
forth a like number. That makes nearly 45,000 men ready to
defend our coasts. Let us keep going, for they'd gather at the
port if warned. We can have some fun and sound the alarm
ourselves."

A light guard was always on duty at the outposts. We
went to where the furthest vedette was posted and seized his
flag of alarm, exposing it so it could be seen from the city. In
less than six minutes — I'm not exaggerating — although the
port lay a quarter league from the city, the infantry we'd left
behind was dispersed in all the outworks and the artillery was
dug in and ready.

"During this run-up to battle," Zamé told me, "we light
fires on the surrounding mountaintops where relays of guards
are posted weekly and designated militias arrive in succession
and with such rapidity that detachments from the furthest city,
situated thirty leagues distant, reach the port within 15 hours
after the alarm is sounded; thus, our army swells in proportion to the threat. If the enemy regroup, after initial attacks
lasting some 14 or 15 hours, intending to continue in spite of

---

* We may not presume to whom the author refers here; but we need only look to history in the early 18th century.

all defensive measures, they will find 45,000 men ready to   0
do battle."

"Such precautions assure you of victory," I said to Zamé.
"Troops that accompany our vessels of discovery are much too
weak and I daresay nothing will ever trouble the tranquility
that your people require to be happily civilized. Only now do   5
we have the celebrated Englishman, Cook, that great man of
the sea with talents as both a statesman and negotiator."*

"If he is English, I'm not afraid of him," said Zamé. "That
nation, at once warlike and honest, would rather facilitate my
accomplishments than seek to destroy them."   10

We returned to the road that led back to the city, escorted by a detachment that along the way executed a variety of
movements and maneuvers, always deftly and with the greatest precision.

100 of these young men, the best and most handsome,   15
were invited to a collation at Zamé's home and, as with the
women the day before, they gave themselves over to games:
boxing and various combats, all with address and agility.

Men on Tamoé are generally well-built and good-looking.
When full-grown they are rarely shorter than 5'6"; some are   20
much taller; but their height rarely unduly affects their body
proportions. Their features are regular and delicate, perhaps
too much so; their gaze is lively, mouth a tad wide but very
fresh, skin pure white and smooth, with superb hair the loveli-
est shade of brown. Their movements are sure, their demean-   25
ors noble; the way they speak is kindly and honest.

"Nature," said Zamé, seeing me examine them with a contented air, "has treated us well in every way."

---

* These letters were composed as their dates indicate; so, we see how Zamé was mistaken as concerns the British.

Sainville, not daring to conclude his provision of details in front of the women, approached Count Beaulé and me, with their permission. In a low voice he told us that Zamé assured him that there existed no country in the world whose men possessed virile proportions brought to such a degree of superiority and that, by another caprice of Nature, the women were so little made for such miracles that the god of marriage never triumphed without help.

The next day our respectable friend of mankind said to me: "I promised to talk to you about the law. Let us take a walk outside the city, where I have Italian poplars brought from Europe planted along the paths. Ideas are grander and conversation better beneath an open sky."

Continued the old man: "The rigor of punishment is one of the things that most revolted me about your European governments.*

"The Celts justified their frightful custom of immolating their victims, saying that the gods could only be appeased for one life by taking another. Is this not the same reasoning that would make you daily eviscerate victims upon the altars of Themis? And when you punish a murderer by death, is it not positively, as with barbarians, to make the life of one man pay for that of another? When will you understand that doubling wickedness is no cure for it? Does duplicating murder gain anything for either the virtue you scorn or Nature that you outrage?"

---

* On this count we expected something human from our first French legislature, but it offered only men out for blood, arguing over how best to slit their brothers' throats. More ferocious than cannibals, one among them brought forth an infernal machine to lop off heads all the faster and more cruelly. Those are the men the nation paid, admired, and believed in.

"But must crimes go unpunished?" I asked. "How otherwise eliminate them under any government not like your own?"

"I don't say we must allow crime to continue. But I claim we ought to better note what truly aggrieves a society and what does it no harm. Once fraud or deception is discovered, we must work to rectify, to extirpate it from the nation; but one does not succeed by punishment. Never must the law, if it is wise, inflict any penalty but that which would tend to correct the guilty party and keep him on the side of the state. A penalty is wrong when it tends only to punish and detestable when it has no objective, giving up on the criminal without instruction, frightening without improving; that is to commit an infamy equal to the crime but with no gain. Life and liberty are gifts man has received from the heavens, favors to compensate for all the wickedness. Yet, as he owes them to God alone, only God has the right to take them away.

"When commerce with the Romans civilized these same Celts, softening them on one hand and relieving them of their harsh customs on the other, the victims they then destined for sacrifice were no longer chosen from among the elderly or prisoners of war; rather, criminals were the only victims to be immolated — still with the absurd conviction that nothing was more dear than human blood spilled at divinity's altars. In making your civilization, rules change but the habit remains. You no longer serve the thirsty gods spattered with blood of sacrifice but you call laws wise because in them you found a specious motive to give yourself over to your ancient customs. The appearance of justice is at bottom nothing but the desire to retain horrible habits you are unable to renounce.

"Men in a pure state of Nature, as Montesquieu says, could only flee without a fight before powerful oppressors or else submit without resistance; laws were established to rec-

tify the balance. Has that happened? Have they enacted the
necessary balance? What have the weak gained from the instauration of law except to see that the rights of the strong, instead of belonging to the one to whom Nature assigned them,
become the prerogative of the man who could raise a fortune?
The unhappy man has thus only changed masters and, still just
as oppressed as before, has won nothing but a little formality.
That would not be so in a state of Nature in which the most
robust was also the most powerful, as must happen when
matters are left to chance. Instead, birth or fortune, placed in
the balance, always favors the class that holds the scale. The
unhappy man is offered only contempt, subjugation, and the
sword. What does man gain by this arrangement? In the frank
state of war in which he lived as a savage, was he any more
inferior than he is under a reign of deceit, injustice, vexation
and slavery?

"The most beautiful attribute of the law, continues your
celebrated Montesquieu, is to confer upon the citizen this
form of political liberty which, under aegis of law, protects
one man from another. But does a man gain anything if he
puts himself beyond the insults of his peers only to expose
himself to those of his superiors? Does he gain anything in
sacrificing one part of his liberty to preserve another if in fact
he ends by losing both? The law of Nature is primary and of
that alone man has real need. In the mind of the evildoer you
will not find imprinted the rule: *Do not do unto others as you
would not wish to be done unto you.* Fear of the law won't stop
him. To embed natural restraint within that heart requires
infinitely greater efforts than those expended to defy the law.
A man truly constrained by Nature would not need other
laws, and if not first constrained by it, fear will fare no better.
Thus, there is little need for law in the first instance and in
the second it is perfectly useless; and now consider the many

circumstances, unnecessary or fruitless, that can render the   o
law extremely dangerous: ready corruption of witnesses and
abuse of depositions, lack of certainty around confessions and
the use of torture to render them still less valid, owing to the
partiality of the judge and the influence of gold and wealth.*
Upon some among this multiplicity of consequences depend   5
the honor, fortune, and life of the citizen. Do you see to what
extent the unfortunate ability conferred upon the magistrate
to interpret the law as he sees fit renders it more the instrument of his passions than a curb upon those of others?

"However pure the law, will it not always become abusive   10
once open to interpretation by a judge? Did the legislator intend to give laws such sense as might open them to the folly
and caprice of the one who applied them? Did he not foresee
these as possible or inevitable? The law is insufficient for some,
useless for others, almost always abusive and dangerous; and   15
here you must agree that whatever a man might gain in putting himself under its protection he loses by all the dangers
he runs in living under it and all the sacrifices he makes in
acquiring it.

"We can go even further. For certainly, few people the   20
world over are actually exposed, more than two or three times
in a lifetime, to an infraction of the law in any of our police-
protected cities. Living in an uncivilized country, a man might

---

* As to lack of certainty, the truth is that a host of absurd rascals who became involved
in something of which they understood nothing decided that for the least offenses the
slightest conjectures sufficed; and so, continued this band of assassins, judges might
put themselves above the law — hence, the less probable, the more that something
must be believed. Can we not see that decisions of these mischief-makers — the
inept among them should themselves be done away with — have no other aim than
to relieve the judge of responsibility at the expense of men's lives? We still follow
these infernal maxims in this century of philosophy, and blood flows by virtue of this
dangerous precept!

find himself exposed that way in the course of his life some 20 to 30 times or more. Thus, the worst case: 20 or 30 times he will regret not being under protection of the law. Let the same man look deep into his heart and ask how often these same laws have cruelly disrupted his passions and rendered him, in consequence, far unhappier. That will give him a precise accounting of the happiness he owes to the law, and his unhappiness owing to its constraints. See if he won't admit that it would be a thousand times better not to be downtrodden by law than to support its weight and rigor, with so much to lose and so little to gain. You mustn't accuse me of choosing from only amongst the lowborn to establish my calculations; I offer them to the honest man and ask only his sincerity in return. If the law offends a citizen more than it serves him, if it renders him 10, 12, 15 times unhappier and neither defends nor protects, is it not thus only abusive, useless, and dangerous as I've just proved, but also tyrannical and repugnant? It would be much better, you must admit, to consent to the limited ill that may result from overturning some of these laws, as a way of purchasing happiness against a smidgen of tranquility.*

"But the most frightful of all these laws is the one that sentences to death a man who has only ceded to an irresistible impulse. Without examining here whether he has the right to cause a fellow's death, without trying to make you see it's impossible ever to receive such a right from God, or from Nature, or from the First Assembly in which the laws were created, with men consenting to sacrifice one portion of their liberty to preserve another — without entering, I say, into such details already considered by so many good minds,

---

* "Why do we see people so often impatient with the press of law? It's because rigor is all on the side of laws that afflict the people while little attention is paid to laws affecting the rich." *Belisaire.*

let's simply examine, the better to convince you of the injus-   o
tice of such an atrocious law, its effect upon men ever since
they've been subject to it. Calculate, on one hand, the number
of innocent victims sacrificed as a result and compare it to all
the victims whose throats were slit owing to crime and villainy. Compare the number of the truly guilty who perished   5
on the gallows with the number of citizens who were actually constrained by the example of condemned criminals. If
I found many more victims of rascality than innocents sacrificed to the sword of Themis while, on the other hand, for
one or two hundred thousand criminals justly immolated,   10
millions were constrained, the law would surely be tolerable.
But if I discover, on the contrary, as has only too often been
shown, that many more innocent victims fall in the house of
Themis than there are murders committed by villains, and that
millions put to death have not been able to stop a single crime,   15
the law is then clearly useless, abusive, cumbersome and dangerous as as just demonstrated. It is also scandalous, absurd
and could never pass muster because it would inflict so much
punishment for villainy yet be authorized by nothing except
custom and habit and force — none by reasons that are natu-   20
ral, legitimate, or any better than those of Cartouche himself.

"What result will thus accrue to a man from the voluntary
sacrifice of a portion of his freedom, and what too will become
of the weakest to have their rights still further eroded in hopes of
counterbalancing those of the strongest? Won't it mean to accept   25
restrictions and live beholden to yet another master? Because,
as before, the strongest will still range against him and the judge
will take their part, whether for personal gain or the secret and
invincible tendency that always aligns us with our peers.

"The pact entered into at society's foundation by which,   30
frightened by the power of the stronger, the weaker man consented to renounce some part of his liberty for pleasure and

peace represented, in fact, the total annihilation of liberty, not preservation of one part of it. You might as well say it was one more trap into which the stronger led the weaker.

"To weaken the strongest would require full equality of fortune and position — not to be accomplished by useless laws. As Solon says, *Gnats perish in the spider's web while wasps always find a way to escape.*

"What injustice and contradictions are to be found in your laws in Europe! They punish an infinite number of crimes of no consequence whatever, which in no way outrage the happiness of society while, on the other hand, they're weak when it comes to the real infamies with consequences infinitely more dangerous — such as avarice, the hard-hearted souls' refusal to help the unfortunate, calumny, gluttony, and laziness — against which the laws have not a word to say although they all belong to the never-ending branches of crime and misfortune.

"Will you not admit that this disproportion — cruel indulgence of the law in certain instances and ferocious severity in others — casts great doubt upon the pronouncements of justice and renders its necessity far from certain?

"With man already so unhappy, so overwhelmed by all the difficulties that arise from sensitivity and weakness, does he not merit a little indulgence on the part of his fellows? Does he deserve it that his fellow man burdens him with so many ridiculous constraints, nearly all useless and contrary to Nature? Before forbidding man to commit what are gratuitously called crimes, it would be well to first examine if doing so accords with rules necessary for the genuine maintenance of society. For if something does not cause serious harm, then society at large, more powerful than the lone individual, and better able to suffer what the latter could not abide were he deprived of some little misdeed he enjoys committing, must surely tolerate rather than punish.

"Let the philosopher-legislator, guided by this wise   0
maxim, review all crimes against which your laws pronounce;
let him detail them all and take their measure, one might say,
for the betterment of society. What sort of retrenchment
would result?

"Solon used to say that he would temper his laws to ac-   5
commodate the interests of his fellow citizens, who would
know that it clearly was more to their advantage to observe
rather than to infringe; and in effect, men would only ordi-
narily transgress upon things that harmed them while laws
wise and mild enough to accord with Nature would never be   10
violated. Why think that impossible? Examine my laws and
the people for whom I made them, and you'll see if they're not
rooted in Nature.

"The best law of all, which would be the least transgressed,
would clearly be that which most closely accords with our   15
passions and the climate in which we're born. Every law is a
restraint, and the best are those we're unable to break. Force
of restraint is not constituted by the number of laws but by
their kind and quality. You think you made your people happy
with more laws while it is rather a question of diminishing the   20
number of crimes. And do you know what multiplies these
crimes? Your government's shapeless constitution, which
gave rise to a swarming multitude that owes more than anything else to the ridiculous importance that fools attached
to petty things. With governments in thrall to Christian mo-   25
rality, you made capital crimes of everything that doctrine
condemns. Gradually you turned your sins into crimes; you
believed yourselves to be imitating the thunder you attributed
to divine justice. And you used the wheel and gallows because
you falsely imagined that God burned and drowned and pun-   30
ished these misdeeds — chimeric in the end, and with which
God in his grandeur was wholly unconcerned. Nearly all the

laws of St. Louis were founded on these sophisms.* We know that and will not revert because it is far too easy to hang a man or thrash him rather than to study why we condemn him —: the one lets Themis's henchman sup in peace at the home of his Phryne or Antinoüs while the other takes him away from his pleasures and makes him spend time in study. Wouldn't he prefer to hang or thrash a dozen unfortunates in his life than give three months to his profession? Thus you added to the heavy constraints upon your fellow citizens, never considering they might live free without barbaric shackles to weigh them down.

"The entire universe would behave in accordance with a single law if that law were good. The more a branch bends, the more easily you can pick its fruits. Holding it high makes them unreachable and the number of those who would steal diminishes. Establish equality of fortune and conditions and let there be a single proprietor, the state, that gives each subject all he needs to be happy for life, and dangerous crime will disappear. The constitution of Tamoé proves it. However, there's nothing on a small scale that cannot be executed writ large. Repeal many of your laws and you'll perforce reduce the number of crimes. With one law there will be only one crime; let this be Nature's law and you will have many fewer criminals. Tell me which is better: to find the means to punish many crimes or to discover a way to give birth to none?"

---

* That several writers over the years have praised that cruel and imbecilic king is something quite singular. Every step he took was false, ridiculous, and primitive. Carefully reading the history of his reign, it is fair to say that France has had few monarchs who more warranted contempt and indignation. Efforts like that of the knave Darnaud aim to make his compatriots revere a fool and fanatic who, not content to proclaim absurd and intolerant laws, abandoned his country to go conquer the Turks and shed his subjects' blood, all for a tomb we would immediately destroy if it were unfortunately located in our country.

"But Zamé," I protested, "your proposal of one fine law is   o
unworkable. Not a day goes by that some unjust person does
not mistreat another in a way he would hate to be treated
himself."

"Yes," responded the old man. "Because you allow the
lawbreaker some interest in breaking the law. Eliminate that   5
and you'll take away the motive for violating it. Here is the
important work of the legislator, and where I believe I succeeded. As much as poor Paul might want to steal from Peter
even though he violates Nature's law in doing something that
would make him angry were it done to him, he would do it;   10
but if I with my system make Paul as rich as Pierre, he would
have no more interest in stealing from him; and the latter for
his part would no longer be concerned about his possessions
and would have many fewer of them — and so on."

I continued to object: "There is a sort of perversity in cer-   15
tain incorrigible hearts. Many do wrong as a matter of course.
Today we recognize that some men give themselves over to it
for the sheer charm it provides. Tiberius, Heliogabalus, and
Andronikos defiled themselves with atrocities that purchased
them nothing but the barbarous pleasure of having commit-   20
ted them."

"That is another order of things," said Zamé. "No law could
contain the men you cite. We must indeed guard against them.
The more you erect barriers to hold them back, the more you
prepare the pleasure they take in breaching them. It is, as you   25
say, the infraction itself that amuses. Perhaps they would not
plunge themselves into these kinds of wickedness if they did
not view them as forbidden."

"Then what law could restrain them?"

"Consider this tree," continued Zamé, indicating one   30
whose trunk was covered with knots. "Could anything make
it well again?"

"No."

"Then leave it as it is. It spreads its branches and provides shade; let us make use of it and not be concerned by it. The men you mentioned are rare; they don't worry me. I'd handle them with care and attention to sentiment and honor; those curbs would be more effective than the law. I would still try to change their habits and ways of thinking; one or the other of these methods would succeed. Believe me, my friend, I've studied men too long and will tell you that I can foil or eliminate every sort of misdeed without use of physical punishment. Maul and abuse are meant only for animals; we must use reason, that powerful resource man possesses, over them all; it is just a question of knowing how.*

"Once again," continued Zamé, "the well-being of the people must concern the legislator; that must be his sole objective. If he simplifies his ideas or limits them to consideration of individual interests, he will do so at the expense of the main work he must never lose from sight, and fall into the same trap as his predecessors."

"Consider for a moment, just as an example, a state composed of about 4,000 subjects. Let half be white, the other half black; suppose further that whites unfairly enjoy a measure of happiness by in some way oppressing blacks. How would

---

* It would be desirable, says a man of genius somewhere, if laws were of greater simplicity and spoke to the heart, which is more closely linked to morality; that they might be gentle and consoling; that their objective, in short, was to make us better without the use of fear but by charm alone that attaches to the love of order and the public weal. Such is the spirit in which laws should be created, and, in place of a despot or harsh judge, rather, a tender father. Would not laws so conceived mean far less punishment? In terms of sentiment, such a precept should bear great interest.

Difficult as it is to believe, the man who spoke thus was the panegyrist of Saint Louis, the Dagon of France, the king who weighted down the code of the realm with a bevy of ineptitudes and cruelties.

the ordinary legislator proceed? He would punish whites in   0
order to deliver blacks from oppression and emerge from this
operation believing himself grander than Lycurgus — but he
would have done something stupid. What difference if happiness accrues to blacks rather than whites? Before punishment imposed by such an imbecile, whites were happy; now,   5
blacks. The outcome is nil because things are allowed to go
on as before. What must happen — but certainly never does
— is to render both groups equally happy and not one at the
expense of the other. But to succeed, one must closely study
the kind of oppression that whites inflict in order to achieve   10
their happiness and to see how much of it is due, as often happens, solely to popular opinion; and if that's the case, to conserve for them as much of the thing as possible to keep them
happy while making blacks understand the extent to which
their complaints are chimeric. That will make it possible to   15
envisage what sort of compensation will provide them some
measure of the happiness that white oppression takes away.
The aim would be to generate equilibrium, for complete happiness is impossible. Thereupon whites would be compelled
to compensate blacks in order to continue oppressing them.   20

"And there you have them, 4,000 happy subjects: whites
made happy by oppressing blacks, who in turn become happy
thanks to compensation they receive; here, then, I say, everyone is happy but no one is punished; here a sort of wrongdoer and a kind of victim, both content. If someone breaks   25
the law, punishment must be applied equally; that is, the black
must be punished if despite the compensation he demanded
and received, he still cannot tolerate the white's oppression;
and the latter will be equally punished if he does not accord
compensation equal to the oppression he's enjoyed inflicting.   30
But his punishment (the necessity for which occurs not even
twice every century) in no way enjoins one individual from ag-

grieving another, which is odious. For justice does not provide a way for one individual to be happier than another; rather, the penalty is brought against him who breaks the law that establishes equilibrium, and from that moment the law is just.

"It is perfectly acceptable, in other words, for one member of society to be happier than another; what is essential to general well-being is that both be as happy as can be. Thus, the legislator must not punish one by seeking happiness for another at his expense because a man, in all this, can only follow Nature's intent; rather, he must examine if one of these men would not be equally happy in ceding a slight portion of felicity to him who suffers hardship and, that being the case, must establish equality so far as possible, condemning the happier to help remedy the sorry state of the other, who might otherwise be forced to crime.

"But let us continue to portray the injustice of your laws. One man let us suppose, after mistreating another, agrees to compensation: equality. The one suffers the blows, the other loses money because he applied the blows; things are equal, each must be happy — but it is not finished. We can sue the aggressor, and although there is no wrong, and he has satisfied the one he wronged and put it to rights, he can nonetheless be pursued under the hollow and scandalous pretext of just reparations. Is that not extraordinary cruelty? The man has made only one mistake and must make reparations once: that must be justice — to keep an eye on satisfactory compliance. From that point the judges have no more to do. Anything else they say or do is only an atrocious vexation for the citizen, at the expense of whom they fatten themselves with impunity and against which the whole nation must revolt.*

---

* Of all the injustices committed by Themis's henchmen, this is surely one of the most blatant: "A tribunal that commits injustices," said the late King of Prussia when ☞

"All other misdeeds may be explained by the same principles and can undergo the same scrutiny." Zamé continued: "Even murder, the most frightful of all, which makes a man more ferocious and dangerous than any beast — murder, which in every country on earth, and in three-quarters of the universe, is still paid for in some way proportionate to the status of the victim.* Nations in their wisdom did not imagine imposing some other penalty than that which could be useful; they rejected doubling the wickedness but did not stop much less repair it.

"Having carefully eliminated everything that can lead to murder, I have very few examples of this monstrous crime on my island. The punishment I call for is simple and fulfills the objective in sequestering the guilty party from society, yet includes nothing contrary to Nature. Every city receives a description of the criminal together with the strict interdiction. I provide the offender with a pirogue stocked with food and supplies for a month. He goes alone with the order to remain isolated and at a distance under pain of death. Let him make out as he can; meanwhile, I've served my country and may not be reproached if he dies. That is the only crime punished in this way; lesser crimes don't call for blood and I must refrain from spilling it. I'd rather correct than punish. The former preserves and improves man; the other loses him to no purpose.

sentence was brought against the prevaricating judges of the millers Arnold, "is more dangerous than a band of thieves. One can defend oneself against the latter but nobody can protect himself from scoundrels who employ the mantle of justice to give full rein to their nefarious passions. They are more malicious than the most despicable brigands in the world and they deserve to be punished twice as harshly."

* The laws of the Franks and Germans taxed murder. A servant could be killed for 30 livres tournois, a priest went for 400; the individual who cost least was a woman of the streets, owing to her bootless, abject status.

I told you about the means I employ, and they almost always succeed. Self-love is man's most active sentiment and there is everything to be gained by engaging it. One of its mainsprings, and I flatter myself for having made adroit use of it, is that a man's heart is moved by just compensation for vices and virtues. It is frightful that in Europe a man who has done 10 or 12 good deeds must lose his life for committing one bad action — and, at that, something often far less dangerous than good acts of no account. Here a citizen's fine actions are all rewarded. If he has the misfortune to succumb to weakness once in his life, we examine impartially the good and bad, weigh them equally, and if good wins out, absolve him. Believe me, praise is a fine thing and reward, gratifying. So long as you fail to use either one to mitigate the heavy penalties your laws impose, you'll never succeed in making citizens conduct themselves as they should. Instead you'll only foment injustice.

"Another of your atrocious customs is to pursue the criminal condemned long ago for a bad act — even though he is reformed and has long led an ordinary life. Inasmuch as good triumphs over evil so rarely, this is still more despicable; you thoroughly discourage men in teaching them that it is useless to repent.

"In my voyages I was told of something a judge did in your country that long made me tremble. 15 years after judgment, he had the guilty party sought out and arrested. The unfortunate man, discovered in his place of exile, had become a saint. Nevertheless, the vicious judge had him dragged him off to be tortured to death. *He* was the real villain, I told myself, deserving of an execution three times more painful than the victim's; and if by chance he prospered, Providence would one day catch up with him. What I said proved prophetic. The judge execrated and had a horror of the French; only too happy to have preserved his own life, which he ought to have

loſt a hundred times over by a multitude of evasions and hor-   o
rors that are easy to imagine after the ſtory juſt cited — ſtill
yet none more shocking than that he became a traitor to
the ſtate.*

"Oh! My good young man," continued Zamé, "the leg-
islator's craft does not consiſt in curbing vice, for that only   5
increases the fervent desire to commit it. The wise legislator
muſt inſtead contend with it by ironing out problems and eas-
ing reſtrictions, for unfortunately it's only too true that the
latter count for much of the charm attracting men to crime.
Deprived of those features, he soon tires of it; by the same   10
token, if we caſt a few thorns upon the path of virtue, man will
finish by preferring it, by taking to it naturally, owing to the
difficulties in pursuing it. Here we see clearly what the adroit
legislators of Greece underſtood only too well: in turning to
good ends eſtablished vices, their attraction for the citizen   15
disappeared with the punishment. The Greeks became virtuous juſt because of the ease of vice and pain of virtue.

"The art of the legislator thus only consiſts in familiar-
ity with one's fellow citizens and knowing how to profit from
their weaknesses; we lead them where we want. If religion sets   20
itself in opposition, we muſt break with it without hesitation;
religion is good only to the extent that it is in accord with
the laws; through unity it creates goodness in man. To reach
this end we may find ourselves forced to change the laws.

---

* We feel obliged to alert the reader that Zamé is mistaken as to the order of things.
He can only be talking about events that date to the beginning of the century while
the flight to exile referred to dates to 1778-1780. We might be required to name the
man but who cannot guess? With talk of a villain, who does not see Zamé can only be
referring to Sartine? To him most assuredly owes this appalling story.

If religion no longer aligns itself with them, it must be rejected.*
Religion, in politics, is superfluous, good only for shoring up
legislation to which it must cede in every case. Lycurgus and
Solon made the oracles speak and always supported their laws,
which were long respected. Not daring to make the gods speak,
my friend, I silenced them and accord them only the status of
a cult in order to help adapt laws made for the happiness of
the people. Any cult that would not ally itself with the code
that assures and continues the general felicity of the people,
I dare say, would be useless or impious. Far from basing my
laws on the largely erroneous maxims of received religion, far
from criminalizing the weakness of mankind, so ridiculously
threatened by barbarous religions, I believed that if God really exists, he could not punish His creatures for faults within
them put there by His own hand. To compose a reasonable
code, I had to be in accord with His justice and tolerance;
hard and fast atheism would be preferable to admitting a God
whose cult opposed the good of humanity. There was less danger in not believing in the existence of God than in supposing
a deity exists as man's enemy.

"But a consideration more essential for the legislator, an
idea that he must not lose sight of, is the sorry state of the
bonds that constrain man from birth. With what gentleness
must we discipline someone who is not free, who has done
wrong only because it has become impossible for him to do
otherwise! If all our actions follow necessarily from first impulse, if everything depends upon the architecture of our organs, of the liquids within and the relative vitality of animal

---

* Frenchman, accept this great truth! Understand that your Catholicism, full of ridiculous absurdities, an atrocious cult of which your enemies take such adroit advantage,
cannot be that of a free people. Never will those who worship a crucified slave attain
the virtues of a Brutus.

spirits, of the air we breathe, of the aliments of sustenance —   o
if all these are linked to Nature's physic such that we have not
even freedom of choice, will not even the mildest law become
tyrannical? And must not the fair legislator do something
other than punish the wrongdoer or keep him from society?
What an injustice, to punish when one is brought to crime de-   5
spite oneself! Is it not atrocious and barbaric to punish a man
for bad acts he could not possibly avoid committing?

"Let us imagine an egg placed on a billiard table with two
balls struck by a blind man. The trajectory of one misses the
egg, the other breaks it. Is it the fault of the ball or the fault   10
of the blind man who launched the egg-destructor? The blind
man is Nature herself, man is the ball, and the broken egg is
the crime committed. Here you see, my friend, how unfair are
the laws of Europe and what care is required of the legislator
who claims to reform them.   15

"Let us not doubt that the origin of our passions and consequently the cause of all our foibles depends solely upon our
physical constitution and, were science what it ought, anato-
my would reveal the difference between the honest man and
the villain: organs more delicate or less, the relative sensitivity   20
of fibers and level of acridity in the nervous fluid, and external
causes of such-and-such a type, life lived with more irritation
or less. These are the things that shunt us ceaselessly between
vice and virtue, like a ship tossed upon the sea, here skirting
the reefs yet now unable to avoid them. We are like musical   25
instruments which, depending on form and proportion, make
a sound that is agreeable or discordant, turned out not by ourselves but by Nature. All is Nature and in her hands we are
never but the blind instrument of her caprices.

"With such minor differences that at bottom owe scarce   30
to ourselves yet which nevertheless, by received wisdom, give

proof to man of such great good and evil — would it not be wiser to return to the cult of Aristippus, who held that he who has committed a fault, however grave, is worthy of forgiveness because whoever does wrong does not do so voluntarily but is forced by the violence of his passions; and that in such cases we must neither hate nor punish; we must confine ourselves to instruction and gentle correction. One of your philosophers has said: *This does not suffice, that we must have laws, they are necessary, even if unjust* — but he offers only a sophism. What is unjust is in no wise necessary; only what is really necessary is just and that is the essence of the law. Any law that is merely necessary, without being just, is only tyranny."

"But you, venerable and respected old man, must agree," I took the liberty of saying, "we must nevertheless put away dangerous criminals."

"So be it," replied Zamé. "But we must not punish them. One must be punished only to the extent one is guilty and unable to stop himself. Put them away then, by banishment, or improve them by compelling them to make themselves useful to those they've offended. But do not inhumanely toss them into stinking cesspools to be surrounded by pernicious brutes such that one can hardly tell what will corrupt them faster — the frightening examples of the jailers or the hardened impertinence shown them by their miserable companions. Still less should you kill them; spilling blood is no solution for, instead of one crime, now there are two. It is impossible for an affront to Nature to serve the ends of reparation."

"If you burden citizens with punishment but aim to leave them in society, avoid chains that debase, for in degrading man you provoke his heart, embitter his mind, and demean his character. Contempt bears a weight so cruel that a man will violate the law a thousand times to avenge himself for

having been its victim; and some go to the scaffold only by   o
way of despair induced by a first instance of injustice.*

"But, my friend," the great man continued, "taking my
hands in his: "So much prejudice to overcome! So many illusory opinions to demolish! What absurd systems to reject!
By principles of its administration, let philosophy spread!   5
Recognize what a multitude of things you've for so long been
constrained to see as crimes — what a task!

"Whoever you are — magistrate, prince, legislator — you
hold in your hands the fate of your compatriots. Use the authority the law gives you to soften its rigor. Consider that only   10
by patience does the farmer domesticate a wild fruit; that Nature makes nothing that is useless, that there is not a man on
earth who's not good for something. Severity is nothing but
abuse of the law; it shows contempt for the sort of human
being who does not regard honor as the only curb to conduct,   15
or shame the only punishment to be feared. Your wretched
laws, barbarous and poorly crafted, serve only to punish and
not correct; they destroy but don't create; they shock but don't
restore. You can never hope for the least progress in the science and behavior of man without discovering the means to   20
correct him without destroying him, ways to make him better
without degrading him.

"The surest way is to act as you see I have done. Oppose
giving birth to crime and you'll need no laws. Stop punishing
other than by ridicule; most deviance offends society not in   25
the slightest, and your laws are superfluous.

---

* O you who punish, by the lights of one man of wit, be careful not to reduce pride to
despair through humiliation, for by doing so you break the back of virtue instead of
strengthening it.

"The laws, yet again to cite your Montesquieu, are a poor way to change manners, customs, and to suppress the passions; that must be achieved by examples and rewards. To what that great man says I add that the real way to bring about virtue is to convey its charm and, even more, its necessity. To trumpet virtue's beauty is not enough; we must prove it. People must see convincing examples dawn before their very eyes and see what they lose by not practicing it. If you want respect for the bonds society forges, make us sense and feel them, and their value and power; but don't imagine you'll succeed by shattering them. Let these reflections render circumspect the choice of punishment to exact from one whom society finds guilty! Laws, instead of returning him to it, will keep him from it or else take his very life — with no middle road. What intolerance! The time has come to detest and destroy such gross stupidity!

"*You vile and despicable and dreadful judge and executioner, abhorred by your own kind, born only take irons and gibbets to be arguments that brook no reply — you and all those who resemble madmen like yourself who, instead of repairing your house, sets it aflame — when will you stop thinking that there's nothing finer than your laws or more sublime than their effects! Renounce those pernicious prejudices that only defile you to no purpose with the blood and tears of your fellow citizens. Dare to let Nature take her course. Have you ever regretted according her your confidence? The majestic poplar that proudly raises its canopy to the clouds — is it less beautiful or proud than scrawny shrubs stunted by the hand of your withering art? The children you call savages, abandoned in the wild, who must crawl back to their mother's womb — are they less fresh or vigorous or healthy than your country's frail newborns, whom it seems you would want to make feel from the moment they open their eyes that they're born only to be shackled? What do you gain in the end by burdening Nature?*

She's never grander or more beautiful than when she bursts ∘
through your dikes and overflows your banks. And those arts
you cherish and cultivate and honor are only truly sublime
when they better imitate Nature's disorders that your absurdi-
ties hold captive. Leave her to her caprices and don't imagine
your vain laws can hold her back. She will ever overpower them 5
as her own laws require and you will become, as will all whom
you enslave, the vile toy of her clever disruptions."

"Great man!" I cried with enthusiasm. "Your words ought
to enlighten the universe; the citizens of this isle are happy
one hundred times over and those legislators a thousand 10
times more fortunate to model themselves after you. How
right was Plato: *Our cities cannot be happy until philosophers*
become kings or those who are now called kings and potentates
shall be philosophers."

"My friend, you flatter me," responded Zamé, "and I don't 15
want that. Because you see fit to praise me with words of a
philosopher, let me prove you wrong with the saying of another. The legislator Solon, having spoken firmly to Croesus, the
King of Lydia, who tried to impress him with his magnificence,
received only harsh words — Solon, I say, was reprimanded by 20
Aesop the fabulist, who told him: 'Either we must never come
before mighty men, or we must try to please them.' But Solon
replied: 'Either we must not come before mighty men, or we
must tell them useful things.'"

When we returned, Zamé prepared another spectacle. 25

"Come with me," he said, "First I brought you to see our
women alone, then our young men. Now you'll see them together."

Opening a vast salon, I saw 50 of the most beautiful women
of the capital together with the same number of young men,
also chosen for their superior size and appearance. 30

"These are all spouses," Zamé told me. "They never go out
into the world except together; and everyone you see here is

married. But no husband is here with his wife nor wife with her husband. That way you can better judge our morals."

Several fresh, simple dishes were served to this amiable group, then each individual displayed his talents, playing several instruments, unknown to us, that the people had created long before civilization; some resembled the guitar, others the flute. Their music, little varied in pitch, seemed unpleasant to me; Zamé had given them no notion of ours.

"I fear," he told me, "that music is made more to soften and corrupt the soul than elevate it; and here we carefully avoid all that might affect morality. I found them with these instruments and let them keep them; in this regard I offer them nothing new."

After the concert the sexes mingled, played and danced together with chaste behavior and modesty ever prevailing. No gesture nor look nor movement could scandalize even the strictest observer. I doubt that a like gathering could take place today anywhere in Europe: no roving hands, hip movements, obscene winks, whispered double entendres, loud laughter — all those things found in our corrupt society that indicate bad form, impudence, disorder, depravity.

"With so few ties that bind," I said to Zamé, "with laws so mild and so few religious restraints, why doesn't licentiousness reign?"

"Laws and religion disrupt morality," said Zamé, "but they fail to purify it. It requires neither shackles nor executioners to make an honest man, neither dogmas nor temples; those are the ways and means of villains and hypocrites and they've never given birth to a single virtue. Husbands of these wives, though absent, are friends of these young men. They're happy with their wives, they adore those whom they've chosen. Why would you want any of them, who also have wives they love, to trouble the felicity of their brothers? They'd at once make

three enemies: the wife they sought, the other whom they'd   o
plunge into despair, and friends whom they'd outrage.

"I joined these principles to education, to be imbibed
with mother's milk. I touch hearts by recourse to sentiment
and sensibility. What more would religion or law do? One of
your European fantasies is to imagine that man, like an un-   5
tamed animal, can only be made to behave if in chains. Such
frightful means enable you to render him malicious by adding
to natural desire the most energetic sort of unrestrained vice.
Nothing gives more pleasure or is a greater honor for these
young people than to be admitted into my home; I take advan-   10
tage of this weakness. Once you concern yourself with conduct, a man's heart is there for the taking; yet so few succeed
because half who try are stupid and the rest have too little
common sense to attain essential knowledge of the human
heart without which they can only act absurdly or live strictly   15
by the rules. The rule is the warhorse of imbeciles. They stupidly imagine the same rule will work for all even though no
two characters are alike; they do not take the time to examine
much less prescribe what is suited for each or reflect that they
themselves would consider a doctor inept who used the same   20
remedy for all ills, that one way alone was right, to succeed or
not. Their thick-skulled consciousness is soothed whenever
the rule is followed and they themselves live *by the rules.*

"If any of these young people failed to behave properly,"
continued Zamé, "he would be excluded from my house. That   25
fear contains them all the more since I know how to make
them love me. They tremble at the idea of displeasing me."

"But when you're not with them?"

"Then they're home, the couples united, occupied in caring for their household, without a thought of going astray.   30
Adultery does exist, but it's rare, concealed, and stirs neither
scandal nor unrest. If matters go further and I suspect a bad

outcome, I separate the guilty parties and make them live in different cities; and in cases still more serious, I banish them for a time. Exile, used for capital crimes, so frightens them that they avoid at all cost anything that could impose such a punishment. When you want to regulate a nation, begin by inflicting mild penalties and you won't need bloody ones."

After several hours of chaste and honest amusements:

"Enough, we're finished," Zamé told me. "I will send back the spouses to where they're awaited — not jealously so, I'm sure, but perhaps with a touch of impatience."

A gesture and a smile brought about a swift departure, unaccompanied, not an arm offered, nor any gesture that could offend decency. The young women retired first; an hour later, the men. All covered their revered father with blessings and thanks — he who loved them enough to enter thus into the fine details of their small pleasures.

"Arise early tomorrow," Zamé told me, "and I will take you to my temple; I want to show you the magnificence, pomp, and luxury of my religious ceremonies. I want you to see my priests as they perform their functions."

"Ah!" I replied. "I'm most anxious to do so, for a people's religion must as pure as their mores. I burn with desire to worship God among you. But you talk of splendor, great man. I know enough to be sure it won't dominate your ceremonies."

"You'll be the judge of that," said Zamé. "I'll be waiting for you an hour before sunrise."

I betook myself to the philosopher's door the next morning at the hour indicated. He was waiting with his wife, children, and daughter-in-law Zilia, all gathered round the cherished man.

"Let's be off," said Zamé. "The morning star will be rising and they'll be waiting for us."

We crossed the city. The inhabitants were already up and about; they gradually joined us as we passed and we thus made our way to the houses, which I shall discuss shortly, where the young were raised. Children of both sexes came out in droves. Led by their elders, they followed us as well; we marched in good order to the foot of a mountain behind the city to the east. Zamé mounted the summit and with his family I followed. The people surrounded us. The greatest silence was observed. At last arose the morning star. All heads bowed, hands raised to the heavens and thereto, it might be said, soared their souls.

"Eternal Sovereign," enjoined Zamé, *"deign accept profound homage from the people who worship you. It's not to you, brilliant star, that we address our desires, but that which moves you and created you. Your beauty recalls to us His image — your sublime workings, His power. Transmit to Him our respect and good wishes. May He deign to protect us so long as His goodness keeps us on earth, that we reunite with Him when it pleases Him to turn us to dust. Let Him direct our thoughts and rule our actions, purify our souls and the sentiments of respect and love they inspire, all in accord with His grandeur. We seat ourselves at the foot of His glory."*

Then Zamé, who was standing straight with hands outstretched while everyone else kneeled, lay his head upon the ground, worshipped a moment in silence, raised himself up, eyes brimming with tears, and brought the people back to the city. He told me once we returned:

"That is all. What more do you suppose the God of the universe may ask of us? Do we need to shut Him up in temples to serve and worship Him? We need only observe one of His most beautiful operations for sublime grandeur to develop in us sentiments of love and gratitude; that is why I chose the moment and place for you to see it. Nature's splendor is all I permit myself; this homage alone pleases the Eternal One.

337

o Religious ceremonies were invented only to focus upon the
flaws of the human heart; I do so to mend that heart in a way
charming to the eyes. Isn't that preferable? Besides, I wanted
to preserve something of the ancient cults. The inhabitants
of Tamoé used to worship the Sun and I had only to rectify
5 their system and prove to them that they were confusing the
work with the workman; that the Sun was a moving thing but
its Mover was what faith must address. They understood and
followed, changing almost nothing of their customs, pagans
though they were; I turned them into a pious people who
10 worship the Supreme Being.

"Do you believe your absurd dogmas and unintelligible
mysteries? Do your idolatrous ceremonies make for happier
or better citizens? Do you imagine that incense burning upon
marble altars is worth as much as the offerings of these good
15 hearts? By distorting the cult of the Eternal One, your religions
of Europe destroyed Him. When I enter one of your churches,
I find it so full of saints, relics, and mummeries of every kind
that I hardly recognize the God I desire. To find Him I must
look deep into my heart — the only place I must seek Him and
20 the only offering to place before Him. The beauties of Nature,
which gave rise to the idea of sanctuary, I contemplate for my
own edification and am moved. I do no more and if I've not
done all I ought, God in His goodness will forgive me; and to
better serve Him I am rid of a host of absurdities around re-
25 ligion and His image that men take to be necessary. I cast out
all that might prevent fulfillment with His sublime essence;
I trample underfoot all that claimed to share His grandeur.
I'd love Him less were He less than unique and grand, if His
strength were divided or could be multiplied, if this simple
30 being had to be worshiped as though He were several. I see
nothing in such a frightening and barbarous system but a
formless assemblage of errors and impieties, the very thought

of which would render Him hateful to my eyes and degrades
the pure Being to whom I address my soul. What more intimate knowledge of this beautiful Being can men have who
all lay claim to be of the illuminati? They only want to abuse
their fellow man. Is that any reason to listen to them — me,
who detests fraud and subterfuge, who has spent his whole
life working to guide his good people along the path of virtue
and truth?

*"If I'm wrong, Sovereign of the Heavens, you'll judge my
heart and not my mind. You know I'm weak and subject to
error; but you shan't punish my error because its source, my
sensitive soul, is pure. You'd not want me, who has sought only
a better way to worship you, be punished for not have done as
convention dictates."*

To me Zamé said: "Come, it's early. These fine children
might take a moment to talk amongst themselves. Such is
their custom on these ceremonial days that they ardently look
forward to and, for that very reason, I accord only two or three
times a year. They should see them as days of grace. The rarer
they are, the more respected. A steady diet breeds contempt.
Follow me — we've time before the dinner hour to visit the
outskirts of the city."

Taking me to see small plots of land, each separated by green
hedges covered with flowers: "Here are their possessions. Everyone has his own parcel of land — not much but by its very
mediocrity I maintain their industry. The less one has, the
more one is interested in cultivating it with care. Each has
what he needs to nourish his wife and himself — in abundance
if a good worker and if less so, he always has the necessities.
Plots for the unmarried, widows and the repudiated are smaller and situated elsewhere, near where they live.

"I myself have only one domain," continued Zamé, "and like them I'm only the usufructuary; my territory, like theirs, belongs to the state. To cultivate it, I choose some from among those who live alone; they also care for and serve me. Having no household of their own, they attach themselves with pleasure to mine; here they're sure to find food and lodging until the end of their days."

Pleasant and pretty paths nicely bordered and connected each domain and I found all of them richly adorned with the sweetest gifts of Nature. I saw an abundance of breadfruit trees, providing the same sort of food as our flour but more delicate and savory. I observed the other products of these delightful South Seas islands: the coconut and palm trees; for roots, yams, and a species of wild cabbage particular to this island, which they prepare in a very pleasing manner by mixing with coconut; several legumes brought from Europe have succeeded here and are highly prized. They also have sugarcane and a fruit resembling the nectarine which Captain Cook discovered in the Amsterdam Islands and which the inhabitants of these English isles call *figheha.*

Such are the foods of these wise, sober, and temperate people; in the past there were four-footed creatures that Zamé's father convinced the people to make extinct; and they never touch the birds.

With these things and the excellent water, the people live well; their health is robust. Young people are vigorous and prolific, the elderly, fresh and healthy, their lives much prolonged beyond the ordinary — and they're happy.

"You see how the temperature in this climate," said Zamé, "is salubrious, gentle, and constant; the vegetation is lush and abundant, and the air is nearly always pure. What we call our winters consist in a little rain during July and August but it never refreshes the air to the point that we must wear more

clothing, such that colds are unknown among us. Nature af-   o
flicts our inhabitants with few illnesses. The passing of years
is the greatest ill to befall us and nearly the only thing that
kills us.

    "You're familiar with our art, I shall say no more; our
sciences similarly amount to just a few things; however, ev-   5
eryone knows how to read and write. My father took care of
that and because many could speak and understand French,
I brought back 50,000 volumes, more for their amusement
than instruction; I distributed these in each village and so
made for little public libraries, which they frequent with plea-   10
sure when their rural occupations permit. They have some
knowledge of astronomy, which I have corrected, and of prac-
tical medicine, good enough for the life they lead and which I
improved with the help of well-known authors. They understand architecture and know the fundamentals of masonry.   15
They understand naval tactics and know how to build vessels.
Some among them amuse themselves writing poetry in their
own language which, if you understood it, you'd find it pleasant and nicely expressed. Regarding theology and law, they
have, thank heavens, no knowledge whatever. That would only   20
happen if I wished to destroy them; to open them up to this
labyrinth of errors and platitudes, all useless. If I wanted them
to annihilate themselves, I'd create among them priests and
men of law, enabling some to talk of God, others of Farinacius,
to decorate the city square with gallows, such as I observed in   25
your country, as eternal monuments to infamy which prove
at once the cruelty of sovereigns who permit them, the brutal idiocy of magistrates that erect them, and the stupidity of
people who tolerate them.

    "Let's go to dinner," said Zamé. "This evening I will you   30
bring you enjoyment with people's talent of which you have
no idea."

Indeed, when the time came, Zamé escorted me to the public square. I admired its proportions.

"You fail to note its greatest merit," he said. "Blood has never been spilled here. Never shall it be soiled by blood."

We continued. About a nicely ordered building set parallel to Zamé's house — both located on the square — I still knew nothing.

"The upper two floors serve as the public granary," said the philosopher, "for the only tribute I impose. I contribute like everybody else. Each year all are obliged to bring here a small portion of the produce they've grown so it can be stored. They will have food in times of shortages. I've always enough to feed the capital for two years; other cities do the same. In this way we never fear bad crop years and, as we've neither administrators nor monopolists, which are one and the same, we'll probably never die of hunger."

The ground level of the building contains a theater. This kind of entertainment, when well-done, is, I think, necessary for a nation. 3,000 years ago the wise Chinese thought the same and nurtured theater; the Greeks, only later. What surprises me is that Rome only took to it after four centuries and the Persians and Indians, never. Tonight's performance is meant for you. Let's go in and you'll see the benefits I reap from this honest and instructive form of relaxation."

The place was vast, artistically arranged, and you could see that Zamé's father, who had it built, brought together the customs of both peoples when he discovered among those still savages a taste for spectacles. He only improved it to provide a form of utility that he thought would work well. Under the roof everything was simple: elegance without luxury, cleanliness without splendor. The room held nearly 2,000 people; it was packed; actors occupied the slightly raised stage. The beautiful Zilia, her husband, Zamé's daughters, and several

young men from the city were cast in various roles. The lan- o
guage of the drama was their own, though written by Zamé,
who kindly explained the scenes as they played out. The story
involved a young woman guilty of infidelity and punished for
her bad behavior by all the misfortunes that can bring down
an adulteress. 5

Near us sat a very pretty woman. Her features, I noticed,
changed as the plot advanced. By turns she reddened, grew
pale, swallowed hard and breathed rapidly. Tears fell and she
grew sadder by the minute until she could no longer contain
herself and rose up, visibly in despair, pulling her hair, and fled. 10

"Well, then," said Zamé, who'd missed nothing of what
transpired. "Do you think it works? Such lessons are the only
punishments a sensitive people need. A French woman, just
as guilty, if confronted in public, would scarcely think it concerned her. In Siam she'd have been trampled beneath the feet 15
of an elephant. Isn't the tolerance found in one country not
just as dangerous as the barbarity of the other? Don't you find
my lesson better?"

"Sublime you are," I cried. "What sacred use you make of
your power and intellect." 20

We later learned that the consequences of this touching occurrence was this woman's sincere reconciliation with
her husband, an apology, confession of her misconduct, and
voluntary separation from her lover.

"How can moralists denounce the theater when these are 25
the results! Your aim might be the same," said Zamé, "but your
souls, dulled by endless repetitions of the same lessons, can
no longer be moved; you laugh at them as though they were
foreign to you; impudence absorbs them and vanity opposes
what you never imagine might have reference to you. You re- 30
press, out of pride, the features by which the ingenious censor
could correct your morals."

o   The next day Zamé brought me to visit the houses of
education: they were comprised of two immense buildings,
taller than others around them, with many bedrooms. We
began at the men's pavilion, with more than 2,000 students
who enter at age two and leave at age 15 to be married. These
5   fine young men are divided into three classes. The first comprises those up to the age of six, whose frail reason requires
they be cared for. From six to 12 begins an evaluation of disposition with an effort to match occupation with likes and
dislikes, preceded always by the study of agriculture, most es-
10   sential for the kind of life to which they are destined. The third
class includes those from 12 to 15 years of age. They alone are
taught the duties of men, in society and in their relationships
with those who gave them birth.

"We talk to them of God, inspire love for Him, and give
15   thanks to the Being who created us. We admonish them, explaining that they are approaching the age at which we will
confer upon them the fate of a woman; we make them feel
what they owe their dear and better half and prove they cannot hope for happiness in this pleasant, gentle society unless
20   they apply themselves and settle well-being upon one who is
part of it, that in the whole world we have no more sincere and
tender friend and companion, to whom we bond more closely,
than a spouse; that no one deserves to be treated more gently
or with more indulgence; and that this sex, naturally timid
25   and fearful, grows attached to the husband who loves and protects her, much as she invincibly hates him who would abuse
his power and authority to make her unhappy only because
he is the stronger; and that, if we possess this captivating authority, much better it be shared and the woman possess the
30   grace and appeal that seduces. 'Would you hope instead for a
heart ulcerated by spite?' We say to them: 'Whose hands wipe
away your tears when sorrow oppresses you? Who helps you

344

when Nature inflicts upon you all its woes? Deprived of men's sweetest consolation on earth, you would have in your house nothing but a slave cowed by your words and intimidated by your desires, who for a brief moment would accede to your desire but who, constrained to be in your arms, would leave your embrace detesting you.'

"We make them work the land, for their knowledge of agriculture makes them indispensable; the domain of this great house is cultivated and maintained by their young hands. Then we acquaint them with advances in military maneuvers. For recreation we permit dance, wrestling and, more generally, all games that fortify and consolidate youth by maintaining their strength, enhancing growth and good health.

"Once they've attained marriageable age, the wedding ceremony is as simple as it is natural. The father and mother of the young man bring him to the young women's house of education and, in front of everyone, they have him choose whom he wants. Choice made, if he pleases the young woman he has weeklong permission to talk for several hours with his betrothed, in the company of the teachers at the house of young women; there they begin to know one another and to see whether they are suited to each other. If it happens that one of them wants to break it off, the other is obliged to consent, because if it is not mutual there is nothing of perfect happiness in this kind of thing; then the process starts over. Once they are in complete agreement the judges of the nation are asked to unite them; consent accorded, they raise their hands to Heaven, swearing before God to be both faithful to each other, to aid one another in mutually meeting their needs, in their work, and in sickness, and never resort to divorce except for reasons necessary and imperative. These formalities complete, we put the young couple in possession of a house, as I said, subject to inspection for two years by parents and neighbors; and they are happy.

"Directors at the men's school are selected from among the bachelors who vow allegiance to the house as others among them do to the legislature. There they take bed and board. We choose from among them the most capable of carrying out their august function, noting that the most extreme regularity of morals is the most important quality."

Directresses of the house of young women, where Zamé and I stopped soon after, are chosen from spouses repudiated only due to age or infirmity, two conditions that do not affect the virtues necessary for that work.

There were nearly 3,000 girls in the house when we visited; they were similarly divided into the classes by age, just as with the boys. The moral teaching is the same; only physical education is reduced, putting aside what does not conform to the delicate sex; its place is taken by needlework, making clothes, and the art of preparing various common dishes. Only the women in Tamoé are involved in this. They make garments for themselves and their spouses; the clothes worn in the men's house of education are made by those in the women's house. Widows and repudiated spouses make those of the unmarried.

"It would be mad to imagine that educating children requires more than what you see here," Zamé told me. "Cultivate their tastes and inclinations, teach them only what is necessary, restrain them by honor alone, make recognition and acclaim their only incentives, with no other penalties than a few privations. By these wise ways we cultivate our delicate and precious plants. We do not irritate them or accustom them to steel themselves to punishment, or extinguish their sensitivity. 'The wildest colts make the best horses,' said Themistocles, 'if only they are properly trained and broken.' Young seedlings are the hope and support of the state. Judge for yourself whether the care we take with them works to our advantage.

"In each of these houses," continued Zamé, "50 rooms are reserved for the elderly, the widowed, the sick and un-married. Old men who are infirm find assured lodging in the men's house of education for the rest of their lives; so do those who've not remarried, become widowers a second time, or never married at all. They live on house funds and are served by the young students in order to accustom the latter to pro-vide the respect and care to which the elderly are entitled. The same arrangements exist for the women; and any among the rest of either sex find safe harbor in my house. My friend, I prefer this to a ballroom or concert hall; I gaze upon these respectable sanctuaries with more lively satisfaction than if the buildings were magnificent and luxurious and used only for hunting parties or as picture galleries and museums."

"Allow me one question," I said. "I don't see how your arti-sans or manufacturers can make a living in a country in which commerce is by necessity internal."

"Nothing is simpler," responded the chief legislator of these happy people. "We have workers of two kinds: those whose posts are temporary, such as architects, masons, car-penters, etc., and those who are always active, such as the ar-tisans of various manufactures. The first possess land like the rest of the citizens and when they're employed by the state, their fields must be cultivated and brought to harvest in order that they have no cares beyond their work. The unmarried perform these tasks. This demands a little clarification.

"There has existed across centuries and in all countries a class of men who, little caring for the comforts of marriage, or fearing such ties for moral or physical reasons, prefer to live alone to the delights of having a companion. This class was so numerous in Rome that, to reduce their number, Augus-tine was obliged to pass the law known as *Lex Papia Poppæa*. Not so famous as the republic that subjugated the world,

o Tamoé too has its unmarried citizens, but we've never made
a law against them. One can easily obtain permission not to
marry on condition that one serves the country in public
works. Clearchus of Soli, a disciple of Aristotle, tells us that,
in Laconia, punishment of men unsuited for marriage was to
5 be whipped naked by women as they circled round an altar.
What use is that? *

"As I am always concerned to eliminate the useless and
replace it with what can result in something good, the only
other penalty I impose upon the unmarried is to demand they
10 help the state since they cannot provide it with more subjects.
We furnish them a house and the means to live in a neighborhood allocated to them; they live as they please, obliged only
to cultivate the land for those employed by the state; they accept this and do not consider the price too high for the free-
15 dom they desire. As you know, they also maintain my domains,
bring relief to the elderly and infirm, preside over and take
care of the schools, and are charged with repairing roads, public plantations, and generally all difficult work indispensable

---

* One purely physical reason must have been the cause of that singular law. Unmarried
men were believed impotent and the ceremony was tasked with recovering the force
they seemed to lack. But the thing was poorly understood; impotence, which can
often only be treated by violence, is not the only or even the main reason for remain-
ing unmarried. If taste and habit cause this or that individual to disdain the chains of
marriage, the means of restoration will act to the advantage of his irregular caprices
without bringing him closer to that which he finds repugnant; thus, the remedy is a
poor one. If it were a question of a dissertation, in addition to this citation, drawn
from the history of antique morality, one could add many others which serve to prove
that, throughout history, whenever man had recourse to powerful means for re-es-
tablishing vigor, the very thing that fools condemn or banter about was an article of
faith among peoples as worthy as they. We know today that a soul awakened by real
or imagined pain — agitated, as Saint-Lambert says — is in all ways more sensitive
and enjoys more agreeable sensations. The celebrated Cardan tells us, in the story of
his life, that when nature did not cause him feel pain, he procured it for himself by
biting his lips and pulling his fingers until he wept.

to a country. And that is how I try to profit from faults and   0
vices to make these people as useful as possible to the rest of
the citizenry. I believe that ought to be the aim of every legislator and I do what I can.

"Regarding workers who are always active and employed
in manufacturing in such a way that they are wholly unable to   5
cultivate their own land, they live off what it produces. When
someone wants fabric for an article of clothing, he takes raw
material drawn from his own resources to the manufacturer,
who uses it to make the product and gives it to the worker, receiving in return a prescribed quantity of fruits & vegetables,   10
more than sufficient to his needs."

It remained for me to learn something about the manner in
which the trial system operated among citizens. Although   15
precautions are taken to avoid them, there are always some.

"All offenses come down to three or four," Zamé told me,
"of which the main one is failure to care for conferred assets.
The penalty, as I told you, is to be given a smaller and infinitely
more difficult plot to cultivate. I showed you that the state   20
constitution has totally abolished thievery, rape, and incest.
We never hear talk of these horrors; they are unknown among
us. Adultery is quite rare in our country; I've explained my
means to limit it and in one instance you've seen the effects.
We have eliminated pederasty through ridicule; if the shame   25
with which we cover those who can still engage in it does not
have its effect, we make such people useful, employing them
such that they alone perform the rudest chores for the unmarried. They are thus unmasked in a corrective way without
locking them away or burning them, which is absurd, barba-   30
rous, and has never rehabilitated a single soul.

"Other quarrels arise amongst the citizens with no other cause than bad tempers in households, and by allowing divorce these are many fewer; once it is clear a couple can no longer live together, they separate. Each party is sure to find subsistence beyond the hearth and another marriage if so desired, provided everything transpires in a friendly manner. All this nevertheless cannot prevent mild disagreements. Eight elders regularly assist me in examining such cases. They assemble at my home three times each week; we see to the everyday affairs and decide them amongst ourselves, with the verdict announced in the name of the state. If one appeals, we consider it a second time; but the third time is final and any decision obligatory. For the state is everything here. It nourishes the citizen, raises his children, cares for him, judges and condemns him; and of this state I am merely the first citizen.

"In no case do we allow the death penalty. I have told you how we treat murder, the only crime which might be judged worthy of it. The guilty party is abandoned to the justice of Heaven to dispose of as He wishes. There are still only two examples in the course of my father's rule and my own. Our nation is naturally gentle-hearted and does not like to spill blood."

Our talk having brought us to the dinner hour, we went back.

"Your ship is ready," Zamé informed me at the end of the meal; "repairs have been made and I've arranged for all manner of provender our island can supply." My philosopher continued: "However, I asked you for two weeks and now just five days have passed. I must request, during the ten days that remain, that you acquire more complete knowledge concerning our island. Much as I would like it if my age and affairs permitted me to be your guide, my son will take my place; he will explain my operations and give you an account of everything, just as I would."

"Generous man," I responded, "of all my debts to you, the   o
greatest is this permission you grant me. It is so kind of you
to multiply my occasions to admire you! I count every one of
them a pleasure."

Zamé embraced me tenderly.

Humanity shines by its most brilliant virtues. The man   5
who has done good wants to be commended; and perhaps he
would do less were he not certain of praise.

We went out early next morning: his son Oraï and his
brother together with one of my officers and myself. The delightful island is nicely cut with canals overhung with palm and   10
coconut trees, and as in Holland, one can travel from one city
to another in charming public canoes that run at two leagues
per hour. They are guided by the unmarried and belong to
the state. Others belong to families and only one person is
required as guide. Thus it was we passed through the other   15
cities on Tamoé — all nearly as large and equally populous as
the capital, constructed all in the same style, with each boast-
ing a public square in their center that holds, instead of the
legislative palace and granaries as in the capital, two houses
of education. Storehouses are located toward the outskirts of   20
the city, situated symmetrically with large buildings that provide dwellings for the some of the surfeit of elderly that Zamé,
in his city, lodges next door to his home. The rest, as in the
capital, live in rooms on the high floors of the houses for children, some 30 or 40 quarters. The unmarried and repudiated   25
of both sexes occupy, as in the capital, a neighborhood around
which they have their small separate holdings, which suffice
for their needs, and they find equal acceptance in lodgings for
the elderly when they become unable to cultivate the earth.

In the end I saw people who were gentle and sober,   30
healthy and hospitable, farmers of land fertile and rich, with
no signs of laziness or poverty. Everywhere was manifest the
gentle influence of a wise and temperate government.

There are no little towns, hamlets, or isolated houses on the island; Zamé wanted all landholdings of every province to be located together in order that a vigilant commandant — an elder who answers to the town — could readily keep an eye upon everyone. In each town he is a kind of officer, representing the chief, having as assistants two old people like himself, of which one is always chosen from among the unmarried, in line with the government's intention to never regard this caste as inferior, but only as a class of men who, unable to be useful to society in one way, serve to the best of their ability in another.

"They are closely connected to the state as members like the others," Oraï told me. "My father wants them to take part in its administration."

"But," said I to this young man, "what if an unmarried man joins this class for no reason except lecherousness?"

"If these vices erupt in public — for we never take action against them — there's no question but that the guilty party may not be chosen to govern the city; but if he is unmarried for legitimate reasons he is not excluded from the administration or operation of the schools, for you have seen the importance my father attaches to them. The city commandants change each year and decide minor affairs while sending others on to the chief, to whom they write daily.

"Thus, just as in the capital, the cities require only a limited police force; there is no need for a rabble of rascals a hundred times more corrupt than those they repress and, to stem the effects of vice, only multiply the contagion.* The inhabitants, always obliged to work in order to live, go in for none of the disorders of sloth and luxury that so afflict your cities of

---

* Asked why he needed so many dishonest police in Paris, Monsieur Bertin replied: "Find me an honest man who wants to do this job." So be it — but an honest man would respond: Is it necessary in the first place to corrupt one half the citizens ☞

Europe. They go to bed early in order to be up at the break of day to cultivate their lands. When the season requires nothing of them, innocent pleasures keep them close to home. Several households come together to dance and make a little music; they chat of their affairs, care for their possessions, and they cherish and respect virtue — for which, stirred by the cult to which they are indebted, they glorify the Eternal One, bless their government, and are happy.

"Theater amuses, too, during the rainy season. In the capital and elsewhere, located above the storehouses, the people give themselves over to that particular pleasure. The elderly compose dramas, always with attention to providing useful lessons, and rarely does the audience leave without feeling more honest."

The pure and gentle mores of this fine people seemed to me, in a word, to recall a golden age. Each of their charming homes seemed like the temple of Astrea. My plaudits, offered upon my return, were born of the enthusiasm inspired in me during this delightful tour; and I assured Zamé that, were it not for the ardor and passion that devoured me, I would ask him, in all grace, to let me end my days beside him.

in order to police the other half? Second, has it been shown that only by doing ill can one succeed in doing good? Third, does the state gain and virtue increase by multiplying the number of scoundrels? Fourth, is it not to be feared that this gangrenous part of the body corrupts the rest instead of correcting it? Fifth, if the way these infamous men set their traps, by confounding innocence with crime in order to reveal it, is that not, I say, quite as dangerous? And does not innocence corrupted by those sorts of people and all others who come after owe to instruction at this school of crime? Is it not the work of these liars? Is it thus permitted to corrupt and suborn in order to correct and punish? Sixth and last, is there not on the part of those who govern a powerful interest in wanting to persuade the King and the nation that a million must be spent to bribe one hundred thousand rascals who merit only the whip and hard labor? Until these questions are resolved, we must doubt the excellence of the French police.

o   At this juncture he asked what troubled me and why I
was abroad. I told him my story, begging his counsel, and assured him that I wanted to fulfill my destiny based on his advice alone. The good man regretted my misfortune and took
the interest of a father in giving excellent lessons concerning
5   the lapses that had enmeshed me in a passion of which I was
no longer master. He ended by insisting I return to France.

      "Your search is painful and fruitless," he told me. "The
information you were given was wrong, perhaps purpose-
fully so. But even if it was correct, what likelihood of finding
10   a single person among a hundred million? You will lose your
fortune and your health — and never succeed. Léonore, more
thoughtful than you, will have made a simple calculation and
seen that the most natural place to reunite with you would be
in your own country. You can be certain she will return there,
15   and that only in France can you ever hope to see her again."

      Yielding before this divine man, I threw myself at his feet
and swore to follow his advice.

      "Come, my son," he told me, taking me in his arms and
raising me up tenderly. "Before you leave us, I want to offer
20   you one final amusement. Follow me."

      Naval combat was the spectacle Zamé intended to show me.

      The beautiful Zilia, magnificently dressed, was seated on
a throne upon the crest of a rock in the middle of the sea. Several women formed her cortege; one hundred pirogues pro-
25   tected her, each manned by four oarsmen; another hundred
were poised to carry her off. Oraï commanded the attack; his
brother, the defense. At a signal, all boats took to the waves
and the battle was joined. Attacks were repulsed with as
much grace as nimbleness and courage; several oarsmen were
30   knocked into the water and pirogues overturned; the defenders finally surrendered, making Oraï triumphant. In a flash he
jumped onto the point of the rock, seized his charming wife

and returned with her to port, escorted by all combatants, to   o
the sounds of praise and cries of joy. "For ten days he hasn't
seen her," said Zamé. "With this little celebration today I'm
trying to spur the pleasure of reunion so that soon I'll become
a grandfather."

"What?"   5

"But no," responded the old man, with tears in his eyes.
"Pretty as she is, his indifference is extreme. He didn't want to
marry."

"And yet you hope?"

"Yes!" replied Zamé briskly. "I employ the method of Ly-   10
curgus. We irritate, we give Nature a hand and constrain her
in order to inspire desires that would never arise without. It
is sure to work. You saw how he went at it with ardor. He
wouldn't have been allowed to see her for two months if he
hadn't succeeded; and if this first victory doesn't bring more   15
in its wake, I'll make it so painful for him to see her and inflame his desire by perpetual force of combat that he'll fall in
love despite himself."

"Or perhaps with another, Zamé."

"No. Were it that, do you think I would have chosen her?   20
Unalterable, his disgust for marriage — perhaps other fantasies, too. You know Nature. Are you not aware of her vagaries
and caprices? But he'll get over it. The opposition is already
vanquished. It's only a matter of redirecting inclinations —
and my methods are sure."   25

And so this philosopher, with his nation as in his family,
working only with the soul, managed to purify his fellow citizens, turning even their faults to the profit of society and inspiring in them, despite themselves, a taste for honest things
no matter their propensities — or, rather, turning bad into   30
good. Little by little, and without punishment, he made virtue
triumph, with sensibility and praise his only resources.

"Let me say to you so you needn't tell me: we must part," said Zamé the next day, as he accompanied me to my ship.

"Wise old man, what a terrible moment! After all the sentiments you've begot in me, I can hardly stand the thought."

"You'll remember me," said that good man, pressing me to his breast, "and recall from time to time that at the ends of the earth you have a friend. You will say: 'I came upon a people who are sweet and sensitive, *virtuous but without laws, pious but without religion,* and their leader is a man who loves me, and there I might find asylum for the rest of the days of my life.'"

I embraced my good friend; it became impossible to let him go.

"Listen to me, Sainville," he said with fervent emotion, "you're surely the last Frenchman I'll ever see. I would like to remain fond of the nation of my origin. Listen to a secret thought that I only wanted to reveal at the moment of our separation. My profound study of the world's governments, and particularly the one under which you live, has very nearly given me the art of prophecy. By examining a people, in closely following its course since it began to play a role in the world, we can easily forecast what is to come. O Sainville! A great revolution is coming to your country. The people are fed up with the crimes of your sovereigns, their cruel exactions, their debauchery and ineptitude. Infuriated by despotism, the nation is ready to cast off its fetters. Free once more, that proud nation of Europe will honor its alliances with all peoples that govern as she does.

"My friend, the dynasty of the chiefs of Tamoé will not last long. My son shall never succeed me; the nation must not be ruled by kings; to perpetuate them would be to prepare the shackles. It will need a legislature; my work is done. Upon my death, the inhabitants of this happy island will enjoy the gentle pleasures of a free and republican government. I'm preparing

them for it; thanks to the virtues of a father whom I've tried to   o
emulate, they are so destined. But crimes and atrocities committed by your sovereigns prepare a fate in kind for France. Made
equal, made free, though by different means, the people of your
country and mine will resemble one another; and therefore,
I ask you, my friend, to mediate with the French to obtain the   5
alliance I desire. Will you promise to carry out my wishes?"

With tears, I replied; "My good friend, I swear to you
that these two nations are worthy of one another. May eternal
bonds unite them."

"I shall die happy!" exclaimed Zamé, "That pleasant hope   10
will let me go to my grave in peace. Come, my son, come," he
continued, and accompanied me into my cabin aboard ship.
"Come, we will say goodbye."

"Heavens! What's this?" Gold ingots covered the table.
"Zamé, what are you doing? Your friend needs only your tender-   15
ness and aspires to make himself worthy of it."

"Could you stop me from offering you the very soil of
Tamoé?" responded the mortal who had done so much to be
cherished. "So that you remember what it brings forth."

"Great man!" I shed tears and fell at his feet, begging him   20
to take back his gold and leave me only his heart.

"Take both," replied Zamé, throwing his arms around my
neck, "as you would have done in my place. I must go now.
Like yours, my heart breaks. My friend, our paths will likely
never cross again but we shall love each other always."   25

With these final words, Zamé quickly departed, disappeared, waved goodbye, and left me drowning in tears, filled
with all the emotions of a soul at once oppressed by pain and
seized with the most profound admiration.*

---

* At this moment of calm — we did not want to interrupt — the reader may permit
us some reflections.

☞

0   Intending to follow Zamé's advice, we left the way we came;
the wind served and soon Tamoé was out of sight.

My finer feelings suffered from my obligation to take with
me, in spite of all, powerful proof of a friend's generosity. But
when I considered that the gold, so precious to us, meant noth-
5   ing to the wise people of Tamoé, I could assuage my sorrow
and give thanks to my benefactor. In memory he'd never be far
from my thoughts.

Our trip was a pleasant one and we made the Cape in
good time. As soon as we sighted it, I asked my officers if they
10   wanted to make land or would prefer to return with me directly
to France. Although the ship was mine, I believe I owed them

One may object that the happiness of the people just described was illusory; that
at bottom they were slaves for they themselves had no possessions. Such an objection
seems to us false; it would be as if to say that the father of a family, a property owner,
is a slave because he is only the usufruitier of the fortune that actually belongs to his
children. We call "slave" one who depends upon a master for everything, a servile
person who is furnished scarcely enough for subsistence. But in the case of Tamoé
there is no master apart from the state, and the leader depends upon it just like the
others. The state owns all assets, not the leader.

But the citizen of Tamoé, one may continue to object, can neither sell nor hire.

And indeed, what need has he to do either? It is to live or to exchange that one
sells or hires; if these things prove useless here, what regret not to have them? To be
unable to do something useless is not to be a slave. One is a slave when one can do
nothing useful or pleasant. What good would it do here to buy or sell, for everyone
possess what he needs to live and if that is all the he needs for happiness?

But one can leave nothing to one's children.

So long as the state can provide subsistence and give them property equal to your
own, what do you need to leave your children? Clearly, it is a great good for parents
to be sure of their posterity, to know their children are destined to be as rich as they
were and that they themselves will never be put to their charge nor their death desired
so their children will become rich in their turn. No, certainly, these people are not
slaves in any way; they are the happiest, richest and freest people on earth, always
sure of equal subsistence as to be found in no other nation — and they are happier
than any nation you could compare them to. One might rather say that the state
voluntarily becomes slave to the people in order to assure the greatest liberty to its
members and, in this case, the best model of government imaginable.

such consideration. As they desired to return to their own
country, they preferred to have me disembark on the coast of
Brittany in order to return to Holland by way of Nantes, then
once home to sell the ship for me. We agreed on all points and
continued sailing; but my health did not permit me to bring
our project to completion. When we reached Cap-Vert I had
a raging fever accompanied by stomach and chest pains, and
could not leave my disgusted bed. This misfortune forced me
to set down anchor at Cadiz where, thoroughly fed up with the
sea, I resolved to return to France by land as soon as I was well.
My considerable fortune enabled me to give up the small sum
I might have gained from sale of my ship, so I made a present
of it to my officers; they showered me with thanks. I had only
praise for them and they ought to have been pleased with me.
Nothing had fraught the harmony that had grown up among
us and we parted with all the reciprocity of mutual esteem.

My health kept me ten days at Cadiz but the air was not
good for me, so I made my way to Madrid, intending to stay
there as long as I needed to regain my strength. On arriving I
found lodging at the Hotel Saint-Sebastien, in the street of the
same name, among the Milanese, who are renowned for the
care they provide foreign visitors. I found that to be partly true
but it cost me dearly!

In no condition to take care of myself, I asked the hotel-
keeper to find domestic help, French if possible and honest as
could be. He immediately produced two tall, sturdy wenches,
one from Paris and the other from Rouen. Both had come
through Spain with masters who had dismissed them because
they refused to continue on a voyage to Mexico from which
they might not return for a very long time; and in such sorry
circumstances they eagerly sought someone to help them re-
patriate. All this being impossible to verify, I took their word
for it, taking them on immediately but resolving not to trust
them. Both served me well during my convalescence, about

two weeks, after which I gradually regained my strength and began attending to the details of my fortune. My eyes turned to the caseful of gold ingots, those precious fruits of my friendship with Zamé; and in examining these treasures my eyes flooded with tears of gratitude. How pure they appeared, formed into bars unmixed with terrestrial impurities. I doubted they could have been mined during my visit to the interior but must have been drawn from the fortune that served Zamé during his twenty years of travel.

I had still not emptied the coffer and when I did so, to count the ingots, I found at the bottom a paper that gave the worth of the gold in French money. It amounted to seven million five hundred thousand seventy livres.

"Great heavens!" I cried, "I'm the richest man in Europe! *Oh, father — might I ease your old age! I could put to right the wrong I've done you; I shall make you content and be happy myself. And you — Léonore! My only love, if Heaven permits and I find you one day, here's what will enrich the feeble gift of my hand in marriage, and satisfy and anticipate your every desire. How tenuous the schemes of men when not submitted to the caprices of fate!"*

"O Léonore, Léonore!" *Sainville interrupted himself* and he wept on his dear wife's breast. "I had everything to make your fortune — enough to repay you for your suffering — yet now nothing left to offer but my heart."

"My heavens," said Madame de Blamont. "And what of all that wealth?"

"Lost, Madame. The essential difference between fortuitous fortune and sentiments of the heart is that the former is evanescent while the tenderness I feel for the one I love will never be effaced from my soul. But let us return to the course of events."

Although I still had nearly 25,000 livres, half in gold and half   o
in money fortunately sown into a belt I never took off, I fan-
cied changing one of my ingots into Spanish quadruples.*
To that end, I betook myself to a director of the coinage as
indicated by my hotelier. I presented him with my gold; he
examined it and quickly realized it could not have come from   5
Peru. Curiosity aroused, his questions became more numerous and pressing and it became difficult for me to control
myself; I visibly trembled with emotion. I saw that I'd done
something stupid and my evident embarrassment redoubled
the fellow's curiosity. His attitude grew severe and he renewed   10
his questions with insolence and effrontery. My heart enabled
me to recover my expression of calm and I responded, un-
troubled, that I had brought the gold from Africa; and it was
mine owing to exchanges in the Portuguese colonies. Here my
questioner examined still more closely, assuring me that in   15
Africa the Portuguese used only gold found in the New World;
and that what I showed him was surely not from there. Now I
betrayed impatience and declared myself tired of his interro-
gations, that the metal on offer was either good or bad; if good,
he might exchange it for me without further difficulty; if bad,   20
let him prove it. He chose the latter course but testing it only
showed the metal was genuine. It became impossible for him
not to give me satisfaction. With a touch of humor, he asked if
I had many more ingots to exchange.

"No," I responded, "This is the only one."   25

Handing off my bags to my people, I returned to my hotel,
where I passed the day not without worry about the number
of questions the director had posed.

---

* About 84 livres in French money. The pistolet being worth 21 livres, there exist
doubles and quadruples.

I went to bed — but what an atrocious wakening! Not two hours later, to a great din the door shot open and my room filled with thirty crispins* — all brutes and friends of the Inquisition.†

"With permission of *Your Excellency*," said one of these illustrious rascals, "you will come with us and directly be brought before the Very Reverend Father Inquisitor, who awaits you in his offices."

By way of response I wanted to throw myself on my sword but was not given the chance. I was not bound; it is one of the tribunal's peculiarities to employ no shackles but only force of numbers in seizing prisoners. I was so surrounded and so put upon as to make any movement impossible. I had to obey. We went down to the street where a coach awaited and these villains brought me to the Palace of the Inquisition. There we were received by the secretary of the Holy Office who, without a single word, handed me off to the Alcaide — the jailer — and two guards conducted me to a locked cell with three iron doors, as dark and humid as could be, never penetrated by the sun. Thus was I left without a word or permission to speak, either to complain or give any orders whatever to my people.

---

* The clothing of such persons is the uniform of these fools.

† Pope Innocent III, with a plan for reinforcing the role of the Inquisition, accorded privileges and indulgences to those who would lend assistance to the tribunal in searching out and punishing the guilty. Easy to see, after instauration of so wise a plan, how their number could only grow. These "friends" were the infamous informers who became part of the Inquisitor's family. The most important seigneurs could acquire impunity for their crimes and so they hurried to enter that noble body. The tribunal of the Inquisition was not the only one to have its "friends" and Spain was not the only country in Europe where its administration was wholly polluted by corruption or toleration of them, with one half of its citizens used to pointlessly torment the other half.

Feeling overwhelmed, absorbed by the most terrible   o
thoughts, you can readily imagine how I passed the night. I'd
traveled the world over and lived amongst cannibals — who
respected my life and liberty. I'd followed a star that brought
me to distant lands across the ocean and came away with
friends and an immense fortune. Only to arrive in Europe —   5
to return to my native land — and for what? To be met by
persecutors!

And as if taking pleasure in the gathering horror of my
fate, I dwelt on it every moment until at last the Alcaide appeared, after a week in that horrible place. He was escorted by   10
two guards. He ordered my head uncovered and I was conducted to the tribunal. I was shown to a narrow hard chair
at the end of a table, where two monks were seated. One was
to interrogate me, the other to write down my responses. I
took my place. Facing me was the image of the Good Lord,   15
redeemer of the universe, in a place where men toiled to
immolate those He had come to save. Before my eyes, thus,
that fair-minded judge and those dastardly men; the symbol
of sweetness and virtue next to that of ferocity and crime.

I sat before the Prince of Peace and men of bloody violence   20
— and it was in the name of the first that the latter would
sacrifice me to their infamous greed.

fig. 8 appears in the left margin at line 20.

They asked my name, my country, and my profession.
Once I answered these initial questions, they demanded I tell
them about the motives for my travels. I hid nothing. When I   25
told them I'd been to an island where I came upon the greatest
of legislators, they asked me if he were Christian.

"He's more than that," I said with enthusiasm. "He's just
and good; he is liberal; he is charitable — and he doesn't lock
up the ill-fated whom chance casts upon his shores."   30

This response was viewed as impious and blasphemous.
The Inquisitor asked if I had baptized this pagan.

"For what?" I replied, outraged. "If Heaven is destined for the virtuous, he will arrive ahead of others who, submitting to vain rites, commit all manner of crime and atrocity."

Another blasphemy! The monk, showing me the crucifix, asked if I took Him as my Savior.

"Yes," I replied, "and if anything revolts Him it's the tyrant who fastens the shackles, not the slave forced to wear them. The Lord you just put before me was unhappy like me, and like me the victim of calumny and men's villainy. He must pity me and condemn you."

At this the Inquisitor, palpitating with rage, told the clerk to write down that I was an *atheist*.

"You put down a lie!" I cried. "I swear I believe in a God that I fear and worship. One who hates the abusers who oppress the innocent in His name."

The clerk, stopped by my response, stared at the Inquisitor.

"Write down," said the latter, "that he insults the officers of the tribunal."

"Let Your Eminence reflect," said the clerk in Spanish, believing I couldn't understand.

"Then write down that he's a slanderer," said the Inquisitor, still furious.

"I thought it was less about your secret observations," I told the atrocious judge, "than of questioning me about facts and confronting me with witnesses."

"Such confrontations never happen in a tribunal directed by the spirit of God. Where the Holy Spirit reigns, formalities are useless. Who owns that gold you changed yesterday?"

"I do."

"Where does it come from?"

"By the kindness of a God-fearing friend who loves men, who serves and never torments them."

"Are there gold mines on his island?"

"No," I answered roundly. (Could I have forgiven myself   o
another response if what I said brought such enemies to the
best of men?) "No, he received the ingots in payment for
commerce done with the English."

"And he made you such a gift?"

"He makes no use of it and has renounced all foreign   5
transactions. Gold has become useless to him."

"Useless? They're worth nearly eight million!"

And suddenly I realized that my whole fortune was by
now in the hands of these rascals.

The Inquisitor redoubled his questioning and did every-   10
thing he could to make me cross or contradict myself, with such
profound skill as can be found only amongst ministers of this
blood tribunal. But I never deviated. My answers were always
the same and foiled him. He wanted geographical details concerning Tamoé; I made them so confusing that it was impos-   15
sible for him to guess where in the ocean the island was located.

When the interrogation ended, I demanded my gold but
was told that further clarifications were necessary to know if it
was mine; and even once it was certain I was telling the truth,
it would still be necessary to deduct the costs of a trial. More- 20
over, the King would be fitting out and sending off a ship to
verify my testimony; I might judge from the money and time
what that would cost; my telling the truth would be essential
to avoid such steps. I guarded against falling into the trap and
changed the subject so as not to give an excuse for a second   25
round. Complaining of my cell, I asked whether, in light of my
wealth, I might not at least be lodged more comfortably. The
Inquisitor asked the Alcaide, who responded that there were
no good rooms available except among the women prisoners.

"Give him one," said his reverence, "and explain the rules." 30

The apartment, located in the women's dwelling, was
infinitely better than mine.

o   "It's an exceptional favor, to be given this room," the Alcaide told me as he brought me there. "You shall conduct yourself with all imaginable prudence and circumspection; the least indiscretion will return you to a dungeon from which you'll never emerge. Cells above and around you hold Jewish and

5   Bohemian women. Keep silent if they ask questions and refrain from being the first to talk."

I promised to comply and the doors shut behind me.

Five days I passed in this new place before one of my jailers invited me to request another audience, as is customary

10 with the Tribunal, replete as it is with ruses and deceit. When the judges want to interrogate the guilty a second time, the audience must owe to pressing solicitation on the part of the victim who might otherwise groan on for centuries without relief or being heard. So I demanded to see my judges again

15 and obtained permission.

The Inquisitor asked what I wanted.

"My belongings and my freedom."

"Have you considered," he asked evasively, "the extreme importance of providing the clarifications we desire?"

20 "I gave satisfaction as to what was required and am content to expect the same."

"Everything is locked away in the Holy Office vault and will go nowhere until return of the ship sent off by His Majesty to gather information. Hasten to give the answers we want.

25 Your freedom will owe to their promptitude and your life to their truthfulness."

But when they saw I was steadfast in my responses, they noted with impatience that one who has nothing to say must not demand an audience, that the tribunal had plenty of busi-

30 ness, and it was not be bothered for minutiæ. I was to make no more demands for freedom unless I decided on truth-telling and submission.

Back in my cell, I confess to feeling near despair. What   o
had I done? How could I deserve a punishment so severe? I
was born sensitive and honest yet they were treating me as
if I were a scoundrel. I possessed virtue yet was being sullied
as a criminal. Of what use my good heart? Had it made me
less a victim? What quality of mine drew their hatred? With   5
vice and mediocrity, I would've found happiness. To win their
esteem, one must be low and vile. If you're afflicted by talent, if fortune shines upon you and Nature serves you, others'
humiliated pride will only set traps; with malice and bitter
calumny, ever ready to crush you, to punish you for being   10
good and to make you repent of your virtues.

Returning to my original error, my greatest crime: to
have loved Léonore. From that first weakness ensued the
whole chain of my misfortunes. If not for that, I never would
have left France. All tragedy followed upon this first fault. Yet   15
what was I saying? Still likely more unhappy than I — alas, and
where was she? Some place alone upon the earth? In taking
her away from her family, had I not destroyed her happiness?
In tearing her away from it, had I not recklessly ruined her
future? Swept away, by culpable imprudence, any happiness   20
she had the right to expect? It was for her alone my tears must
fall; I must feel sorry for her alone. My own misfortune was
well-deserved because it had brought about her own.

"O Léonore! Léonore! All that has gone wrong for you is my
handiwork alone. Those bursts of pleasure my love excited in   25
you were like those deceptive gleams that mislead the lost traveler, swallowing him forever in the abyss." I continued, weeping: "And as to you, my benefactor, why did I leave you? Why
did I not find Léonore on your island and why did we not both
settle in that enchanting land? And as for this vile tribunal in a   30
nation subjugated by imposture and superstition, what rights
do you have over me? What allows you to hold me prisoner
and make me the unhappiest of men?"

A week passed and then I was summoned for a third audience. But this time I was not compelled to request it. The rascals had begun to see I suspected the trap they desperately wanted me to fall into. With recourse to only slander and dread, they hoped to obtain confessions by which they could unfairly find me guilty while appeasing any remorse they might have felt in robbing me with such impunity.

This time I was received in what they called "the place of torments" — a frightful underground, reached by descending an endless staircase, a place so remote that no cry from within could ever be heard. It is there, without respect for either modesty or humanity, without distinction as to age or sex or position, those infernal vultures came to feed with their barbarities and atrocities. Here honest young women, abashed as they are stripped naked under the eyes of these monsters, are pinched, burned, placed upon the rack — and, spurred by ferocity, they awaken lust in perverse hearts. In order to obtain ever more confessions for the realm, they annually defile 50,000 souls. All the instruments of torture were laid before my frightened eyes; missing only were the executioners. The same monks, seated in huge chairs, ordered me to take my place on a wooden stool, facing them.

"You can see," said the one who had previously interrogated me, "what methods we have to obtain the truth."

"They are useless," I responded with courage. "They may frighten the guilty. But the innocent victims see them and do not tremble. Let your assassins come, I shall withstand their tortures, pity you, and console myself."

"Your unwonted pride and the stubbornness by which you conceal the truth may cost you dearly," said the Inquisitor. "Is there any reason to pretend? We know everything already. Your hotelier and your people, imprisoned like you" — this was false — "and everyone around you, has deposed against you.

We surprised you as you went about your scheming; we saw   o
you invoke the Devil. In a word, you are a chemist and sor-
cerer, which we regard as the same thing."*

Anywhere else, I confess, laughter would be my only response to the foolishness of these people. You cannot imagine
the contempt that such a judge inspires when, renouncing the   5
wise austerity of his minister, he demeans himself whether by
libertinage or stupidity to contend with trifles, with senseless
dishonesty. We can no longer see him as anything but a villain
or imbecile, motivated by foolishness or a taste for debauch,
worthy of nothing but the rigors of law and public indignation.   10

No matter: I contained myself; but my feelings for such
pitiful false-hearted men could not be concealed. The two of
them exchanged looks without knowing exactly what to say that
would support their stupid accusations. Finally, I told them:

"If I was as powerful as the Devil, believe me, the first   15
thing I'd do would be to take myself out of the hands of his
own henchmen."

"But if it is certain," said the Inquisitor, unfazed by my response, "that you fabricated this gold, it could only be by the use
of chemistry — and chemistry, by our lights, is a diabolical art."   20

"No chemical process makes gold," I said, quickly interrupting this imbecile. "Those that spread such foolishness are
as stupid as those who believe it; the earth is its sole matrix
and cannot be imitated. I explained the provenance of these
ingots; I acquired them by means that could not weigh upon   25

---

* Accusations of chemical sorcery cannot astonish in a century that saw the famous
trial of the priest of Blénac. The Parlement of Toulouse, in 1712 or 1715, accused the
unfortunate curé of commerce with the Devil. As a result, he was scandalously dis-
robed for all to see whether his body bore marks of such commerce; and as several such signatures were found, the facts were no longer in dispute. He was lanced
and each of the signatures was burned to see whether it was the work of Nature
or the Devil. Such served as the spiritual school for those who murdered Calas.

my conscience. You can torture me to death, I'll never tell you more. Keep my gold if it tempts you. I lived before I had it and will not die having lost it. But give me back the freedom of which you've wrongfully deprived me, impelled by only greed."

"So you recognize," the liar added, "that this gold is the fruit of your own labors?"

"I recognize it was given and belongs to me. You want to put me to death so you can steal it."

"The height of impudence!" said the monk, rising, furious and sounding a little silver bell he kept next to him. "We shall see if it persists when you're at death's door."

Four assassins appeared, masked like penitents in our provinces of Midi. They made ready to seize me.

"My God!" I cried. "Forgive my executioners and lend me power to endure the torments of their foolish rage."

At these words the Inquisitor sounded the bell a second time and the Alcaide appeared.

"Return this man to prison," he told the monk. "There he shall end his days, for he confesses to nothing. Let him understand that his freedom depends upon it and he can confess when he likes."

I was taken away and leave you to imagine my feelings for the notorious scoundrels clearly intending nothing but thievery and murder.

Anxiety alone occupied me the first day but the next I fell into somber reflection and a state of melancholy that made me intend to end it all. Terrible pain followed as a result and did such violence to my soul as to put a stop to such dire plans.

Yes, I told myself while in my slough of despond, here is a tribunal: one that never issues a pardon, corrupts the probity of its citizens, the virtue of women and innocence of children. Like the tyrannies of Ancient Rome, it makes compassion a crime and finds wrongdoing in a show of tears. Suspicion signifies guilt, denunciation means proof, and wealth is suspect.

It is a tribunal that defies all laws, human and divine, while
covering its impudence, greed, and lust with hypocritical
claims to divine love and decency; a tribunal that forgives
the crimes of those who serve it and assures impunity to its
henchmen; a tribunal which, combining the greatest horror
and impudence, condemns and corrupts heroes,* destroys
ministers of state,† robs the nation of its finest possessions,‡
and cashiers the government. Such a tribunal, is the clearest
proof of the feebleness of the state that abides it, the most certain sign of the danger posed by the religion that protects it,
and the clearest manifestation of God's own vengeance. ✠

Monarchs beware — both those who tolerate all this and
those who, while rejecting it, consent to soil their nation's tri-
bunals with the atrocious declarations of this band of thieves.
The barbarous citizen, mad or inept, who would abuse his position to instill such views, would be an infernal instrument
invoking celestial anger to undermine the power of empire;
and if this rascal, less imaginary than one might suppose,
managed to raise himself for a moment above the vile state
to which Nature reduced him, heaven would permit it only
to prepare him for the shame of falling from a higher place.

The boil lanced, now came new ideas. My 25,000 livres in
gold remained intact in my belt; it was extremely tight around
my waist. I was glad it had escaped discovery when they
searched me when I first was taken into custody. That happy
circumstance made me think that fortune had not entirely

---

* Charles V.

† Count d'Olivares had made a fortune for more than 4000 people when the atrocious
tribunal summoned him before it, and he could find not a single friend who dared
come to his aid.

‡ The Netherlands, etc.

✠ The watchword of this tribunal is: "We would rather burn you as guilty than let the
public think we had locked you up innocent."

0   abandoned me but proffered a hand to liberate me from my
unhappy fate. So little is needed for one so miserable, hope
came alive. No longer did the prison walls seem to be those of
my sepulcher. My eyes measured them anew with a view toward escape; I examined them carefully, sounded their thick-
5   ness, scrutinized the windows; not as high as those of other
cells. I thought that with a little patience and work it ought
to be possible: the bars were doubled and quite thick but that
didn't put me off. I saw that the window seemed to give out
onto a small isolated courtyard bordered by nothing more
10   than a single wall with no more than 20 paces separating it
from the street. I resolved to put to work that very moment. A
steel tinderbox, always found in such places, served me well.
Chipping away with it against a rock, I managed to make a
sort of file and by the same evening had succeeded in making
15   deep cuts in the bars.

     Courage! I told myself. *O Léonore! I kneel before you.
No, death won't take me here. To work!*

     In order that my jailers suspect nothing, I affected great
agony; I took the ruse to the point of even refusing food and
20   in this way gained a little pity and allayed suspicion. The
consolation amounted to nothing much; the art of soothing
the wounds of an afflicted soul is unknown among those vile
enough to accept dishonorable employment as prison guards.
But in any event I deceived them and that was what concerned
25   me. Their blindness was more useful to me than their tears;
for more than touch their hearts, I wanted to divert their gaze.

     My work advanced. Soon my head could pass through the
opening I'd made in the wall. Each evening I had to put things
in order so that it remained unseen, but all went according
30   to plan until one day, toward three o'clock in the afternoon,
I heard knocking above my head in a place where the ceiling
seemed weakened and through which voices could penetrate.

I listened: more knocking. 0

"Can you hear me?" It was the voice of a woman, speaking French badly.

"Quite well," I replied. "What do you want of an unhappy companion in misfortune?"

"Pity and consolation. I'm a prisoner too and innocent like 5 you. For a week I've been listening and believe I've guessed your plans."

"I've none whatever," I replied, fearing a trap. I knew about the vile ruse of placing a shackled spy next to an unfortunate prisoner with the aim of winning his heart to pilfer a 10 secret that would instantly betray him — an execrable artifice that once again proves, instead of honest and legitimate work that would presume innocence, the frightful intent to create criminals.*

"You're mistaken," replied my fate's companion. "I'll allay 15 your suspicions as best I can. As concerns me, they're misplaced. If we could see one another, I'd convince you of my honesty. Will you help me? Let's each of us pierce this spot and we'll hear each other better and see one another. I dare think that with just a brief talk we'll be both convinced that 20 we've nothing to fear in confiding in each other."

Here my situation became quite embarrassing. Clearly I had been discovered and in such circumstances there was

---

* By this awful practice judges never see the accused except as guilty and so commit terrible and bloody mistakes. A host of causes can bring enemies down upon a man. Gossip and calumny are so often employed that it would seem that, for any honest soul, the first impulse should always be favorable to the accused. But where are the judges today who practice that virtue? What would become of all their arrogance and severity, and insolent and stupid inflexibility, if, instead of the hangman's noose and the wheel, we passed our lives proving innocence and absolution. A man to be hanged, guilty or not, is to a berobed judge just as necessary as the fly to spider, the sheep to the roaring lion, the fever to the physician.

perhaps less danger in according the woman what she wanted than irritating her by refusal. If she was false, she'd assuredly betray me; if not, my rudeness could determine her to do so. Thus, I accepted without further ado; but as the hour when the jailers made their rounds came near, I counseled my neighbor to put off work until the next day. She agreed. Repeating as she bid me good night:

"We owe you much gratitude."

"*We?*" I replied. "Are you not alone?"

"Yes, I'm alone," came the response. "But in the cell next to mine is a companion with whom I speak very freely through an opening we've made, and she'll find a way to enter my cell in order that we both can pass into yours when the work you and I've begun is complete. The favor I implore is as much for this poor woman as for me. If you knew her, you'd find her most interesting. She's from your own country. Young, innocent, and beautiful, it's impossible not to like her. If pity doesn't speak in my favor, have some for her sake!"

"What! The one you speak of is French?" I replied eagerly. "How can it be?"

But we had no time to say more as we heard noise that put an end to our conversation.

After supper I plunged into serious reflection on what course to take. Certainly I was gratified by the idea of breaking the yoke of our villainous captors, myself, and two more like me; but, on the other hand, what of the risks in being saddled with these two women? How undertake such a dangerous operation with an outcome so uncertain? If it failed, I would've only made matters doubly worse for them and brought down upon us all still greater tribulations than those that already awaited. By myself it seemed possible; with them, it seemed certain to fail. I equivocated no longer and closed my heart.

In order to not entertain personal regrets in so cruelly refusing to help my two unfortunate companions, I determined to
escape immediately.

I waited until midnight. Inspecting my work, I found the
opening large enough to pass through. Tying a bedsheet to one
of the undamaged bars, I used it to slip out and down into the
courtyard. But a new quandary arose as I dropped into a kind
of chasm, with still more frightful darkness, the space narrow
and high, leaving me with 20 feet of wall to climb and nothing
to help me do it. I immediately regretted what I'd just done;
for death, in a thousand ways, confronted me as punishment
for my imprudence. Bitter sorrow invaded my heart for having
harshly disappointed the hopes of the two women whom I'd
abandoned. I was ready to remount to the cell when, scroung-
ing around in the courtyard — suddenly I came upon a ladder.

Great heavens! I told myself: *You're saved — doubt not.*
Providence serves you better than you do yourself and wants
to rescue you. Follow its voice; take courage.

Seizing the precious ladder, I threw it up against the wall.
But then more distress: it barely made it halfway. Still, my
lucky star had not deserted me. In the courtyard I discovered
an elevation that my ladder could reach and once upon this
parapet I pulled up the ladder and placed it against the wall —
which put me on the ledge. But was I really better off? I had
to go down the same way I'd come up and nothing on the far
side seemed promising. The ledge being wide enough to walk
upon, I went around it in search of anything that might help. I
finally noticed a pile of manure, about six feet high, in the corner of a little street abutting the wall. Without further reflection I jumped into it and from there onto the street, pleased
not to have hurt myself.

Thereupon, as you might imagine, I promptly took to
my heels.

A man in flight from the Inquisition will find help nowhere in Spain, where the kingdom teems with collaborators
and spies for the tribunal, ready to seize you wherever you
might be. Nothing is more vigilant than the Hermandad, or
Brotherhood — the band of rogues that lends a hand to the
Inquisition from one end to Spain to the other and spares no
expense, using every scheme imaginable to arrest and return
whomever the tribunal pursues. That much I knew and it
was perfectly clear that the only thing to do was get out of
Spain and if possible make my way, without stopping, to the
French border.

Thus I set out to flee — yet who was she? The one whose
hopes I'd just betrayed? Who was the charming young woman
for whom a tender friend had solicited my pity? Whom did
I betray? From whom did I flee?

Léonore, my dearest. 'Twas she whom fortune let slip
through my hands yet a third time — she whose chains I refused to break and whom I left in thrall to a monster more
thunderous than Venetians or even cannibals — she, from
whom I distanced myself as fast as my feet could run.

"Oh! So unfortunate!" *exclaimed Madame de Blamont*: "Henceforth I shan't believe in love's intuition. Oh! Madame," she
continued, kissing Léonore, "how all this redoubles our desire
for you to tell us about *your* adventures. How interesting they
must be!"

"Let Monsieur de Sainville finish," said the Count de Beaulé.
"Terrible to deal with women. We take curiosity to be their
burning desire. But we're wrong. They just want to talk."

"Exactly who keeps us from listening?" asked Aline gently,
addressing the Count. "Only you, it seems to me."

"Very well," he replied. "But if you interrupt once more, either of you, I shall take Sainville and Léonore to Paris, and deprive you of the rest of their story."

"Come, come, listen and be silent lest the General do as he says," said Madame de Senneval. "Continue, Monsieur de Sainville, I beg you. For I much desire to know how you were reunited with your cherished love."

"Alas! Madame," replied Sainville. "There remains little interesting to tell you between this last circumstance and our happy reunion. Your eagerness to hear what Léonore has to tell you will make me abridge the details."

I walked fast, avoided cities and larger towns, and slept in the countryside. If I met someone, I passed myself off as a deserter from the French army. Six days on foot brought me across the mountains. I arrived in the village of Pau in a most pitiful state, but there at least found tranquility and could pay for comfortable accommodations. But calm after so much agitation provoked illness; hardly had I settled into a bourgeois home, rented in order to rest, than I was gripped by a burning fever and for a week lay close to death. Fortunately, I was among honest people who provided care I shall never forget; but my convalescence took four months and I no longer thought about returning home. Toward summer's end I bought a coach, took on several domestics, and went to Bayonne; but I was still not well enough for exhausting travel and so made my way in short stages to Bordeaux. There I resolved to spend two weeks recuperating and was as relaxed as the state of my heart permitted — until one evening I sought some distraction and decided to attend a performance of *Le Père de la Famille*. The play, a comedy I'd always liked, was to feature a debutante in the role of Sophie, and she was also to play Julie in *La Pupille*.

0   The talented young woman, said to possess all the graces, was just come from delighting audiences in Bayonne.

As was customary, shortly before the performance, young people chatted on stage with the actresses. I did so, too, intending a closer look at the young and captivating woman to decide for myself if she deserved such lavish praise. Having already met an actor named Sainclair, whom I'd previously seen on stage in Metz, in the same role he was to reprise as the tender and spirited Saint-Albin, I asked if he would point out to me the goddess he adored in the play.

"She is dressing," he told me. "She will be down in a moment; I'll make certain you see her when she appears. This is my first time on stage with her; I saw her only for a moment this morning; she arrived just yesterday. We rehearsed the tragic scenes and she's indeed most interesting. Pretty figure, charming voice — and a sensitive soul."

"And you've not fallen in love?" I joked.

"Oh my!" responded Sainclair, "Don't you know we actors are more like confessors? We never hunt in our own backyard; it's bad for talent. *Illusion* goes to the devil when one sleeps with a woman. To adore her on stage must not the illusion be complete? Besides, this young woman is as wise as she is beautiful. In truth, all our friends say so. Your own eyes will do infinitely better than any portraits I might sketch. But here she is now — how do you find her?"

I was in no state to reply. Great God! How my limbs trembled! Cruel anguish froze my senses for a long moment before — suddenly grasping the situation — I rushed to her.

"O! LÉONORE!" I cried. *Overcome, I fell at her feet.*

I don't know what happened or what was done. I only regained consciousness in the tiring-room backstage. When I opened my eyes I found myself in the care of Sainclair and several actresses, with Léonore on her knees beside me. Her hand pressed to my heart, she called my name, overcome with tears.

Our delirious kisses interrupted questions posed and unan-   0
swered a thousand times. Mutual tenderness and joy at having
found one another after no many tribulations drew tears from
all around. The debutante, it was announced, had fainted and
Le Père de la famille was canceled while the troupe closeted
themselves with us backstage. Léonore explained who I was,   5
the bonds of marriage that connected us, and how impossible
it would be for her to continue in her role. I offered to pay the
expenses but the actors would not hear of it. Few people know
what delicacy and sensitivity are to be found among people of
the theater. How not be honest and sensitive if you spend half   10
your life on stage! One renders poorly emotions one doesn't
feel; yet even without an inclination for virtue, borrowed sentiments quietly accustom the soul to be moved by them alone.*

When the indisposition of the actress was announced,
the public demanded *Les Trois Fermiers* to go on and all was   15
well; after that, I only wanted to leave the theater.

"Let's go now," I said to Léonore. "We'll surrender ourselves in peace to the sweet charms of reunion. Let us go, my
dearest, and celebrate the happiest day of our lives!"

"Just one moment. I mustn't leave without expressing   20
thanks to two persons you see here," said the adorable young
lady. From the company that had helped us, she pointed out a
man and a woman. "Their many kindnesses have made them
as dear to me as my own parents and, indeed, taken their place."

She embraced them and received tender caresses while   25
I joined with her to give these honest people some sense of
my own heart's effusions. After we said our goodbyes, we left

---

* For such a notion, exceptions should be understood. If it supposes that actors in
roles implying treachery and duplicity resemble the characters they play, that's not
the case. But those roles are comparatively infrequent; a play features more honest
characters than villains, which aligns in support of Sainville's assertion.

Bordeaux the same evening for Livorno, where we remained several days. After communicating to my dear spouse my intoxication at having found her, and 24 hours spent attending to nothing but the enjoyment of a thousand proofs of love and happiness, I begged her to tell me of all that had happened to her — beginning with the fatal moment of our separation. "But the further tale of our adventures, Mesdames," *said Sainville,* as he finished recounting his own, "will be more charmingly told by her than by me. Permit her, if you will."

"Most assuredly," said Madame de Blamont, speaking for all. "We will be delighted to hear them and —"

Great God! How can I possibly go on? What sudden thunder has just shaken the whole house to its foundations? O Valcour! Is heaven dead set against us? The doors — they're breaking down the doors — the windows are rattling. The women are fainting. Goodbye, goodbye my unhappy friend. What next? Will I ever be able to recount anything besides horrors and misfortune?

Endnotes

Our translation, in accord with the 1990 Pléiade publication, takes the third state of the 1795 edition of the novel as the canonical text, into which Sade had introduced a small number of significant changes after the novel's first printing. Modern French editions, beginning with Jean-Jacques Pauvert's 1966 edition for *Cercle du Livre Précieux*, include useful contextual information, and we are indebted to the work of Michel Delon, editor of the Pléiade edition, and to Jean-Marie Goulemont for his notes to the 1994 Livre de Poche edition. Our own endnotes and brief explanations, which bear witness to Sade's encyclopedic mind, are designed explicitly for an Anglophone audience.

19   170.3: Saint Ultrogote, dating to the 6th century, is depicted as dressed in an elaborate gown.

20   176.9: Venice, in decline during the 18th century, was indeed by then only the shadow of a republic, its vaunted democratic character more myth than reality. Malamocco village is located on the Lido of Venice, a barrier island that connects the city to the Adriatic.

21   182.14: *"we caught sight of"*: Corfu Island, off the coast of Greece in the Ionian Sea. The Cape of Morée probably refers to the Morea Eyalet, a province of the Ottoman Empire. *Shores of Pera*: a reference to a suburb neighboring Constantinople (İstanbul).

22   182.26: Sublime Porte: The term of diplomacy for the central Ottoman Empire

23   185.22: Fort St. Elmo, a bastion built in the 16th century, located in the capital city of Valletta on the island of Malta.

24   187.8: *"Æsop's fable"*: A dog with a bone loses it by mistaking its shadow (or reflection in water) for another dog with a bone more scrumptious.

25   187.23: Cap Bon, a peninsula in Northeastern Tunisia, is today a popular resort.

26   188.13: The historic city of Salé, indeed once a haven for pirates, had been controlled by the Sultan of Morocco since 1668 and so, too, the old imperial city of Meknes.

27   189.21: Safi, a major seaport in Morocco.

28   190.17: Island of Saint-Mathieu: Sade here refers to a phantom island that appeared on maps as early as the 16th century and as late as the 20th, but does not exist. James Cook attempted to discover it during his second voyage.

29   192.10: Cape Negro Bay, today part of Angola, was a southern outpost of the Portuguese empire.

30   194.0: Sade locates the Kingdom of Butua in what today forms part of Zimbabwe, the interior of southern Africa, where the Portuguese had established a colonial presence beginning in the 16th century; they also encountered Africans whom the Dutch called Hottentots. The Lupata Mountain chain has today disappeared from geography texts, but it was near the eastern coast and included Mount Kilimanjaro to the south. The Portuguese applied the term "Jagas" to fierce warriors — often described as savages, cannibals, and idolaters.

31   196.24: *"route to their own colonies"*: The Portuguese established the Colony of Benguela in 1617; today it would be part of Angola. Zimbawbe was a major trading center with a complex history of rule. Zanzibar by the 18th century was under a sultanate. Monomotapa refers to an ill-defined region historically sketched by the Portuguese (today, parts of Southern Africa) and often cited on maps of the period.

32   196.31: Abbé Raynal (1713–1796) was a highly popular man of letters and considered a prophet of the French Revolution.

33   196.12: *"his brow"*: A paraphrase of Raynal, whose *l'Histoire des deux Indes* (parts of which were written by Diderot and

others) was an examination of topics such as commerce, slavery, and religion. The book was considered incendiary and banned in 1779.

34   198.3: When the imperial gaze of Empress Livia, wife of Augustus, was exposed to a group of naked men, she saved them from death by saying that to a chaste woman they were like statues.

35   201.12: The Empire of Monoèmugi is mentioned in Diderot's *Encyclopedia*.

36   203.7: *"Sultan's handkerchief"*: A ceremony in which the Sultan would throw his handkerchief, a sign of his authority, before one of the slaves in his harem, who would prostrate herself before him and serve as his bedmate.

37   204.16: The Portuguese encountered cannibalism among the indigenous Tupi when they arrived in Brazil in 1500. And an early father of the church, Saint Jerome (c. 347–420), discussed cannibalism in pagan Ireland, referring specifically to the Attacoti tribes in his *Against Jovinianus*. Cook's second voyage (1772–1775) took him to Australia and islands in the South Pacific.

38   206.32: Cornelis de Pauw (1739–1799), a provocative Dutch philosopher, also discussed cannibalism and sacrifice. See, for example, his *Philosophical Researches on the Greeks* (1788).

39   213.26: Antoine de Sartine (1729–1801) served as Lieutenant General of Police of Paris. His secret police used criminal informants and spied on Sade himself, among many others.

40   214.11: The Ilotes were helots (slaves) in Sparta, which was also known in various contexts as Lacedaemonia.

41   218.6: *"just as the Turks"*: Venice fought the Ottoman Empire in the wake of the loss of Constantinople in 1453.

42   218.7: *"Turks long ago supported the Pope"*: After the fall of Constantinople, the Ottoman Empire made numerous

efforts to keep Christian Europe divided. Even in the context of the Crusades, Popes were not averse to alliances with the infidels.

43 218.23: The famed Cape of Good Hope was first known as the Cape of Storms (Cabo das Tormentas), named by the Portuguese explorer Bartolomeu Dias in 1488.

44 219.8: When under the House of Braganzia the Portuguese freed themselves from Spanish rule in 1640, high-ranking officials in the Catholic Church, including the Grand Inquisitor, Dom Sebastião de Tello, conspired against the dynasty and its new rulers. See e.g. H. Morse Stephens, *The Story of Portugal* (1895).

45 222.24: A figure of the French Enlightenment, Bernard Le Bovier de Fontenelle (1657–1757). The third volume of his *Dialogues of the Dead* includes this interchange, which Sade actually paraphrases but cites (wrongly) as a direct quotation. We translate his paraphrase. In Fontenelle's dialogue, the character of Juliette expresses horror that love is not reciprocated, and Soliman replies as Sade describes. Michel Delon (Pléiade, p. 1268), characterizes the reference to Montesquieu, Helvétius, and La Mettrie as a "dubious assertion."

46 224.3: *Isolism* is a term that signifies for Sade the positive value of Stoic indifference; surely reflective of Sade's experience in prison, it appears frequently in *Juliette*.

47 227.31: Dramatic demonstrations of air pressure were popular in the 17th century.

48 228.21: "*the age of reason*": In the Catholic Church, seven years of age. See also p. 797.

49 229.0: "*The old feudal government*": Sade is referring to the period of fragmentation in Poland that dates to the 12th century.

50 231.31: Sade refers to the story of Nehushtan, told in the biblical Book of Numbers (21:8–9), in which, on orders from God, Moses creates a serpent in bronze.

51 234.8: The African Kingdom of Juida, in English, Ouidah, located in what is currently Benin, was ruled by a tribal monarch and served as a major conduit and transfer point for European slave traders.

52 235.6: Themis was the goddess of divine law and order.

53 238.11: Solon (c. 638–558 BC) and Lycurgus (7th century BC) were lawgivers in Athens and Sparta, respectively.

54 238.30: A *philosophe* and friend of Voltaire, Jean Sales (1740–1816) was imprisoned owing to his multi-volume encyclopedia, referenced by Sade, which was judged to be anti-religious. Like Sade, he was imprisoned during the Terror but escaped the guillotine.

55 244.31: Louis-Antoine, Comte de Bougainville (1729–1811), created a sensation with accounts of his circumnavigation of the globe, published in 1771.

56 245.32: Sade refers to Cornelis de Pauw's discussion of the poison curare in his *Recherches philosophiques sur les Américains* (1770).

57 254.25: Monomotapa: see note 135. The Bororès and Cimbas are peoples mentioned in 18th century texts such as *Géographie Moderne et Universelle* (1777).

58 259.14: The Berg River, located near present-day Cape Town, was indeed settled by the Dutch, who used the term "Hottentot" to describe the people today known as Khoikhoi. *Yellow nation*: also a reference to the Hottentots.

59 262.17: "Land of Van Diemen" refers to the island of Tasmania, off the southeast coast of Australia; "New Holland" refers to mainland Australia.

60 264.8: *"land once sighted by Davis"*: a reference to Edward Davis, the English buccaneer who in 1684 apparently first sighted what would later be named Easter Island.

61 265.12: *"Chief's Palace ... Chief's residence ..."*: Sade evidently made changes in this paragraph and several others that reflect political considerations in the wake of the 1789 revolution, with a view to eliminating sensitive tropes associated with royalty.

62   265.25: Egyptian Pharaoh of the 12th Dynasty, Sesostris (or Se-
nusret I) ruled from 1971–1926 BC and was said to have
conquered the world. Sade would have been intrigued
by the story from Herodotus according to which, in the
wake of victory over a rival, Sesostris would erect a pil-
lar resembling a vagina in the capital of the vanquished,
presumably to indicate the army was weak and "fought
like women."

63   277.7: *"emperor of Russia"*: Russian Tsar Peter the Great (1672–
1721) famously traveled to Europe as a young man and
studied ship-building, navigation, and advances in science and technology.

64   277.29: *"to those who worship"*: Fo-Hi (many orthographic vari-
ants) of Chinese legend was the first human and sometimes described as a sun god. Ali, Muhammad's cousin
and son-in-law, is the central and key figure for the various branches of Islam.

65   279.24: Philosopher Diogenes of Sinope (412–323 BC), famously
carried a lighted lamp during the day while in search of
an honest man. Apicius, who lived during the 1st century
BC, was known as a lover of luxury; his name is associated with a book of Roman recipes.

66   279.31: Sejanus (20 BC–31 AD), a powerful soldier and leader of
the Praetorian Guard, was said to have sold his body, as
a youth, to Apicius. The story comes from Tacitus. See
also note 159.

67   280.2: *"If you wish to live"*: Michel Delon notes (Pléiade, p.1277)
that the Greek philosopher Porphyry of Tyre (234–305
AD), a vociferous opponent of Christianity, thus characterizes the thought of Epicurus in his letter to his wife.
Sade paraphrases but could not have read the letter itself,
which was known only through various citations and
paraphrases and not discovered until 1816. See Porphyry,
Letter to his wife Marcella (1910).

68   281.8: Place de Grève in Paris was known as the site of most public executions.

69   281.31: Sade again cites Abbé Raynal, whose work *Histoire des deux Indes*, published between 1770 and 1780, was a comprehensive account of European colonization from the point of view of the Enlightenment. The second edition of this popular work was translated into English as *A Philosophical and Political History of the Settlements and Trade of the Europeans in the East and West Indies* (1798).

70   281.17: Massacres in the French city of Mérindol and the commune at Cabrières-d'Avignon took place in 1545 in the context of the Reformation, with hundreds to thousands of victims, crimes that won the approval of both the French monarchy and Pope Paul III. Accused of conspiracy, Huguenots were hanged and decapitated in a bloody scene at the Chateau d'Amboise, in the Loire valley, in 1560. Marking a a turning point in the French Wars of Religion that exacerbated tensions between Catholics and Proestants, the St. Bartholomew's Day Massacre (*Massacre de la Saint-Barthélemy*) took place in 1572.

71   281.29: Sade here refers to the Hussite Wars, which began in 1419, several years after the Catholic Church executed Czech reformer Jan Hus (1369–1415). The "two species" refers to the bread and wine of communion, a source of the conflict.

72   282.22: *"massacred for pride... I told myself"*: The first state of *Aline et Valcour* included at this point an extended historical digression, a clear distraction which was eliminated in subsequent printings. We have not translated this section but it can be found in Pléiade, pp. 630–637.

73   285.0: Abbeville, in northern France, was a center for superfine cloth beginning in the Middle Ages.

74   285.31: The issue of famine and near-famine in agro-rich France was much discussed, often with rumors of conspiracy, in the years leading up to the Revolution.

75   286.2: Romulus, the eponymous founder of Rome.

76   288.21: *"priestlings of his temple ...":* Judges and justices.

77   301.8: Draco (c. 7th century BC) refers to the first lawgiver of Athens, whose code is noted for its harshness. Sade makes the contrast with Persian or Achæmenid legal systems, which indeed had the character of a more co-operative search for justice, as opposed to an adversarial system.

78   312.18: The Celts of Gaul did indeed engage in considerable human sacrifice and exceptional cruelty, the extent of which was described by Tacitus and others. Roman rule put an end to such practices as immolating prisoners of war and divination by the entrails of victims.

79   315.3: *"the use of torture":* Physical torture of prisoners at justice was a long-standing and common practice in the ancien régime and, indeed, in most European countries until the time of the French Revolution.

80   316.31: *Bélisaire* was a banned novel by Enlightenment figure Jean-François Marmontel (1723–1799), in which the title character, a Byzantine general, represents the virtues of mercy, and it stands as a plea for religious tolerance.

81   317.21: Cartouche: See note 16.

82   318.5: *"Gnats perish":* As ruler and lawgiver to the Athenians (see p. 238.11), Solon was a reformer. The quotation, found in Plutarch and elsewhere, is actually attributed to the 6th century BC philosopher Anacharsis, from a conversation with Solon.

83   319.22: *"Your government's shapeless constitution ..."* Zamé refers to the pre-revolutionary "constitution," which was understood to consist of judicial laws, ordinances, royal edicts, etc.

84   320.4: Phryne (4th century BC) was a celebrated courtesan in
      ancient Greece; Antinous (2nd century BC) was a lover of
      the Roman Emperor Hadrian (76–136 AD).

85   320.27: Sade alludes to the failed 7th Crusade (1248–1254), dur-
      ing which Louis IX (St. Louis) was taken prisoner, and
      he makes reference to the Tomb of the Patriarchs. —
      "Darnaud" refers to novelist and playwright François-
      Thomas-Marie de Baculard d'Arnaud (1718–1805).

86   321.18: The atrocities committed by Roman Emperor Tiberius
      (42 BC–37 AD) are described by Suetonius; Heliogabalus
      (Cæsar Marcus Aurelius, c. 202–222) resides in history
      as cruel and depraved; Byzantine Emperor Andronikos
      I Komnenos (1118–1185) was also known for his cruelty.

87   322.31: The eloquent panegyrist whom Sade refers to is prob-
      ably Jean-Sifrein Maury (1746–1817); "Dagon" was a
      primitive deity worshipped by Philistines, represented
      as half-man, half fish.

88   324.32: In a celebrated legal case, Frederick the Great intervened
      on behalf of Christian and Rosine Arnold, upholding
      their property rights, and he sent the justices in the case
      to prison, setting a powerful legal precedent supporting
      equal rights without regard for class although, by both
      contemporary and later accounts violating "rule of law."
      For a contemporary reevaluation, see David M. Luebke,
      "Frederick the Great and the Celebrated Case of the Mill-
      ers Arnold (1770–1779): A Reappraisal" in *Central Euro-
      pean History* 32(4) 379–408.

89   325.31: Salic and Germanic law did indeed impose fines on mur-
      der based on social status and gender. The livre tournois
      (Tours pound) dated to the Middle Ages.

90   327.28: Another reference to Antoine de Sartine who, after serv-
      ing as Lieutenant General of Police of Paris (and Sade's
      bête noire), was made Secretary of State for the Navy.
      He was dismissed in 1780 but accorded an extravagant

pension. For his liberal use of the *lettre de cachet* and secret police to spy on ordinary citizens, he became widely detested during the Revolution. Sartine was Spanish by birth; hence his "horror" of the French.

91 330.1: Aristippus of Cyrene (435–365 BC) founded a school of philosophy, known only by anecdote, based on pleasure and accommodation to circumstance.

92 330.6: *"One of your philosophers..."*: According to literary historian Jean Deprun, Sade refers here to Jean Le Rond d'Alembert's 1759 *Essai sur les éléments de philosophie*, ch. 7, concerning morality.

93 331.31: The "man of wit" has not been identified but Pléiade (p.1291) suggests Cesare Beccaria (1738–1794), the influential figure of the Enlightenment who wrote extensively on crime and punishment.

94 332.0: Sade paraphrases Montesquieu from *De l'esprit des lois*, and Pléiade cites Book XIV, ch. IV.

95 333.18: In his *Lives*, Plutarch tells the story of Solon and Æsop at the court of King Crœsus.

96 340.19: *figheha* (and several variant spellings): Sade here and elsewhere makes use of Cook's own accounts of his voyages, which were translated into French and published in France in 1778. Cook landed on the Tongan Islands first in 1773; owing to his reception, he named them the "Friendly Islands" — ironically, as is understood today, for a plot was afoot to murder him. Sade cites the French edition of Cook's work, the first volume of *A Voyage Towards the South Pole and Round the World*.

97 341.24: Farinacius: see also p. 140.9. In 1778, Sade successfully appealed his death sentence by the court at Aix.

98 346.29: Plutarch's *Lives*, Themistocles. We use the 1910 revised Dryden translation.

99 347.31: The *Lex Papia Poppæa* was instituted in 9 AD.

100 348.3: Clearchus of Soli (4th century BC), Greek philosopher. Laconia was the region of the city state Sparta.

101 348.30: *"agitated, as Saint-Lambert says"*: The poet cited is Jean-François de Saint-Lambert (1716–1803), whose popular and well-received 1775 poem *Les Saisons* cites the extreme masochistic behavior of the famed medieval lawyer, astrologer, and physician Jérôme Cardan (1501–1576).

102 352.31: Statesman Henri Bertin (1720–1792) served as head of the Paris police from 1757–59; he emigrated during the French Revolution.

103 353.17: Astrea, in Greek Myth a celestial virgin, was associated in the 18ᵗʰ century with renewal and visions of utopia.

104 355.10: Lycurgus, the lawmaker of Sparta, represents a clear model for Zamé. See also note 53.

105 359.5: Cap-Vert is the westernmost point of the African continent, a rocky promontory off the coast of today's Senegal.

106 362.2: *"with thirty crispins"*: Sade adopts the name for a character in French comic theater, dating to the 17ᵗʰ century, a valet portrayed as cowardly and gluttonous.

107 362.17: *"the Alcaide"*: The Alcaide in Spanish terminology referred both to a leader of a fortress or district and the administrator of a prison.

108 369.33: In 1762 Protestant merchant Jean Calas was convicted of murdering his son, allegedly because he was considering conversion to Catholicism. His son probably committed suicide. The cruel execution of Calas, who was broken on the wheel, became a symbol of religious intolerance. We have not discovered any information concerning Blénac, the priest Sade cites.

109 371.27: Charles Quint (Charles V) (1500–1558), Holy Roman Emperor from 1519 to 1556, advanced cultural life and the causes of humanism but also controlled the Inquisition and attempted to persecute Protestants.

110 371.28: Gaspar de Guzmán, Count-Duke of Olivares (1587–1645), powerful minister to Philippe IV of Spain, lost his

powerful post in 1643 and was summoned by the Inquisition in 1644, shortly before his death, charged with a variety of absurd crimes.

111   371.31: The Netherlands: Sade refers to the long and determined resistance of the Dutch (1548–1648) against Spanish (and Catholic) rule.

112   374.3: Members of the Santa Hermandad, or Holy Brotherhood, were active in Spain until 1835. Their reputation was as Sade implies. See also p. 524 and p. 573.

113   375.16: The commune of Pau is about 80 kilometers from the Spanish border, set against the Pyrénées.

114   377.30: *Le Père de famille*, a 1758 play by Denis Diderot. *La Pupille*, a short simple comedy by Barthélemy-Christophe Fagan (1701–1758).

Illustrations

"Ah! I knew it," the man continued. *"She could not survive the tempest."*

fig. 5 ⟡ p. 186

Her skin dazzled, and every part of her body was formed by the hand of the gods.

fig. 6 ⑤ p. 256

"Sometimes I receive friends; courtesans, never."

fig. 7 ☙ p. 267

I sat before the Prince of Peace and men of bloody violence.

fig. 8 ⑧ p. 361

COLOPHON

ALINE AND VALCOUR
was handset in InDesign CC.

The text is set in *Adobe Warnock Pro*.
The illustration captions are set in *IM Fell Pica*

Book design & typesetting: Alessandro Segalini

Cover design: CMP

Cover image: Federico Gori, "Sade" (2019),
36 × 23 cm, ink & enamel on paper,
federicogori.org

ALINE AND VALCOUR
is published by Contra Mundum Press.

Contra Mundum Press   New York · London · Melbourne

CONTRA MUNDUM PRESS

Dedicated to the value & the indispensable importance of the individual voice, to works that test the boundaries of thought & experience.

The primary aim of Contra Mundum is to publish translations of writers who in their use of form and style are *à rebours*, or who deviate significantly from more programmatic & spurious forms of experimentation. Such writing attests to the volatile nature of modernism. Our preference is for works that have not yet been translated into English, are out of print, or are poorly translated, for writers whose thinking & æsthetics are in opposition to timely or mainstream currents of thought, value systems, or moralities. We also reprint obscure and out-of-print works we consider significant but which have been forgotten, neglected, or overshadowed.

There are many works of fundamental significance to *Weltliteratur* (& *Weltkultur*) that still remain in relative oblivion, works that alter and disrupt standard circuits of thought — these warrant being encountered by the world at large. It is our aim to render them more visible.

For the complete list of forthcoming publications, please visit our website. To be added to our mailing list, send your name and email address to: info@contramundum.net

Contra Mundum Press
P.O. Box 1326
New York, NY 10276
USA

OTHER CONTRA MUNDUM PRESS TITLES

SOME FORTHCOMING TITLES

THE FUTURE OF KULCHUR
A PATRONAGE PROJECT

With bookstores and presses around the world struggling to survive, and many actually closing, we are forming this patronage project as a means for establishing a continuous & stable foundation to safeguard our longevity. Through this patronage project we would be able to remain free of having to rely upon government support &/or other official funding bodies, not to speak of their timelines & impositions. It would also free CMP from suffering the vagaries of the publishing industry, as well as the risk of submitting to commercial pressures in order to persist, thereby potentially compromising the integrity of our catalog.

CAN YOU SACRIFICE $10 A WEEK FOR KULCHUR?

For the equivalent of merely 2–3 coffees a week, you can help sustain CMP and contribute to the future of kulchur. To participate in our patronage program we are asking individuals to donate $500 per year, which amounts to $42/month, or $10/week. Larger donations are of course welcome and beneficial. All donations are tax-deductible through our fiscal sponsor Fractured Atlas. If preferred, donations can be made in two installments. We are seeking a minimum of 300 patrons per year and would like for them to commit to giving the above amount for a period of three years.

Part tax-deductible donation, part exchange, for your contribution you will receive every CMP book published during the patronage period as well as 20 books from our back catalog. When possible, signed or limited editions of books will be offered as well.

Your contribution will help with basic general operating expenses, yearly production expenses (book printing, warehouse & catalog fees, etc.), advertising & outreach, and editorial, proofreading, translation, typography, design and copyright fees. Funds may also be used for participating in book fairs and staging events. Additionally, we hope to rebuild the *Hyperion* section of the website in order to modernize it.

From Pericles to Mæcenas & the Renaissance patrons, it is the magnanimity of such individuals that have helped the arts to flourish. Be a part of helping your kulchur flourish; be a part of history.

To lend your support & become a patron, please visit the subscription page of our website: contramundum.net/subscription

For any questions, write us at: info@contramundum.net

9 781940 625324